# THE HANDS OF GRAVITY AND CHANCE

**Books by Thomas Ogden**
(available at www.karnacbooks.com)

**Fiction**

*The Parts Left Out: A Novel*

*The Hands of Gravity and Chance: A Novel*

**Non-Fiction**

*Projective Identification and Psychotherapeutic Technique*

*The Matrix of the Mind: Object Relations and the Psychoanalytic Dialogue*

*The Primitive Edge of Experience*

*Subjects of Analysis*

*Reverie and Interpretation: Sensing Something Human*

*Conversations at the Frontier of Dreaming*

*This Art of Psychoanalysis: Dreaming Undreamt Dreams and Interrupted Cries*

*Rediscovering Psychoanalysis: Thinking and Dreaming, Learning and Forgetting*

*On Not Being Able to Dream: Selected Essays, 1994–2005* (available only in Hebrew)

*Creative Readings: Essays on Seminal Analytic Works*

*The Analyst's Ear and the Critic's Eye: Rethinking Psychoanalysis and Literature* (co-authored with Benjamin Ogden)

*Reclaiming Unlived Life: Experiences in Psychoanalysis*

# THE HANDS OF GRAVITY AND CHANCE

## A Novel

Thomas H. Ogden

**KARNAC**

First published in 2016 by
Karnac Books Ltd
118 Finchley Road
London NW3 5HT

British Library Cataloguing in Publication Data

A C.I.P. for this book is available from the British Library

ISBN-13: 978-1-78220-357-5

Typeset by V Publishing Solutions Pvt Ltd., Chennai, India

Printed in Great Britain

www.karnacbooks.com

*In loving memory of*
*Elizabeth K. Ogden*
*1920–2015*

# ONE

It is a large house, once grand, but no longer. A turn-of-the-century, Midwestern farmhouse that almost certainly, at one time, was trailed by fields of corn and soybean, like an enormous regal cape. There must have been a barn and silos and other outbuildings, but no trace of them remains. The house now is confined to less than an acre of land. The front porch is sorely in need of repair, as is the lichen-spotted, wood-shingled roof. The most attractive feature of the house is the forest-green shutters that stand out in bold relief against the chipping white paint surrounding them.

On both sides of the house are 1950s-style ranch houses, one with a television dish attached to its side, the other crowned by an elaborate antenna sporting eight or ten thin, aluminum rods pointing upward and outward, gesticulating in the wind.

The house is set back farther from the road than are the neighboring houses, giving it a quality of reserve. This effect is compounded by the steep set of brick steps with several landings, which rise abruptly from a road that at one time was a dirt thoroughfare connecting the farmlands and the city.

On entering the house, one finds oneself in a dimly lit front hallway with a staircase to the left that rises sharply to a narrow second-floor landing. The stairs and banister are uncompromising in their refusal to soften their straight lines with even the slightest widening or turning of the bottom step.

To the right is the living room in which a couch and an array of armchairs hint at something softer, though far off, as if hidden in a mist. On the left is the dining room, at the center of which is a long rectangular table with three linen place mats carefully arranged on each side. To its right is a walnut serving table.

Late on an otherwise ordinary February afternoon, the light in the front hall seemed to become momentarily brighter, illuminating the motes of dust in the air. Time seemed to slow almost to a halt for the three children playing on the landing atop the staircase, and for their mother and aunt who were chatting just to the right of the foot of the stairs. Without a sound being uttered, all eyes turned to the top of the staircase, where Catherine began to tilt forward, her feet still touching the lip of the landing. Something had been set in motion that could not be reversed. Catherine's thin-framed, early adolescent body, tilted forward on the uppermost stair, was now fully in the grip of gravity and chance.

Catherine's older brother, Damien, was standing behind her with his arms stretched out toward her shoulders, which were just out of reach. The tips of his fingers grazed her upper back. The eldest child, Erin, raised himself from the floor of the landing, his eyes fixed on his sister as if trying to draw her back with the force of his gaze.

Catherine's mother, Rose, turned her head toward the movement at the top of the stairs, finding herself in the role of an observer of the unthinkable. Catherine seemed, to Rose, startled by a sudden sensation of weightlessness, which quickly gave way to a powerful downward force. Rose watched as Catherine tried to pull her head and shoulders back in an effort to see what was coming. She could feel on her own cheeks and forehead the movement of the air that lifted Catherine's hair as she fell.

A look of terror swept across Catherine's face. She extended her right arm and hand toward her mother, though Rose was now out of her field of vision. She was confused by the fact that her mother's hand was not taking hold of hers, as it always had when she needed it, a hand that was not hers, but nonetheless a part of her. Rose extended her own hand toward Catherine's, and like Catherine, wondered why their fingers were not touching.

Catherine lowered her right arm to reposition herself in anticipation of the collision of her head with an edge of one of the banister's white spindles. She reflexively extended her left arm to absorb the impact, but her arm almost immediately collapsed at the elbow as her head collided with one of the four right-angled corners of the spindle.

The blow to the side of Catherine's head was strangely silent, as was the downward movement of her body across the staircase, which caused her ginger hair to sweep across her face, covering her eyes.

As Catherine careened across the width of the stairs, Rose thought, Catherine's hair is too long. I told her she'd look darling in a pixie cut. It would bring out the beautiful bone structure of her face. She'd burst into tears and stormed out of the kitchen, yelling, "Do you have to make me feel bad about *everything*, even the length of my hair?"

Catherine's collision with the wall sent her rolling down the stairs in what looked like a failed attempt at a somersault. Her new sneakers seemed to follow her, thumping down stair after stair, her right shoulder leading the descent. Rose remembered Catherine worrying that the iridescence of the stripe on her sneaker looked too boyish. "Nothing," Rose recalled telling her, "could make you look remotely like a boy." Catherine, with her beautiful, lightly freckled face, her thick, soft hair, the graceful lines of her torso, would look radiant in anything she wore, Rose thought.

3

The end of the fall was marked by the sound of the slap of Catherine's forehead against the dark, oak-planked floor at the foot of the stairs, and by another sharp twisting of her neck. With her cheek pressed to the floor, the momentum of the remainder of her body pushed her head forward and downward, bunching her shoulders up over her head. Catherine's body lay absolutely quiet and still, her legs splayed across the bottom two stairs.

Rose made her way toward Catherine as if slogging hip-deep in water, which prolonged the ache of not yet having Catherine in her arms. Rose's fear that Catherine was dead was momentarily allayed by her fleeting belief that what she had witnessed was a nightmare from which she was unable to awake. She dropped hard to her knees just to the right of Catherine, whose left ear was pressed to the wooden floor, her eyes closed. Rose released Catherine's head from its sharply downturned position, and gently laid her cheek on the floor. She put her ear to Catherine's back to see if she could detect the sound or slight movement of shallow breathing.

"I can't hear anything," Rose murmured, her voice trembling.

Margaret, Rose's older sister, kneeled down on the other side of Catherine's body and pressed two fingers to the right side of Catherine's neck, searching for a carotid pulse. Erin and Damien, Rose's two sons, who had watched helplessly from the landing as Catherine fell, were now standing with their shoulders slumped forward, a few feet from Catherine's body, not knowing what they should be doing.

"I can feel a pulse," Margaret said in a matter-of-fact way. "Erin, get the phone in the kitchen, dial 911. I'll talk to them as soon as they pick up. Damien, run upstairs and pull the blankets off Rose's bed and cover Catherine with them as fast as you can. Rose, just keep doing what you're doing, letting Catherine know you're here with her."

4

It was calming for Rose to hear Margaret take over and enlist the boys in helping her. Margaret had always been the smart one, the definite one, the one who knew what to do.

The ambulance lights splashed the front hallway with alternating red and blue light as the paramedics silently and methodically checked Catherine's pulse, blood pressure, and pupillary response, before fastening a thick yellow brace around her neck. They then carefully turned her over and lifted her onto the collapsed gurney. The odor of the steel frame of the gurney filled the entryway of the house as the paramedics performed their well-choreographed but utterly impersonal dance.

Margaret helped Rose up from the floor and out the front door into the damp, cold, early-evening darkness. They walked together, arm in arm, down the front steps to the street. Rose climbed unsteadily into the back of the ambulance, where she took a seat on a metal bench to the right of Catherine's gurney, which was locked into place.

Catherine's arms and hands lay limply on the thin foam mat atop the gurney. Rose took Catherine's cold hand in both of hers, trying to transfer what little warmth there was in her hands to Catherine's. The ambulance flew through the streets, its siren screaming. Rose's eyes were riveted to Catherine's face, hoping to see her eyes open. "It's all right, Catherine, Mommy's here," Rose said, her voice hardly audible amidst the wailing of the siren and the cacophony of metal parts knocking against one another somewhere inside the ambulance. "You're going to be fine, I promise." It was a promise Rose knew was beyond her power to vouchsafe, but one that mothers make, and children need.

Rose startled at the thunk of the turning of the handle of the rear door of the ambulance. Catherine was quickly wheeled out, the lower structure of the gurney dropping down hard onto the concrete ramp leading to the sliding glass doors of the emergency room. Rose, now sitting by herself in the empty ambulance, had no memory of getting into the ambulance or traveling to the hospital. Through the haze of shock, Rose felt the full weight of responsibility for all of what had just occurred, though the specifics of how she was responsible were beyond her at the moment.

## TWO

The front door and storm door were still open, letting in the cold evening air. The storm door wheezed as it moved in the strong breeze. Margaret and her nephews, Erin and Damien, stood stunned in the front hall for quite some time without saying a word. The pale yellow blankets that had covered Catherine remained in a heap on the floor.

As they stood there, they could feel that something in them had been changed by what had happened, but none of them had a name for that change. Something that had been silently imminent had finally occurred.

A gust of wind slammed the storm door shut with such force that the blast shook the three of them out of the half-sleep in which they'd been enfolded. The entrance hall felt as if it had been gutted.

Margaret closed both doors and switched on the lights. The boys squinted as if coming out of a cave into bright sunlight. For Erin, the dark brown stairs took on a purple hue, and the yellow walls appeared to be awash with large, swimming patches of orange and green. Damien kept his eyes closed as he walked clumsily into the unlit living room.

When Damien returned to the front hall, where Margaret and Erin were standing, the three stood silently, awkwardly, making no eye contact. Even as Catherine was falling, Margaret had asked herself, How does a thirteen-year-old girl fall down a flight of stairs? Did she trip? Was she pushed? If pushed, by whom, and why? Perhaps Catherine had fainted or had a seizure. She had a distinct feeling that if Catherine had been pushed, it could only have been Damien who pushed her—an unkind thought that she felt ashamed of.

As Catherine fell, Margaret's gaze had moved from one child to the next, as if digging deep into each of their faces. She could see most of Erin's face through the spindles of the railing as he rose to his knees four or five feet to the right of Catherine. His mouth was open, and he winced each time she collided with the banister or the wall, seemingly trying to cry out, but finding himself unable to summon the breath with which to do so. He pulled himself up from the floor of the landing during the fall, and then sprang to his feet when Catherine's head hit the floor at the bottom of the stairs.

The expression on Damien's face was still vivid in Margaret's mind, but difficult to interpret. He was standing behind Catherine and seemed surprised that he was not able to reach her with his outstretched arms. Along with surprise, she thought she detected guilt or remorse in his eyes. But was he feeling sorrowful for pushing her or for not being able to get hold of her, or both? Impossible to tell. She also saw in his face that innocent, uncomprehending look she'd seen so often when he was very young. Why is this happening, his large brown eyes had asked her, but she had had no answer for him.

In the emptiness of the front hall in which Erin, Damien, and Margaret found themselves after the departure of the ambulance, the boys, without speaking a word, walked up the stairs with slow, heavy footsteps; Margaret silently turned and walked into the living room to read.

The boys took their usual positions on the floor of the TV room—knees up, backs against the front of the couch, about five feet from the television screen. Neither of them turned it on. The room was misshapen, long and narrow, giving the impression of having been lopped off the end of a larger room. The couch—a huge, well-worn, brown corduroy thing—sat stolidly against one wall, equidistant from the double-hung window at the far end and the door to the hallway at the other. The dull white built-in cabinets and shelves that lined the wall opposite the couch were filled randomly with metal trucks, children's books, board games, and other remains of an earlier era of the life of this family.

Both boys remained stunned as they sat in silence. Damien eventually turned to his older brother, Erin, and was startled to see his face blanched and expressionless. He blurted out more loudly than he'd expected, "Erin, you okay?"

"Yeah," he said unconvincingly.

"Really?"

"I said yeah."

"But you don't sound it."

"It's the whole thing."

"Come on, what whole thing?"

"You won't remember, but it's just like when Dad had his accident."

"What are you talking about?"

"I told you you wouldn't remember."

"How could I? I was only two or three when it happened."

"They called and told Mom about the accident, and she went to the hospital, and Margaret stayed here with us."

"You think Catherine's going to die, like Dad did?"

"No."

"So why are you saying it's like when Dad died?"

"Forget it."

"This always happens! You start telling me something and then you clam up. Just tell me—what's so secret about what happened when Dad died? Was it his fault or what?"

"I don't know whose fault it was. It was a motorcycle accident. He got hit by a car that went through a stop sign ..."

9

"I know that," Damien blurted out. "Everyone just keeps repeating that, but there's a secret that everyone's in on—except me, and maybe Catherine."

"It's not like there's some big thing everyone's hiding. Mom went kind of crazy when Dad died. She was out of it and did weird things like chewing on rubber bands and cardboard. She was pregnant with Catherine and everyone—mostly Margaret—was scared she'd do something that would hurt the baby, so she went to a mental hospital. Margaret made up stories about where she was, but I knew she was lying. I heard her talking on the phone about a psychiatric ward in a hospital. Even after Mom got home, they kept lying about where she'd been."

"So what's the big deal about being on a mental ward?"

"It's not a big deal."

"Were you scared when Rose was in the hospital?"

"What do you think? I was only five, Dad was dead, and Mom was in a mental hospital," Erin said, his voice cracking.

"Sorry I got you upset."

"I'm not upset."

"Okay, let's talk about something else."

"All right, but I don't want to talk about Catherine either. She's in the hospital by now, and they're doing whatever it is she needs to have done, and us trying to guess what's going to happen won't change anything."

"Why are you jumping all over me? I didn't say I wanted to talk about her."

"I could tell that's what you wanted to talk about."

"No, it wasn't. Why don't we just watch television?"

They sat quietly as they watched a program neither of them paid attention to. Damien's right shoulder was pushed up against Erin's left arm.

Damien was first to hear Margaret calling upstairs, "Erin, D, would you like some hot chocolate?"

"Nah, I'm not hungry," Damien yelled back.

"Then come down and keep me company. It would help me with the waiting."

Erin said to Damien, "We should go down."

Margaret was surprised to see Damien walking slowly into the kitchen, a stride behind Erin. He usually wouldn't sit in the same room with her.

The two boys sat across from one another at the round kitchen table. Damien's gaze was fixed downward on the square foot of checkered tablecloth in front of him.

After pouring a cup of hot chocolate for Erin, Margaret said to Damien, "You sure I can't pour you a cup of hot chocolate?"

"Yeah."

"'Yeah,' you'd like some, or 'yeah,' you're sure you don't want some?"

"Yeah, I'll have some," he grumbled.

"D, you've had a weak spot for hot chocolate since you were small. You used to call it 'choco-treat.'"

Damien gruffly pushed his chair back from the table and said as he stood up, "I've changed my mind. I'm not hungry. And please don't ever call me 'D' again."

Margaret betrayed not the slightest bit of emotion, though she felt painfully exposed as a failure, once again, in her effort to be motherly to Damien, who was her son as well as her nephew.

# THREE

Rose had been standing in the waiting room for an hour, maybe two. She was too anxious to sit. The plate glass windows traversing the full length of the room were now completely black, throwing back at her a reflection of herself surrounded by orange vinyl couches and armchairs. She quickly averted her eyes after glimpsing her reflection. She hated the sight of herself.

A female voice calling Rose's name barely pierced the din of the two enormous television sets hanging from the ceiling, facing the family groups that were gathered like Bedouins under blankets. Children played at the feet of multiple generations of adults. Rose made her way over the extended legs of the adults and through the clusters of squirming children on the floor. In the small piece of unoccupied space near the twin doors to the room, Rose saw a dour-looking woman in a white nurse's uniform, impatiently waiting.

The nurse, after verifying that Rose was in fact the person whose name she had called, told Rose that Dr. Weber, the director of the Pediatrics ICU, would see her now. The nurse led the way down the hall toward the ICU and stopped at a door with DR. WEBER printed on a badly scratched, stainless steel nameplate, which had been slipped into a horizontal metal holder. The nurse knocked on the door.

A man inside said loudly and distractedly, "Come in," as if the pressing work in which he was absorbed were being intruded upon. The nurse opened the door and with her eyes directed Rose to go in. Dr. Weber, sitting behind a gray metal desk, said, "Mrs." and then broke off midway to look at a medical chart before saying, "Keane, Mrs. Keane. I'm Dr. Weber."

Dr. Weber was a man who looked to Rose to be in his mid-forties—a good-looking man despite the cratered surface of his cheeks and chin, probably scars left by severe acne. He was about six feet tall, with thinning, straight blond hair, pallid complexion, and piercing blue eyes. Looking toward her, but without actually focusing his eyes on her, he asked Rose to sit down in one of the two metal chairs in front of the desk.

"I'm glad to be able to tell you that Catherine has regained consciousness. You'll be able to see her when we finish talking." Thumbing through the chart, he spoke without looking up at Rose. "Your daughter's fall has resulted in a bad concussion and some contusion. It's the possible bleeding associated with contusion that most concerns me. I want to keep Catherine in the Pediatrics ICU at least a couple of days to keep close tabs on her. I'd like to be able to tell you that your daughter is out of the woods, but it's not so."

"I don't understand a lot of the terms you've used, and so I'm not sure I understand anything more than 'she's not yet out of the woods'—that part I understood."

Dr. Weber closed the chart in front of him and looked at Rose for the first time. The person he saw was a charmingly self-deprecating, very pretty woman with soft green eyes. A good deal of what made Rose so immediately endearing to him was the innocence in her face. The trace of an Irish accent in which her words were wrapped made her all the more appealing to him. He saw in the chart that Rose was thirty-nine, but he thought she looked much younger.

14

Rose could feel his eyes sizing her up, which was a very discomfiting feeling for her. She felt that she'd been a cute little girl and a pretty young woman, but she'd aged terribly after Brian died, and was now just one more invisible middle-aged woman.

"I'm sorry I've used so many technical terms, so let me try again. Your daughter, … Catherine, has suffered a concussion and a contusion. A concussion is a blackout that occurs when the brain, which floats in fluid in the skull, slams into one of the walls of the skull, as happened to Catherine when she fell down the stairs. It doesn't cause permanent damage unless it's severe. A contusion is a bruising of the brain that may cause the brain to swell or bleed. Only a small amount of swelling has shown up on the scan so far. And in terms of prognosis, it's too early to say for sure, but we seem to be headed in the right direction."

Tears rolled down Rose's cheeks. Dr. Weber looked for a box of tissues, but couldn't find one. Rose could see that he was embarrassed by the fact that he couldn't even locate any tissues in this office space that he shared with countless other doctors who slid their nameplates into the metal holder on the door as soon as he left the room. He was a hospital employee, a replaceable part in a machine. Rose imagined that he wished he had an office of his own that would instill in his patients, the moment they entered the room, a feeling that they were in the right place, in good hands. She was aware that she was inventing this doctor, as she did most strangers, and would hold onto her invention, much preferring it to the actual person.

"So, let's go see Catherine," Dr. Weber said, giving up his search for tissues. "I should warn you that all the beeping and flashing lights of the machines can be frightening if you're not used to them. And there's quite a bit of bruising on Catherine's face, which will be painful to the touch for the next day or two. Only a child's tendons and ligaments are flexible enough to allow someone to fall down a flight of stairs without breaking a single bone. We're trying not to use painkillers because we don't want to mask changes in her level of alertness.

"After you spend some time with Catherine, you could spend the night in the waiting room, if you choose, but the hospital sleeps too, and not much goes on here. I recommend that you go home and get some sleep. The ward secretary has your home number. I'll tell her to call you if there are any new developments. I know that those words, 'new developments,' are the stuff nightmares are made of, but we'll have to live with that for a few days."

Rose liked Dr. Weber's manner of speaking—formal, but with a note of genuine concern. She particularly liked the fact that he used the word *we* when talking about waiting to see what would happen to Catherine.

"Yes, I'd very much like to see Catherine," Rose said. "Will you be bringing me to her or will you have a nurse do that, if that's not what doctors do. I apologize. The words aren't coming out right."

"Mrs. Keane …"

"Please call me Rose."

"I'd be pleased to, and I'm Michael."

Michael Weber smiled at Rose warmly. She walked next to him toward the large, padded doors of the Pediatrics ICU, which swung open when he pressed the large red button on the wall to the right of the doors. Passing through the inward pointing doors, escorted by Dr. Weber, Rose felt the way she had as a young girl when walking at her father's side, before he deserted the family.

Dr. Weber had been wrong. It wasn't the flashing lights and cacophony of beeping sounds that would upset Rose; it was the faces of the children. There were five or six beds on each side of the room, spread fairly far apart. The child in the first bed on her left must have been comatose. He looked nothing like a sleeping child, more like a child who had just died. Rose closed her eyes in an effort to remove the image of the boy's face from her mind, but his face was still there as if imprinted on the inner side of her eyelids. From then on, she tried to keep her eyes out of focus while walking beside Dr. Weber. She could not keep from hearing the sound of another child—his voice hoarse, calling for his mother.

The ICU was blanketed in semi-darkness. An odor that seemed to be a mixture of urine, alcohol, and ammonia hung thickly in the air. Dr. Weber picked up his pace and was now walking ahead of Rose. Through squinted eyes, Rose spotted Catherine lying on her back in her hospital bed, her eyes closed. As Rose approached, she could see that Catherine's face was swollen, with large reddish-purple blotches on her forehead, right cheek, and the area around her right eye, extending back past her ear and disappearing under her hair. Rose became momentarily disoriented, realizing that Dr. Weber was no longer there. Catherine opened her eyes, sensing her mother's presence.

Rose, greatly relieved by the sight of Catherine's eyes, leaned over the round metal bars on the right side of Catherine's bed, trying to get her arms around her shoulders without pulling out the IV needle or the electrical leads. She leaned down as far as she could to kiss Catherine very lightly on the unbruised portions of her cheeks and forehead. Catherine lay still as if tolerating a dog's rough tongue licking her face.

"Sweetheart, they've finally let me come and see you. Are you in a lot of pain?"

"Mom, you're always making a big deal about everything."

Rose smiled, delighted to hear Catherine chastise her.

"You're right, the only things that have happened are that you fell down the stairs, got knocked out, and were brought to the hospital in an ambulance."

"You're always making things sound worse than they are."

"I don't care if you roll your eyes, you've been through a lot. How long have you been awake?"

"On and off for a while. What time is it? What day is it? Why don't they have any windows in this place? You can't tell if it's day or night."

"It's 10:30 at night," Rose said looking at her watch. "It's still Sunday, the same day you fell."

"Will they let you stay with me here, or will they make you leave? I don't want you to leave. It's so much better since you got here."

"I've been in the waiting room the whole time you've been here, but they don't like parents getting in the way."

"So they're going to make you leave soon?"

"I don't know how soon, but they're going to make me leave the ICU so you and the other children here can get some sleep. I don't think they want the children who don't have their mothers here to feel even worse than they do already."

"That makes no sense at all. Since there are some children whose mothers aren't here, everybody should feel as bad as they do?"

"Catherine Keane, you're a very smart girl, and you can argue a case better than I can argue against it. You'll make a very good lawyer when you grow up."

"You're always doing that. You're changing the subject from the stupid rules they have here to me becoming a great lawyer."

"I'll ask if I can stay."

"No, don't just ask, because that would be acting like a sheep asking directions to the slaughter house. You have to act confident. Tell them, 'I'd like to stay with my daughter, Catherine. I'll be very quiet so no one will notice me.' Can't you do that?"

"I'm more like the sheep who's asking for directions."

"Will you at least try?"

"I will, but don't get your hopes up."

Rose looked around the ICU to see if Dr. Weber was still there. She caught sight of him talking quietly with a nurse at the foot of the bed of one of the children.

"I can't bring myself to ask to be treated differently from all the other mothers."

"So stay in the waiting room. Do they have bunk beds there?"

"No, it's just a room filled with vinyl chairs and couches. I'll do whatever would make you feel better."

"Don't leave it to me. I'd feel bad about you lying on a plastic couch all night. I don't want to make the decision for you."

"All right, I'll make up my mind when the time comes. I'm here now, so let's just talk. You must have been terrified falling down the stairs, not being able to stop, not knowing what was going to happen."

"No, it wasn't like that. It was like it was happening in slow motion. It wasn't me falling, it was me watching myself fall. It's hard to explain. I saw the stairs and the banister moving, not me moving. Every once in a while I saw the banister hit my head, but it didn't hurt. I saw you at the bottom of the stairs. You were very still, and you were trying to get our eyes to meet, and I was too, but things were moving too fast to be able to do it. While it was happening, I thought it was weird that I wasn't feeling scared. The next thing I remember is beginning to wake up here."

"Catherine Keane, you are a good little storyteller. You got it just right. It was something like that for me, too. It was in slow motion with lots of time to think of other things, like your haircut, and the time when we were buying the Nike sneakers you were wearing."

Rose decided to sleep in her own bed at home. She was relieved that Catherine didn't cry when she left.

Margaret heard Rose's car in the driveway and met Rose at the door in her bedclothes—not a nightgown, but pajamas that looked like men's pajamas. It was almost midnight. Erin and Damien thumped down the stairs to see what was happening.

"Catherine woke up and seems to be returning to normal," Rose said as they stood at the foot of the stairs where Catherine

19

had lain unconscious six or seven hours earlier. "She's in the ICU. Her face is badly bruised, but she didn't break any bones. The doctor said that she's not out of the woods yet, but there are encouraging signs. She was herself when we talked, correcting everything I said, in the way she does, but not at all in an angry way. We'll just have to wait. I'll fill you in on the details in the morning. Now, I just have to take a bath and try to get some sleep."

As Rose lay in bed after her bath, it was Damien, not Catherine, whom she was haunted by. She went over and over in her mind, as she had for more than a decade now, what she had done to him. She knew now that she was lying to herself if she told herself she'd had no choice other than to do what she'd done. She'd had choices. She could have asked Margaret for help earlier, but she hadn't. Why hadn't she? Because keeping secret what she had done had been more important to her than Damien's welfare. It hadn't felt as if she'd had a choice at the time; it had felt as if she were caught in a current so strong that she couldn't do anything but let it carry her. "Enough," she said out loud. "Stop the excuses. You were the mother of a child in terrible distress. It was your responsibility to comfort him, and the fact is, you didn't. You did the opposite."

She tried, as she'd done countless times in the past, to interrupt this relentless cycle of self-accusation by confessing it all, by laying it all out on the table, not allowing herself to hold back a single detail of what she had done. When he cried in the middle of the night, you didn't go to him. You put him in the guest room in the far corner of the house, so his screaming wouldn't keep Catherine and Erin awake all night. Sometimes Erin came to the side of your bed saying, 'Mommy, can't you hear Damien crying? Go pick him up.' After listening to him screaming for hours, you went to his room. He'd be standing in his crib, holding onto the top edge, purple-faced from crying and shouting for you. Tears and snot and sweat covered his face and neck. You shrieked at him, 'Shut up, let me sleep,

I can't stand it! I wish you'd never been born. It's not asking too much to ask you to let me sleep. Won't you give me just an hour's sleep?'"

It was agonizing for Rose to complete her confession, but she forced herself to continue to say what she had never told anyone, and never would. "You hit him, hard. Not so hard as to leave marks, but much harder than a spank. After hitting him, you hated yourself for what you'd done, but an hour later, and the next night, and the night after that, you'd do the same thing." Rose sought no forgiveness as she spoke these words. Who was there to forgive her? Certainly not Damien, and not even Margaret.

The images in her mind and the memory of the words she'd yelled at Damien were a constant presence for her. During the day, these thoughts were like sleeping bats. At night, as she tried to sleep, they awoke and flew at her from all angles. In vain attempts to escape them, she'd get out of bed and sit in the kitchen.

The night of Catherine's fall, after chain-smoking at the kitchen table while waiting for the call from the hospital telling her something awful had happened to Catherine, she stood, opened the cabinets under the sink, and reached to the back where she hid the bottle of bourbon. She took a juice glass out of the sink and poured herself a drink. Rose hated the taste of it. She drank it in three gulps, which sent a shudder through her. And then, miraculously, she felt calm. The relief was always a surprise. She'd grown to like the burning in her throat that lingered. She wasn't an alcoholic, she told herself. She really didn't care if she was or not. The bourbon ended the self-torture. The accusations ceased—the bats returned to the crevices in which they slept, as if waiting for the fog brought on by the bourbon to clear.

That night, the bourbon silenced the screaming in her head, but couldn't numb the terror that the phone would ring.

In the very early hours of the morning, the phone did ring.

21

# FOUR

Erin and Damien were relieved to hear that Catherine had regained consciousness and that she was getting better. They returned to their bedroom and got back into bed, neither boy saying a word. They fell asleep listening to the soft rumbling of their mother's bath water and the sound of someone talking, which didn't surprise them. They'd grown accustomed to Rose's talking to herself at night.

Later that same night, Erin was awoken by Damien, who was rummaging for something across the room in the dark. Erin switched on the table lamp next to his bed, which filled the room with yellowish light that cast thick black shadows across the walls and floor.

Erin, at first, could only make out the outlines of Damien as his eyes adjusted to the light.

"What are you doing?"

"Looking for my radio."

"Why?"

"Can't sleep."

"How come?"

"I just can't."

Damien began to cry and turned to leave the room. Erin, whose bed was closer to the door, jumped out of bed and

23

planted himself squarely between Damien and the door. Considerably larger than Erin, and not wanting to knock his brother down, Damien tried to outmaneuver him like a football player sidestepping a defender. Erin was able to get an arm around Damien's waist as he tried to get by. Though Damien could have twisted free, he didn't. He just stopped where he was in Erin's half-embrace. He didn't turn his head because that would have brought his face too close to Erin's.

"Damien, what's going on?"

"Nothing."

Erin let his arm drop from Damien's waist. He turned and walked to his bed, and with his eyes still focused on Damien's face, sat on the side of his bed.

With sleep still in his voice, Erin said, "Come on. Sit down on your bed."

Damien inhaled deeply, and with his cheeks full, exhaled slowly as he sat down. As Erin watched Damien, he had the thought that his body was three sizes too big for his age and his maturity.

"Is it about Catherine?" Erin asked.

"Yeah."

"Is it about seeing Catherine fall down the stairs?"

"No, it's not that. It is, but it's not what you think."

"It's about her falling, but it's not?"

"You wouldn't get it."

"Get what?"

"I pushed her. I tried to get my hand on her shoulder to pull her back, but I couldn't."

"You think it's your fault that she fell?"

"I don't think it, I know it."

"What do you mean, you know it?"

"I told you. I pushed her."

"You didn't push her. I was there. I saw what happened."

"Just listen to me. I pushed her, on purpose. I don't know why I did it. I wasn't angry at her or anything like that. She

24

wasn't being a pest like she sometimes is. I just pushed her for no reason. I tried to pull her back, but I couldn't reach her."

"I don't understand what you're talking about."

"We were chasing around, remember?" Damien said impatiently. "And you caught up with me on the landing. I forget exactly what happened, but we were down on the floor wrestling, near Catherine. I got up while you were still on the ground and I pushed her."

"You did not push her," Erin said, enunciating each word slowly.

"I know I pushed her. I could feel the tips of my fingers touch the thin shirt she was wearing."

"We both know what Catherine's back feels like. We've both lifted her up so she could reach something, we've pushed her out of the way, and other stuff. So the fact that you know what her back feels like doesn't mean anything. I was there. You didn't push her."

Damien was now shivering and his teeth were chattering. Erin moved over to Damien's bed, and sat next to him. He put his arm around Damien's broad back. The force of the rattle of Damien's body ran through Erin's arm, and deep into his chest and abdomen.

Erin calmly asked Damien, "Have I ever lied to you, except when we're playing some game and we're both making stuff up?"

Damien was silent.

"Have I?"

"No, you don't usually lie," Damien said, begrudgingly.

"What do you mean I don't *usually* lie? I *never* lie when it comes to something serious. You know that's true, don't you?"

"Yeah, I guess."

"You guess? Admit it, I'm right about that."

"Yeah, you're right, you don't lie, but I know I did it."

Erin kept his arm around Damien's back until he stopped shivering.

# FIVE

Rose dressed quickly after receiving the call from the ward clerk and arrived at the hospital at about quarter to five in the morning. A faint turquoise streak had begun to form at the horizon as she pulled into the visitors' outdoor parking lot. She'd had another couple of swallows of bourbon before leaving the house. Walking from the lot to the main entrance to the hospital, she could hear the sound of distant highway traffic. Several night workers in dark blue jumpsuits were standing outside one of the back exits of the hospital, talking loudly and laughing together. Rose couldn't stop herself from endlessly recounting the voice of the ICU ward clerk saying that the doctor had asked her to notify her that there had been a change in Catherine's condition. Those were the words the ward clerk had used—"a change in Catherine's condition." The woman said she didn't know what change had occurred. Rose didn't believe her.

The doors to the Pediatrics ICU remained closed when Rose pressed the red button that Dr. Weber had used to open them. She stood there paralyzed by fear that Catherine was dead. The doors opened, as if by magic, for a thin black man in scrubs pushing a metal cart with loose, squeaking wheels. Rose walked next to the man as he pushed his cart into the ICU.

Once inside, Rose was unable to find Catherine, which confirmed her fear that Catherine was dead. She had never in her life felt the depth of panic she was feeling now. Waves of nausea passed through her. Her legs felt as if they were about to collapse, but she had to find out what had happened. She made her way slowly to the glass window of the nurses' station.

"Excuse me," Rose said, apologetically.

No reply. Not even a glance in her direction.

"Excuse me," Rose said a little louder.

Still no sign of recognition.

"I've been called at home about my daughter, Catherine Keane. Will someone please help me find her?"

Rose wondered if no sound was coming from her mouth. Had she become mute? She left the nurses' station and walked the length of the ICU, peering through the dim light at the children, one by one, hoping not to find Catherine on a respirator or some other life-support device, but fearing her absence even more.

From behind her, Rose heard the voice of a woman saying with great annoyance, "Ma'am, visitors aren't allowed in the ICU except during visiting hours without doctors' authorization. Would you please leave now."

Rose turned and saw a diminutive, officious looking nurse, staring at her with an expression of exasperation and disgust, as if she'd sighted a pool of urine on the linoleum floor.

"I have doctors' authorization," Rose replied, surprising herself with the strength of her voice. "A woman who said she was the ward clerk here called me at home at four-fifteen in the morning and told me that the doctor had asked her to call to tell me that something had happened to my daughter, Catherine Keane. I don't know if that qualifies as doctors' authorization, but if it isn't, it's a very good way to scare the shit out of a mother."

"Why didn't you tell this to someone at the nurses' station?"

"I tried to, but no one ..."

"Follow me. Your daughter is in one of the isolation rooms at the rear of the ICU."

The words "isolation rooms" couldn't refer to anything good, Rose thought, but she was so relieved to hear that Catherine was alive that the words were beautiful music to her. As she followed the nurse, the clamor of the beeping machines faded. There were two rooms on each side of the darkened hallway into which they walked, each with a large plate glass window through which Rose could see a child sleeping in a hospital bed, beside which stood a set of monitors lazily blinking their red and yellow digital numbers. Catherine's room was the first on the left.

A large black woman stood outside Catherine's room. The nurse, addressing no one in particular, said, "This is Brenda Williams. She's the nurse's aide assigned to the isolation rooms tonight." Without another word, the nurse turned and walked briskly in the direction from which she'd come.

Brenda said, "Sweetheart, let's go see little Catherine. Even though she's asleep, she'll know you're here."

Brenda opened the door to Catherine's room and told Rose to go in ahead of her so she could close the door behind them. As Rose approached Catherine's bed, she was terrified by what she saw. Catherine was lying on her back, absolutely still, with her eyes closed, her face devoid of color. A large white bandage that looked like a turban was wrapped around her head. Rose's knees began to buckle. Brenda was able to get her arm around Rose's waist before she fell. She slowly walked Rose to the chair next to Catherine's bed and helped her get seated. Rose tried to talk, but no words came from her mouth.

"I'm sorry, I should have prepared you before you saw Catherine. Just sit there for a while till you collect yourself. I'm not going anywhere."

Rose sat for a few minutes and then looked up at Brenda. "Please tell me what's happened. No one will tell me anything."

Brenda picked up a metal chair with a cushioned seat and placed it close to Rose's. She said, "No one but doctors is supposed to tell patients or their families 'bout their medical conditions, but it's not right to call you in the middle of the night and not tell you why they called. I'll tell you what I know to tide you over till one of the doctors come to talk with you. I listen very carefully to what the doctors say when they talk about a patient among theirselves or give orders to an RN. Around two this morning, I was talking with Catherine out in the main room of the ICU, trying to help her get as calm as someone can in a place like this. I was talking to her 'bout where I grew up, and this and that, hopin' the sound of me talkin' on and on would put her to sleep. She did fall asleep, but when I came back to check on her a few minutes later, she didn't look right to me. I tried to wake her by talking to her, and then by holding her hand tight, and finally by pressing hard on her chest with my knuckle, but she didn't stir. She couldn't wake up, so I told the head nurse and she called Dr. Richards. He examined her and after only a few minutes she was taken by gurney to surgery. She wasn't there all that long, only a couple of hours. She only got back here an hour or so ago. She was awake, but groggy when she got back, which I can tell you is a very good sign. Don't be scared by the gauze wrapped 'round her head. It's keeping clean the place where they drained the blood. Catherine's here, in an isolation room, to protect her from infection."

"I don't understand."

"What don't you understand, hun?"

"Why they took her to surgery?"

"Because a bleed right inside her skull was pressin' down, creatin' too much pressure, and they had to drain the blood through a small hole they made in her skull."

"Were they able to drain the blood?"

"Yes, and they left in a tube in case they have to drain more blood some time. The gauze 'round Catherine's head is protecting the tube from infection."

"Is she all right?"

"Only the doctors can tell you that."

Brenda paused before adding, "I've seen lots of children come and go from this hospital. The thing that's impressed me most is the fight they got in them, and none of them's had more fight than I've seen in little Catherine—that's more important than any medicine they have here to give these children. They hold onto life stronger than adults, maybe 'cause they haven't had their chance yet. There's lots of praying done on the children's ward, but I don't go in much for praying. The faith I got is in the children theirselves."

Brenda took Rose's right hand and held it between her two big hands. Tears rolled down Rose's cheeks. Brenda reached for a tissue and blotted the tears around Rose's eyes and cheeks.

"You look awful tired, sweetheart. Having a child in the hospital takes it out of you. My two boys were never in the hospital, but both of them were in Vietnam: Both did two tours. They wrote me when they weren't out in the jungle fighting. Those years are a blur to me. It seemed like forever they were gone. I was raised religious, Southern Baptist, but what I saw of the war on television changed all that. I don't know how I got from one day to the next, so I don't have any secrets to give you about how to get through this. You just kind of hold your breath, I guess, is how I'd put it. That's how it was for me. You'll find your own way, I know you will."

Brenda continued to talk to Rose about her two boys, even after she saw that Rose had stopped listening to the words. Rose's eyes got heavy and then closed. Brenda carefully removed Rose's hand from between her own, and placed her hands on her lap. After wrapping a blanket around Rose's shoulders and arms, Brenda quietly left, but kept close watch from the hallway.

Rose sensed movement beside her and opened her eyes to find Brenda waking Catherine, as she did every half-hour during the night to monitor Catherine's mental state.

31

Catherine turned to Rose. "Mommy, what's happened to me?"

"You blacked out again, and they had to do a surgical procedure."

Just as Rose began to try to repeat what Brenda had told her, Dr. Weber knocked on the door before he and his entourage of doctors and nurses filed into the room. After saying good morning to Rose and Catherine, he gave Catherine a neurological examination that took about ten minutes.

Turning to Rose, he said, "Catherine had a bleed into the space between her skull and her brain last night. The surgeons drilled a burr hole in her skull on the right side, behind her hairline, and drained the blood. They made sure that no further bleeding was occurring. They left in a small, temporary catheter. We'll use that to monitor Catherine's intracranial pressure, which will tell us if there is any further bleeding, and if there is, we'll drain the blood through the catheter. Catherine was semi-conscious by the time she got back from surgery and continued to regain consciousness during the next few hours. I expect Catherine to fully regain consciousness by the end of the day, but there can be plateaus and even setbacks along the way. We just have to let the body do its work of healing. That's easy to say, but agonizing to do."

An hour or so later, while Catherine was sleeping, Dr. Weber asked Rose to come into the hallway outside Catherine's room. "I didn't want to frighten Catherine when I explained what was happening. There is more that you should know. The tube the surgeons left in will be useful to drain small quantities of blood, but if there is a major subdural bleed, the surgeons will perform a craniotomy to drain the blood and staunch the bleeding. A craniotomy involves removing a part of the skull and then reattaching it after the bleeding has been stopped."

"How much danger is Catherine in?"

"She has what's called an acute subdural hematoma. It has to be monitored extremely closely because it can result in a major bleed that is very difficult to stop. I don't want to frighten you unnecessarily. I don't think that that is going to happen, but you should know the truth about Catherine's condition."

By evening, Catherine was able to talk coherently, but with slightly slurred speech. Since Catherine was in an isolation room, Rose was allowed to sleep in her room in a cot they set up next to the hospital bed. Catherine and Rose spoke and then dozed, spoke and then dozed.

## SIX

During the hours that Rose sat next to Catherine's bed, her mind was drawn to the past. The details of particular days felt as clear and immediate now as they'd been when they occurred. Rose's thoughts most often were drawn to that evening when she had called Margaret and asked her to come to the house after the children were asleep. The torpor of that hot, humid day in July had been shattered by a thunderstorm in the late afternoon, leaving in its wake thick, cool evening air.

Once Margaret arrived, they sat in the living room, which was strewn with plastic toys, wooden blocks, and bright red metal trucks and cars. A dark wooden coffee table stood askew between the peach-colored couch and the fireplace. Margaret cleared the drawing books and crayons off one end of the couch to make a place to sit, while Rose turned on several floor lamps, straightened the coffee table, and slid one of the armchairs close to the end of the couch where Margaret was sitting.

Rose began by saying, "I can't manage."

"I'm surprised to hear you say that. I think you've been doing very well under the circumstances. Brian died only six months ago."

"I've been a terrible mother since Brian died, and even before he died. You don't know how terrible, and I'm too ashamed to tell you."

"Don't you think things will get better as time passes?"

"You're not listening to what I'm trying to tell you. It's not a matter of a widow grieving her lost husband, it's much, much worse than that. I'm all alone here and I'm not doing well at all, and I keep getting worse as a mother, not better."

"I hope you know that you always have me."

"I do know that. You're the only person I have. I'm going to say something that you'll find deplorable, but you're the only person I can tell."

"You think you're the only one who does terrible things?"

"Just hear me out. Catherine has been a good baby. She doesn't demand a lot, she's easy to nurse, and she sleeps through the night almost every night now. But she's still a baby. Erin is very independent. He doesn't ask for much, but he needs me all the more now that he's lost Brian, whom he worshipped. The problem is Damien. No, that's not right—I'm the problem, the way I've been treating Damien."

"All four of you are missing Brian …"

"Margaret, hear me out. Damien was a very difficult baby. Even now he doesn't sleep through the night. Things were never right between Damien and me. It wasn't like it was with Erin, who was so easy to love, or with Catherine, who is such a sweet baby. It didn't get easier with Damien as he got older, it got worse, and it's been intolerable since Brian died. But it's not just Brian not being here, it's that Damien and I never made a connection with one another. I know this sounds terrible, but he feels like a stranger in my house. Really, he always has. Even when Brian was alive, I wasn't good with him. That's an understatement: I've done things to him that are unforgivable. What I'm about to ask you will come as a shock to you, and I'm ashamed to be asking it. It's hard to say it." Rose paused as she struggled to get the words out of her mouth. "Would you consider taking Damien?"

Margaret didn't know what to say. The question confused her.

"It's just an idea," Rose said. "All I'm asking is that you think about it. I know it's asking you to change everything, to change the way you live your life. I'll try to stop talking so you can say something."

"I'm not sure what you're asking."

"I know this sounds appalling, and I'd be horrified if I heard another mother say these words, but what I'm asking you to think about is taking Damien and raising him as your own child."

Margaret was stunned by Rose's request. She felt profound sadness for Rose and Damien. She knew that Rose had been struggling, but she had no idea that it had come to this. As she tried to imagine what it might be like to be a mother to Damien, images and memories and thoughts vied with one another for first entry onto center stage—images of watching Rose bathing and dressing and comforting her dolls while she looked on, feeling freakish for having that empty space in her where the feelings that Rose was having ought to be; images of their father fussing over Rose while she stood there only a few feet away, invisible to them; images of that day when she was six or seven, when she had gone to the bathroom, locked the door, taken off all her clothes, and looked at herself in the full-length mirror attached to the back of the bathroom door, to see if she was a boy or a girl. She hadn't known what a boy looked like down there, so she couldn't be sure if she was a boy or a girl. What she did know was that she didn't like the things Rose and other girls liked—trying on their mother's shoes and dresses and jewelry and make-up, listening to stories about princesses and unicorns, decorating their hair with glitter, and having stars painted on the ceiling of her room.

None of it interested her. She hadn't liked the things boys liked either—guns and trucks and bats and tackling one another. All of that seemed ridiculous to her. Even after her body changed in adolescence and her hideous periods began, she didn't feel feminine in the way Rose was. This was one of the few secrets she kept from Rose, though she thought Rose knew anyway.

Margaret said that she wanted to be certain she understood what Rose was proposing. Rose explained that she was asking her to have Damien come live with her and to raise him as her own child. Margaret had long ago given up the idea of ever having children of her own, which had not felt like a great loss. In fact, she'd felt an enormous weight lifted from her when she accepted the fact that having children would not be part of her life. She and Rose had settled into their different ways of living their lives—Rose enjoyed her children, while Margaret enjoyed her career. After her brief marriage, she found that living alone suited her very well.

Margaret broke the silence by saying, "I know that something horrible is happening between you and Damien. The question is whether giving him to me is the best solution to the problem."

Rose responded dejectedly, "No, you don't understand. This isn't a problem to solve, this is an emergency, a house in flames. It's something that has to be done *now* for Damien's sake. He's a good-hearted boy and should not be subjected to the way I treat him. No child should. I feel so ashamed of what I've done that I can't tell you the specifics of it. You just have to take my word for it."

Margaret was silent for quite some time before saying, "Rose, we both know that I've been much more focused on achieving things in a man's world than achieving things in a woman's world. I've acted as if, and even believed, that I don't miss the female things I haven't had, but sometimes I do. Sometimes when I leave your house, I miss what you have with your children and the marriage that you had with Brian."

"I'm sorry to interrupt again, but you overestimate my marriage. This isn't the time to go into it, so go on with what you were saying."

"I was trying to be honest with you about my feeling that something's missing in my life that I can't get vicariously from you and your family. That's not a feeling I have most of the time, but when I feel it, I feel it strongly. So the idea of raising Damien is something that I'm open to considering."

Rose chose her words carefully as she said, "You must be asking yourself why I think that you'll do better with Damien than I have. Some children simply are not a fit with their parents. Damien is one of those children, for me. From the moment he was born he didn't feel like my child. I think Brian felt that way too, though he never said those words out loud. No child is born unlovable, but a child may be born to parents incapable of loving him. You've spent time with Damien. What am I saying? You took care of both Erin and Damien while I was in the hospital right after Brian died. You know what a sweet boy he is. You'll do fine with him, and you'll both come to love each other very much."

As Rose spoke, Margaret wondered if she were capable of loving Damien—or any child, for that matter. Rose was the only person she had ever loved. If it weren't for Rose, she wouldn't know what the word meant. She had depended on their mother when she was very small, but that's a different thing from loving her, she thought. Margaret remembered feeling, while still in elementary school, that their mother was pathetic for believing their father's lies. And, she couldn't blame Martin for trying to wring love out of her, and becoming enraged with her and divorcing her. She wondered if Rose really believed she'd do better with Damien than she'd been able to. Rose didn't lie about important things like this, so she probably believed what she was saying. Most of it, anyway.

They both were tired and felt that there was nothing more they could say that night. Margaret looked at her watch and said, "It's getting late. I'd better go."

Rose called Margaret on a Sunday morning, a few days after she'd asked Margaret to take Damien. She said that the situation with Damien was getting much worse. They arranged to meet that evening at Rose's house, after the children were asleep.

When Margaret arrived and they were seated in Rose's living room, Margaret began, "At times it feels to me as if we're playing God with Damien. But it's our job to make decisions like this for him. To tell you the truth, I'm not at all sure I have it in me to be a good mother to him."

Interrupting, Rose said pleadingly, "I need to know. Please, tell me what you're going to do."

"You know I'm not good with children."

"Margaret, stop it. Are you going to take Damien or aren't you?"

Margaret nodded and said, "I will. I've decided that's what I want to do."

"I …," Rose said, trying to complete the sentence she had in her head, but finding it impossible to continue, the words seeming to be caught in a constriction of her throat. She made several more attempts to complete the sentence, and then put up her hand as a way of asking Margaret to give her time to finish saying what she wanted to say before Margaret said anything more. After a minute or so, Rose, brushing away the tears that had gathered at her chin, said, "Margaret, I feel as if you've saved Damien's life, and mine. I genuinely believe that this is best for him, and I hope it's best for you, too."

After a long pause, Margaret said, "There's something I've been afraid to talk to you about, but there isn't any way around it. I've been thinking about how to make it real between the three of us—between you, me, and Damien—that I'm Damien's mother, not for a day or a week or a year, but for as long as he and I live, and even after I die. I don't think I could open my heart to Damien unless I know for sure that my heart won't be broken. I couldn't bear it if in a few months or a few years, you changed your mind and wanted Damien back. If that happened, I'd have to choose between him and you, and I never want to be in that position because whatever I chose, I'd lose one of you, and probably both of you."

"I don't want that either," Rose said.

"It's my turn to say, 'This may sound horrible.' But I think that the only way I could really feel that I'm Damien's mother, for sure and forever, is if I adopt him, legally. Does that sound coldblooded?"

Rose took a deep breath, clearly taken by surprise. "To be honest, the idea never occurred to me, but I can understand how you feel."

"Are you sure you're going to be able to bear hearing him call me Mommy?"

"I've been blurring in my mind what I'm asking of you by referring to it as raising him," Rose said.

"Yes, that does blur the truth of what we're thinking of doing."

Rose could feel her face blanch and her hands become cold. She was reminded of fairy tales her mother had read to her as a child in which a character grants a wish on one condition that sounds minor, but turns out to be the equivalent of selling your soul.

Rose's tone of voice was different when, after some time, she said, "You're right, I'm not asking you to raise him, I'm asking you to be his mother forever. I hadn't been honest with myself, but that's what I'm asking of you. Adopting him makes sense."

"That's what bothers me about this. I'm not sure that you really know what you want. You're asking that the two of us do something that can't be undone. It could, I suppose—legal adoptions can be reversed—but I'm asking that that be ruled out, no matter what happens. You'd be giving up being Damien's mother forever. When he wins a race at school, he'll be bursting to tell me about it, not you. Are you sure you could take that, really sure?"

"I'm not absolutely certain, but I'm as certain as I can be about anything. Damien deserves a mother who loves him, who's proud of him, and looks forward to seeing him, and a mother who will fight with all her strength to hold on to him if someone tries to take him away from her. If there are times when I have any doubts about giving him away, and I know there will be, I will be able to get through them by reminding myself that I did this because I sincerely believed that it is what is best for this little boy."

And so the conversation ended, and the adoption process began. Rose and Margaret planned to make Damien's move from Rose's house to Margaret's a gradual one. They hoped that if Rose and Damien spent increasing amounts of time at Margaret's house, he would adjust to the change without quite knowing what was happening. But Damien did not like spending time at Margaret's house, probably because he desperately wanted something from Rose, not Margaret. It was not that he actively disliked Margaret; she was irrelevant. When Rose left him at Margaret's house for a visit on a Saturday or Sunday afternoon, he would immediately begin intoning, "I want to go home. I want to go home." At home, his temper tantrums became more violent; he broke his own toys, and

Catherine's, by throwing them against a wall or tearing them apart, something he'd never done before. He awoke even more frequently during the night, allowing Rose almost no sleep.

Very early one morning, shortly after the adoption had been approved, Rose phoned Margaret in tears, saying, "I've been up all night with Damien again. He knows what's happening and he's frightened and angry. I'm sorry to force this on you, but I have to leave him with you ..." Rose stopped speaking, not because she was sobbing, but because she was unable to hold in mind what she was trying to say.

"Margaret, I am so exhausted ..."

"We've been preparing for this long enough. When you get Erin off to school, we'll make today the day that Damien stays here with me. Just drive him over here with Catherine."

Rose arrived at Margaret's house later that morning with Damien and Catherine. They chatted while the children played, as they had done so many times in the course of the previous months. But Rose, Margaret, and Damien could all feel that something was different this time. As Rose stood up to leave, Damien wrapped his arms around her legs and held onto her as tightly as he could. Rose picked him up and said to him, "Damien, I've been too angry and too harsh with you, and that's not good for you. You deserve much more than I've been able to give you. Margaret loves you very much. She will be a much better Mommy to you than I've been."

Rose knew that Damien did not fully understand what she was saying, but she could see in his face that he understood that this parting was different from all the other times she had left him with Margaret. As Rose and Catherine made their way to the door, Damien stood motionless, staring at them with a blank expression on his face. After Margaret closed the door, Damien walked over to the living room couch, climbed up on it, put his head down, and went to sleep. Margaret covered him with an afghan, tucked him in, and sat on the couch at his feet while he slept.

# EIGHT

After Rose and Catherine left, Damien slept deeply on Margaret's living room couch, saliva dripping from his mouth. Margaret felt oddly tranquil. Despite the fact that she and Damien had begun to get used to one another during the visits he'd made to her house, she knew that Damien had not experienced her house as his home, nor had he, in any sense, come to view her as his mother. She stroked his shin as she read, the shin of a frightened little boy, now her own. He was an endearing child lying there in his blue short pants, short-sleeved orangey-yellow T shirt, and black and green striped socks. He didn't like long pants because they were too scratchy, Rose had said. Margaret had no doubt that Rose had chosen with great care this particular combination of colors and styles, just as she'd dressed her dolls when she was a girl.

When Damien eventually began to stir, after almost two hours, Margaret girded herself. Damien slowly sat up, his eyes unfocused. On his right cheek, the cheek on which he'd been sleeping, there was a perfectly round, dark red spot, about an inch-and-a-half in diameter. He surveyed the room, looking for the familiar.

"Where's Mommy?"

"She's gone to her house. I don't know if you remember what she said when she left, so I will tell you again."

"Where's Mommy?"

"Mommy said that she thought that you and I could grow to love one another more and more as we got to know each other better. I'm sure that's so, but I also know that what's happening now must be very confusing."

"I want Mommy."

"She's at her house now."

"I want to go home."

"Damien, that's what's confusing. This house is your home now. It's home for me, too."

"I want to go home," he said, his voice becoming more insistent and desperate.

"Damien, let's take a look at the toys in the corner where we play. I think I can see a new one poking its head out from behind that armchair. Can you see it?"

"Call Mommy."

Margaret moved closer to Damien on the couch. "Will you let me sit next to you and put my arm around you like we do sometimes?"

Damien moved away from Margaret, pushing himself into the large, floral pillows at the end of the couch.

Margaret felt out of her depth. "Damien, I'm going to have a look at what's behind that big yellow-striped armchair. Will you come with me?"

She got up and walked slowly toward the armchair, trying not to startle him with sudden movement. Margaret could feel his gaze on her back.

"Damien, I need your help. I want to push this big chair out of the way so I can see what's behind it, but I'm not strong enough."

Damien burst into tears. "I want Mommy … Call her … I want to go home."

His face was covered with a thick mixture of tears and mucus. Margaret returned to the couch and sat down near Damien. He cowered as she approached. He looked deeply into her eyes as he cried; his eyes, the color of dark chocolate, were rimmed with tears. She slid next to him and put her arm around his little shoulders. He pulled away. Margaret felt stunned by the enormity of what was being forced on this little guy. His mother was not going to take him home with her ever again, and he was being asked to switch not only mothers, but also families. What could that possibly mean to a child his age, or to any child? Damien and Rose had fought with one another fiercely for years but, for a child, being "given away" could not have been part of the "rules of engagement," as he understood them. How could it be? She, as a child, had only in nightmares imagined such a punishment. And yet that was exactly what she and Rose were doing to Damien, in the belief—or was it a rationalization—that they were "saving his life," and Rose's.

As Damien demanded to be taken home, Margaret, too, was tempted to take him back to Rose's house and tell her that she felt like a kidnapper and could not go through with it. Margaret looked around her living room with new eyes. This was a house not for a child but for an adult, with its Persian rugs, antique furniture, pristine white linen couch (with a saliva stain where Damien's head had been resting). She only now recognized that she had not made room for Damien in her house, much less in her heart. She had allocated to Damien a part of the house—"his room"—where he could be as messy and destructive as he wanted to be. She would not mind if he scribbled with crayons on the walls, spilled paint or ketchup on the carpeting, accidentally cut his sheets or blanket with scissors, wet his bed, or did any of the other things that children did. Margaret had gone to great lengths to "childproof" her home, but she now realized that what "childproofing" had meant to her was protecting the house from a child, rather than protecting a child from the house. She had removed everything from the living room and bedroom tables, and even from the mantelpieces in case he was so clever as to use a chair as a step stool to get his hands on the objects displayed there that she didn't want broken or damaged.

After being ignored by Damien, Margaret lifted him from the couch and placed him on the floor next to the new robot with battery-powered lights and wheels, and the red metal fire truck. He refused to even look at them.

"I want Mommy to pick me up."

"Damien, hon, you and I are going to live here, and I'm going to take good care of you, and we'll have a good time together, you just wait and see."

In speaking to Damien, Margaret was careful with the verb tenses and the ways she named, or did not name, people and things. She avoided using the past tense when speaking of Rose or her house. She made no mention of Erin or Catherine. She did not use the word Mommy. She tried not to refer to "the house where you lived" or to something "you used to do at home." Neither did Margaret refer to herself as Damien's "new Mommy" because she felt that that would be presumptuous on her part. She hadn't earned that name yet. What she was to Damien currently, Margaret did not have a name for, and neither did he.

As the afternoon turned into evening, Damien alternated between periods of torpor and despair, and fits of anger. Margaret quickly exhausted the first-line strategies with which she had hoped to lure Damien into giving her a chance. Her second-line strategies aimed simply at making it clear that the two of them were going to have to make the best of the situation. They were stuck with one another, whether they liked it or not. Life was to be endured as best they could manage. Joy should not be expected by either of them, for the time being. Loneliness would have to be endured. Margaret could not expect to feel that her maternal instinct was of any value to Damien, if in fact it existed at all; Damien could not expect to feel that he was sufficiently lovable to deserve a mother. Margaret would have to settle for the role of manager and referee so that things did not get out of hand. While there would be fear and loneliness and desperation on both their parts, no physical harm would come to anyone or anything. There would be anger and animosity, but not cruelty. In the absence of love, there would be civility. Love would come much later, if at all. Affection would be withheld, but withholding of recognition of the other's existence would not be tolerated. Each time Margaret spoke to Damien, she made a point of using his name; Damien never used Margaret's name and rarely made eye contact with her, but he did not pretend she didn't exist. It was a pock-marked connection, but not a mutilating one.

Neither Margaret nor Damien ate much of anything during their first week together. Margaret did not cook—she had never really learned to cook—she bought frozen or prepared dishes at a delicatessen in town and heated them in the microwave. They both slept fitfully through the night, each in their own room, and took naps during the day. Damien would fall asleep so quickly and unexpectedly, regardless of time of day or location in the house, that Margaret worried he was suffering from some kind of seizure disorder. When he fell asleep in this way, whether it was on the floor, on the couch, or in the cabinet under the staircase, he could not be awoken by jostling him or even by pinching him. When Damien collapsed into this strange form of sleep, Margaret would carry him to his bed, tuck him in, and lie down next to him. Those were the most intimate moments of their early days together.

Even in the absence of love between the two of them, Margaret, having set her mind to making this work, would not be diverted from her goal. But at the same time, she was not one to be a martyr. She had a very good job at the bank, which she thoroughly enjoyed, and had no intention of giving it up. Damien was to be an addition to her former life, not a replacement of it.

By the end of their first week together, Damien had come to accept Margaret a bit more, though he wasn't at all sure who she was. The coexistence that the two of them worked out had come more easily than Margaret had expected. Having achieved that equilibrium with Damien, Margaret felt that the time had arrived for her to hire a nanny to look after Damien while she was at work. She placed ads both in the *Chicago Sun Times* and the local newspaper, *The Gazette*: "Live-in nanny wanted. Must be of strong will and kind heart. In-law unit with separate entry provided. Generous pay."

The morning the ad appeared, the phone began ringing at five-thirty. Margaret eliminated the callers who began by asking about wages, as she did those who took deep drags on cigarettes between sentences. Margaret scheduled three interviews later the same day and three the following morning. She made a point of having Damien at the interviews, which she held in the living room. In each interview, she chose a moment to leave the room on one pretext or another. Margaret would then listen from just outside the living room. Damien obliged by doing something he knew was off-limits to him. One of the applicants ignored Damien, even as he took the brass shovel from beside the fireplace and used it to try to dig holes in the wood flooring. Another told him to behave like a good little boy and stop being destructive to his mommy's beautiful house.

One applicant surprised Margaret, not altogether pleasantly. She was a diminutive black woman named Sybil Wentwood, who spoke with a Jamaican accent that made every sentence she uttered sound like a song. When Margaret left the living room, Damien began to pull books, one at a time, from the built-in bookshelves that spanned half of one side of the large room. Sybil walked over to the shelves, got down on the floor next to him, and asked if he needed any help.

Damien looked at her dismissively. He then continued what he'd been doing as if she weren't there.

"Damien, would you let me show you how I did this when I was a girl about your age? I wasn't as big and strong as you are, but my heart was in it."

He ignored her.

From the other end of the bookshelf that Damien was emptying, Sybil reached behind a row of books as far as her arm could reach, and sent the books flying all over the floor, some sailing as far as six or seven feet from their places on the shelf, and making more ear-jarring noise than Damien's books had achieved. Damien was clearly impressed by the explosiveness of the act, but nonetheless was annoyed by this woman who refused to be ignored. Much as he would have liked to, he couldn't refrain from trying out her method of emptying the shelves. What he lacked in the reach of his arm, he made up for in the force with which he flung the books. After he'd emptied a few rows of books, he looked at her as if to see if she had any other ideas.

Sybil began carefully piling the books that now littered the floor, one on top of the other, until the tower began to teeter. She looked at Damien as if to say, "You know what to do now." And he did know. He threw himself at the tower, embraced it, tackled it, and then lay on the floor amid the books in momentary peace. He then got to his feet with a serious expression on his face. Sybil, in turn, built another tower of books, and when she was finished, she looked at him, nodded, and he once again tackled it. Margaret was impressed by what she was seeing, but at the same time saddened by the fact that in all the time she had spent with Damien, both before and after he moved in, she had never once felt she had succeeded in engaging him as passionately as this stranger had.

When Margaret walked back into the room, it was as if a bubble burst. The intensity, the seriousness, the importance, the joy of the game that Sybil and Damien were playing went into hiding, as if they'd been engaging not in a form of mischief, but in a form of intimacy that should be kept private.

Sybil said to Damien, "Your Mommy and I have to talk now."

"She's not my Mommy."

Margaret and Sybil sat on the couch and talked for almost an hour. Damien played on the floor, pretending not to be listening. Margaret said that she knew she was asking a lot, but she needed someone to take care of Damien, shop for groceries, prepare meals and keep the house in order, deal with the gardener and the snow plow, the garbage pick-up and the water bills, the telephone service (which was terrible), and the house repairs—roof leaks, broken vacuum cleaners, and such. She asked Sybil about her experience in taking care of children. Sybil told her that she had taken care of her younger brothers and cousins in Jamaica, but had not worked as a nanny. At the end of the interview, Margaret offered Sybil the job.

Instead of gratefully accepting the offer, as Margaret had expected, Sybil said, "I don't mean to talk out of turn, Mrs. McCardle, but I think that what you're asking can't be done. I mean it could be done, but young Damien here would be just a piece of furniture who was in the way of the person you hire while they do all the things you want done."

"I don't know anything about raising children, so I'd be grateful to you for your thoughts about how to arrange for Damien's care while I'm at work."

"I'd feel funny giving you advice. You are a kind person, and that's what matters most with children." Without having to be told, Sybil understood the situation Margaret was attempting to deal with.

"I thank you for thinking that of me, but even if I were to deserve that compliment, that doesn't mean that I know how to go about raising a child. It's a very difficult thing to do, at least I expect it will be for me. So I would very much like to hear what you think."

"I'm not sure what you're asking."

"I'm asking what you think is needed to raise Damien. I know that's too big a question, and I have no right to ask it of you. It's unfair to ask you how I should go about doing right by him. I very much want to do that. His life has been very hard so far."

Sybil said, "I'll tell you what I think, but I don't want to be disrespectful by having the nerve to give my opinion about something that's none of my business."

"I want you to tell me honestly what you think, and I promise I won't take what you say as disrespectful. I can tell that you're not a disrespectful person."

"I feel strange telling you what I think, but I'll try. Mind you, I'm no expert myself. All I know I've learned from taking care of my younger brothers and some cousins in Kingston where I grew up. But I'll tell you what I'm thinking if you want me to. First, all the things that you want done require more than one person to do them. One person can't take care of Damien and play with him and do everything a child needs, and at the same time do all of the rest. I think another person has to help out. I feel strange saying this ..."

"Please go on."

"I think you should hire a man who can drive and has a car of his own. I don't know how to drive. I say I think it should be a man because there will be things that are too heavy for me to lift and things that need fixing. The man should also know his way around, if you know what I mean, and be good with numbers, if he's to deal with all those people you want him to be talking to. That way I can be looking after Damien all the time when he's not taking a nap. I think he needs a nap in the afternoon. My younger brothers and cousins, when they were as young as Damien, were grumpy all the time, rubbing their eyes, unless they had a nap in the afternoon. Listen to me go on as if I have a degree or something."

As Sybil was talking, Margaret found herself wondering how old Sybil was. It was hard to tell. She had soft, shiny, café au lait skin that had hardly a line in it, which made her look young, perhaps in her mid- to late twenties, but there was something about her—a combination of wisdom and acceptance acquired from hard experience—that bespoke many more years than that. And there was sadness visible in her dark brown, black-flecked eyes, and audible in the beautiful music of the sound of her voice, even when she laughed—especially when she laughed.

Margaret hired Sybil, and with the help of an agency, hired part-time a tall, lanky black man named Edward, who drove an old but well-cared-for black Lincoln Town Car. He was a quiet man, well acquainted with the world, who molested Damien. Margaret fired him immediately after Sybil sensed that something was wrong and told Margaret about it.

## NINE

Rose watched Catherine sleep in the semi-darkness of her isolation room in the ICU. She'd had another bleed, this time a much larger one, that had required an emergency craniotomy to drain the blood and staunch the bleeding. Catherine's head was now wrapped in an even larger turban of white gauze. As Rose stood at her bedside, there was no mistaking the droop of the left side of Catherine's face. The cloud-shaped bruise marks on the right side of her face had turned from bright purple to reddish brown. Rose did not know how many days had passed since Catherine had been admitted to the ICU. As in dreams, time did not pass, it disappeared.

Rose dozed by the side of Catherine's bed and then stood to look out of the window, only to be reminded that the ICU has no windows. Though Rose had spent many days and nights in Catherine's room, it came as a slap across the face each time she was denied even a momentary glimpse of the outside world. Rose, at this point, had to deduce virtually everything having to do with time—whether it was day or night, when she had last slept and for how long, the day of the week, the season, when she last ate, the last time she'd bathed, whether Margaret had just left or was just about to arrive, the number of subdural bleeds Catherine had had, how long it had been since the last bleed, the degree of clarity of Catherine's consciousness, how long it had been since Catherine was last awake, and so on.

To live in the absence of measures of elapsed time and the natural cycles of the sun and moon and stars and seas and seasons is to live as a character in someone else's dream, a dream that is strange and unearthly, a dream that is not merely supernatural, it is anti-natural, and as such, it leaches away one's humanness.

When Catherine opened her eyes from sleep—or was it merely a brief period of rest?—she was lying flat on her back. She slowly looked around the room, first at the picture window in front of her that, like an unblinking eye, stared into a hallway. There was a wall to her right that was blank, except for a dry eraser board made of shiny, kitchen-appliance-white material, marked with pink numbers arranged in sloppy columns, probably a long-out-of-date medication schedule or listing of one vital sign or another. A collection of IV stands stood huddled in the corner, like a group of people silently sheltering one another as they waited in the cold for a bus in the early hours of the morning.

"Mommy, where am I?"

"You're in the hospital and I'm here with you, sweetheart. You fell down the stairs, do you remember now?"

Catherine tried to say something more but became terrified by the fact that it was very difficult to form the words. She said in ill-formed words, "My face feels like it does when the dentist gives me novocaine, and I talk funny."

A moment later, "I can't move my arm ... or leg ... this one ..." Catherine let out a shriek so filled with horror and sadness that it cut deeply into Rose's heart.

Rose stammered, "I know, I know." She released the two catches on the left side of Catherine's bed, which allowed the round metal bars to descend. She let her shoes drop to the floor as she climbed onto the bed. Rose pressed her lips to Catherine's pale cheek as she lay down next to her. She slid her arm under Catherine's back and pulled her body tightly against Catherine's.

Catherine's body heaved as she sobbed, while tears silently rolled down Rose's face.

In sloppily articulated words, with saliva bubbling at the left corner of her mouth, Catherine said softly, "I'm a freak … I'll never be the same again … I can hardly remember who I used to be."

"No, sweetheart, you're not a freak, you're my Catherine, you'll always be my Catherine, and you'll be back to your old self before very long. I promise."

"No … I'm not. I'm not me. I … can't talk the way … I …"

Catherine, abandoning her effort to speak, let out a scream different from the first one, a scream of anger and frustration; she used her right hand to punch herself in the face with terrific force, the first blow landing with a dull thump on the gauze wrapped around the upper part of her forehead. She delivered the second punch lower, just above her nose. Rose reached across Catherine and tried to hold Catherine's right arm, but Catherine was so crazed with desperation that she was able to throw Rose's hand aside and, in quick succession, delivered three more powerful punches to her forehead. Catherine ceased pummeling herself when her body lacked the strength to continue. She lay next to her mother in desolate silence.

Both Catherine and Rose fell asleep—for how long, neither of them knew or cared. They were startled by the sound of Dr. Weber knocking on the door frame as he asked, "May I come in?"

Rose felt the absurdity of Dr. Weber's question. He didn't need permission to enter the room—he must know that. Neither she nor Catherine held dominion over a single square inch of the room they occupied. More to the point, he had no intention of entering into the reality of what was actually happening in the room. He seemed intent on continuing the charade of the family doctor making a house call on a family he's known for decades.

Rose, now standing next to Catherine's bed in her bare feet, asked Dr. Weber bluntly, "Why can't Catherine move the left side of her face or the left side of her body?"

"As you know, Catherine had an emergency craniotomy last night in order to deal with another bleed, this time a major one. The surgery went well, I'm glad to say, and it's common for there to be muscle weakness after an invasive surgery of the sort Catherine had. I know that when I say something is common, it is not at all common to either of you. Having a craniotomy is a harrowing thing, and its aftereffects can be very frightening. I know they would be for me. Before I can say anything more specific, I want to examine Catherine myself. I know this is no time for either of you to be subjected to the intrusion of this herd of staff, but they have to know Catherine's current neurological status so that they'll have a baseline for any change that might occur."

Rose thought that Dr. Weber's tone had become slightly officious for the first time. Gone was any trace of the brief flirtation they'd had.

A group of doctors and nurses filed in, taking their places around three sides of the bed. Catherine silently obliged Dr. Weber as he asked her, in sequence, once again, if she would allow him to check her pupils and eye movement, her ability to move her tongue, squeeze his hands, lift her legs, and push her feet against his hand as hard as she could. He tapped her here and there with his hammer, poked her skin with a sharp instrument, asking her to nod if she could feel the jab or the vibration. He tried to get her to smile by acting as if he were using the handle of his tuning fork to remove wax from his ears. Neither Catherine nor Rose was the least bit amused. He ran the end of the handle of the reflex hammer upward on the soles of her feet. The staff stood silently around Catherine's bed, the doctors in their long, stained white lab coats, the nurses in their crisp white uniforms.

Dr. Weber jotted notes in the chart and then slowly placed it back on its metal hook at the foot of the bed.

He said to Rose, "Catherine is experiencing muscle weakness on the left side of her face and body, which may be a result of the pressure of the blood on her brain, or a result of the trauma of the craniotomy and the removal of the blood and the sealing of the blood vessels. None of this is surprising, given the severity of the head trauma Catherine suffered."

As Rose listened to Dr. Weber speak, she thought that he sounded more like a lawyer than a doctor. Everything was "common," everything was "to be expected," and it was unspoken, but certainly implied, that no one could do more than he and his staff were doing.

"It's important that Catherine continue to be watched closely. There is every reason to be hopeful that she'll recover most of her muscle strength with the help of time and physical therapy."

It was not lost on Rose or Catherine that Dr. Weber had used the words "hopeful" and "most" as if they meant "definitely will" and "all."

Catherine, in poorly formed words, said, "Dr. Weber, I have two questions. Why are you talking to my mother as if I'm not here? And why are you lying to us?"

Caught by surprise, Dr. Weber looked hard at Catherine for a moment before saying, "Catherine, I apologize for talking to your mother as if you weren't here. As to whether I was lying, I would rather say that I was putting things in a way that I hoped would allow you and your mother to feel less frightened about the muscle weakness you're experiencing. Frightening a patient or their family never does anyone any good, so I try not to do it."

Catherine began to cry.

Dr. Weber asked, "What did I say to make you cry?"

"That's just it, you didn't say anything. Why won't you talk to me?"

"About what?"

"About the fact that I can't talk without saliva dripping from the side of my mouth, the fact that I can only see through one eye because one eyelid won't open, and I can hardly move my left arm and leg."

"I would be glad to answer your questions."

"So, go ahead and answer them … *gladly*."

"All right, let me tell you how I go about talking to myself about what's happening. We've been able to determine with as much certainty as is possible in medicine—which is not absolute certainty, but it's what we have to work with—that you had an acute subdural hematoma. We …"

"Stop it. I can't stand it," Catherine yelled as loudly as she could through lips that felt two inches thick, "So many words, and you haven't said anything I don't already know. Who are you protecting with your carefully selected words? It's not me. I get frightened when someone is lying to me because I don't know what they're covering up or why. Can you understand that?"

"What do you want me to say?"

"I want you to tell me the truth."

"The truth is that the second bleed was much more extensive than the first," he said with sadness in his voice that Catherine could feel was genuine. He continued, speaking now only to Catherine, "I really wasn't expecting it. I asked the ward clerk to call me at home if they were going to do a craniotomy. I came in and went with you to surgery last night. I don't know why it felt important for me to be there, but it did."

"I believe you. Now please tell me the truth about my face and arm and leg. Am I headed for life in a wheelchair?"

"No, I don't think you are. Your face and arm and leg are not paralyzed, they're weakened. The CT scan shows that your spinal cord has not been severed, which would cause paralysis

60

of a part of your body. Your brain has swelled, and as a result, it is under greater pressure than it should be, which limits its functioning but does not cut entire nerve pathways. But the pressure does kill some cells. Neighboring cells take over the work of the dead ones, but they do so very slowly, and only if their development is guided by physical therapy. Time and intensive physical therapy will allow us to tell how much you'll recover of the strength you've lost. I can honestly say that I think the odds are good that you'll get back a lot of your strength, but probably not all of it, and that what you don't recover won't be so great as to be an encumbrance to the way you live your life. Do you know what encumbrance means?"

"You were doing so well, right up until the end. Why did you have to go and spoil it? When you talk like that, it makes me feel that I can't believe what you've said."

Dr. Weber thought for a while. The other doctors and nurses looked on in disbelief.

"I think that the only place where I was being less than fully honest was in the way I slid over what is involved in physical therapy. That's going to be very hard, and at times very discouraging. It's a slow and demanding process. You are a strong-willed girl—and I'm certainly telling the truth when I say that—and your determination will be of enormous help to you. I also have left out a fact that you are aware of, but is frightening, so I don't know if it helps to talk about it."

"Yes, talk about it."

"You've had two bleeds, the second worse than the first. There's no guarantee that there won't be another one." Dr. Weber paused. "There's still one more thing. I may not tell the truth as often as I should, but as a doctor, I have a good eye—not much escapes me. I'm not blind to the fact that your face is freshly bruised. I can only guess that you've punched yourself in the face. I hope I'm wrong, but I don't think I am. You're not the first to have done that in this ICU, and no one but you can prevent it from happening again. I won't ask you whether I'm right or not, but I will ask you to try not to do that to yourself again. It's a very dangerous thing to do right now."

"You think I don't know that?" Catherine said.

"If you know it's dangerous, why do you do it?"

"Why do you think?"

"I can only imagine that you don't care what damage you do to yourself."

"There you go," Catherine said, with tears in her eyes, and saliva on her chin.

# TEN

Margaret would never forget the triumphant sound of Damien's grunts and muted screams as the books flew out of the bookcases and crashed to the floor, or the delight in his face as he tackled the towers of books that Sybil stacked to the height of his chest. It was obvious to Margaret from as far back as she could remember that Rose was far better than she was with children, and far better with adults, too, except at work. Anywhere other than work, Margaret felt as if she was made of cardboard.

While watching Sybil and Damien that first morning, Margaret tried to make sense of the event she was witnessing. It seemed that Sybil was inviting Damien to join her in gloriously subversive activity, a joyful protest, a tearing down of the castle walls, an embracing of anarchy, an active rejection of the rules, an assertion of freedom and independence. And what most astonished Margaret was the fact that what she was seeing did not feel the least bit dangerous, out of control, or destructive. Sybil retained her authority as an adult, while seeming to be an equal partner with Damien. This was a sleight of hand that Sybil performed masterfully. She was at the same time a rebel and the law. She made it work.

Margaret felt grateful to Sybil for giving Damien a chance to experience undiluted joy, something she could not remember ever having felt as a child or as an adult. It was not that Damien's worries and fears had evaporated in the heat of this rebellion, but there could be no doubt that he was transported into a place where his problems—the fact that he was without a mother, a family, and a home—were, for a moment, eclipsed by something new and completely unexpected. In that moment and in that place, he was no longer a child in the hands of adults who had the power to do anything they liked with him, whenever they wanted to. The terrible imbalance of power between children and adults no longer existed: It was *as if* he were on an equal footing with adults. He could send grown-up things flying, and he could throw his body at adult things and flatten them. He could destroy them in his mind and in his body. He could interrupt the silence that adults so adore and cling to. Sybil intuitively understood all this. She created for Damien the setting in which to create the particular illusion that he needed more than any other map of the world at that time.

And so it went for the weeks and months that followed that morning when Margaret, Sybil, and Damien, out of nothing, began to form something of a family. In that embryonic family, Margaret served as the father. She went to work early in the morning and came home most evenings at seven, except when she had to stay at work to complete a project or was on a business trip. At eight, Sybil helped Damien get ready for bed. Margaret read him stories once he was in his bed. For both Margaret and Damien, bedtime was their favorite time together.

Sybil served as the mother. She looked after Damien, played with him, cooked for him, cared for him from morning to night. She comforted him in the afternoon if a bad dream woke him up with the feeling he was lost or bad to the core, or had lost track of who he was and who Margaret and Sybil were. But she did not love him as she would love her own child. To do so would make unbearable the eventual end of his tenure in her life and her tenure in his.

Damien awoke each morning to the sound and smell of Sybil making breakfast. His days conformed to a routine that barely changed. There were no surprises; nothing unexpected occurred, which is not to say that these predictable rhythms were devoid of the fantastic. He and Sybil lived in a world of the imagination in which anything could happen, but the worst things never happened, and things always turned out well—of that he was certain. Sybil dressed him, invented games with him, drew in coloring books with him, and gradually taught him the beginnings of reading and writing. Sybil and Margaret decided that Damien was not sufficiently mature for school, so they postponed his enrollment.

Damien and Sybil spent a good deal of every day—regardless of punishing summer heat, spring rains, or biting winter cold and wind—outside in the backyard and in the acres of woods and fields behind Margaret's house. Nothing was too much for them. Sybil understood Damien better than anyone had ever understood him, so she was well aware that he was a severely wounded child. She had known almost immediately upon meeting him that she could play with him, comfort him, even love him, but she could not save him from what had already been set in motion. She recognized the depth and intensity of his anger, and knew that if she were to genuinely accept him, she would have to accept his anger. He often became cross with her, which she usually deflected with humor, but never ignored. She occasionally became cross with him, but expressed it in a way that was devoid of the threat of leaving him. She knew that that threat in particular was poisonous to him, though her leaving him was inevitable. That was the central paradox of their lives together.

Damien and Sybil traveled the world together. She took him to Kingston to see the house in which she grew up, and to meet her mother, grandmother, brothers, aunts, uncles, and cousins; they went to Africa to see the lions, giraffes, and elephants; and to Antarctica to see the penguins. Their travels and adventures took place in the seemingly endless expanse of the fifteen acres behind Margaret's house.

Because, for all of Damien's life with Rose, Rose had had to take care of two children—three, when Catherine was born—she could not give any one child the undivided attention that Damien received from Sybil. To skew matters even more, Damien had no memory of his father, so at Margaret's house, for the first time he could remember, he was cared for by two adults, each quite different from the other, and yet firmly allied in the task of taking care of him.

Damien would never forget Sybil explaining to him that when sending a letter to a grown man, you address it to "Mister," and when sending it to a young man, like Damien, you address it to "Master." Sometimes, when they played together, Sybil called him "Master Damien," if the occasion was a formal one, such as receiving a knighthood. He enjoyed her calling him Master Damien because it made him feel very important, a feeling that was, for him, rare and ephemeral. Sybil liked to tell Damien that he was different from other children. There was something dignified about him, and about Margaret, which set them apart. Though Damien didn't know any other children except Erin, whom he remembered only very dimly, he liked to believe that what Sybil said was true—that he was different from other children—and he could feel that Sybil believed what she was saying.

The family that Margaret, Sybil, and Damien created was one in which the division of power and responsibility was clear and consistent. Sybil decided such things as what they would have for supper, at what point Damien no longer needed to take an afternoon nap, and whether he was too feverish to go outside on a particular day. Sybil and Margaret together made decisions concerning Damien's education, such as when to begin putting aside time each day for learning to read and write, and how long to postpone Damien's going to school. Margaret made the most important decisions by herself. She changed Damien's surname from Keane to McCardle, her ex-husband's surname, which she had retained after the divorce. The most critical decision that Margaret made was to precipitously and decisively end Damien's contact with Rose, as well as with Erin and Catherine. Margaret firmly believed that her tie to Damien, and his tie to her, could take hold and grow only in the complete absence of Rose. If given a choice between Rose and her, Margaret felt certain that Damien would choose Rose. What child wouldn't?

On Saturday mornings, Margaret took walks by herself in the woods behind her house. During these walks, she did not know, nor did she care, when she was silently thinking and when she was speaking her thoughts aloud. On one walk, Margaret was quite agitated. She went over and over in her mind the question of whether hiring Sybil had been another of her many mistakes in the realm of dealings with other human beings. Sybil was so far superior to her as a mother that it was no wonder Damien instantly became more attached to Sybil than to her. Without Sybil's help, she wouldn't have lasted a month with Damien. He had hardly eaten or drunk anything during the week that she'd been alone with him. He had lacked vitality, even the vitality necessary for anger or grief. Sybil was a genuinely good-hearted person, Margaret felt. She had never done anything to undercut Margaret's connection with Damien. Sybil had a way of soothing Damien, and soothing her, that they both badly needed. But Margaret couldn't keep herself from imagining that Sybil, very subtly, was driving a wedge between her and Damien.

During Damien's first year with her, Margaret hadn't felt jealous of Damien's bond to Sybil. She felt that this was an honest appraisal. She had been able to accept playing second fiddle to Sybil, so long as she had some role to play. She had enjoyed reading books to Damien and watching television with him in the evening, the two of them propped up next to one another in her bed, Damien snuggling under her arm. She had never experienced physical closeness like that in her entire life, with anyone. Sex was far less intimate than snuggling with Damien.

Margaret's thoughts turned to the house in which she was living—a "large, Tudor affair," the real estate agent had called it. She was well aware that the interior decoration of the house looked as if she'd inherited it, with all of its furnishings, from her aged parents or grandparents, and hadn't moved a single stick of furniture from the place it had occupied. In a sense this was true. She had bought the house fully furnished—the children of the elderly couple who had lived there didn't want the massive, gloomy furniture or the threadbare Oriental carpets. Margaret remembered how she had recoiled from the suggestion that she hire an interior decorator. She would be the first to admit that she had no sense of style, but she abhorred the idea of living with someone else's aesthetic. That would feel like using a stranger's toothbrush. It would sound silly to anyone but her, but the thing that most appealed about the house was not the house itself, but the tortuous, poorly paved driveway, lined with birches, that separated the house from the outside world. The house itself was an imposing two-story affair, with large leaded-glass windows on the first floor, and on the second, four dormers poking out of a dusky purple slate roof. The house was now like an old friend.

It was November, always a sad time for Margaret. "The holiday season"—the season of arguments between her parents, her father relentlessly belittling her mother's parents and brother. "No man has survived your grandmother," he would tell her. "Your grandfather and your Uncle Phil have been neutered. I would have thought that your grandfather was deaf and dumb if I hadn't heard him ask me to pass the gravy last Thanksgiving. Phil is a spectacular loser, and he doesn't seem to mind."

Her mind seemed to exert a constant force drawing her thoughts back to Sybil. She wasn't sure whether to use the word *love* to describe what she thought Sybil and Damien felt for each another, but she didn't have a better word for it. She tried not to blame this on Sybil. Sybil had not once stood between her and Damien. Quite the opposite. If Damien held on to Sybil after dinner, when it was time for Damien to say good night, Sybil would say, "I'm a tired old woman who will be no fun at all tonight. Your mother is a much better story-reader than I am. She told me she has some stories in mind to read to you, but she didn't tell me what they are. You tell me tomorrow." Sybil referred to Margaret as "your mother," but the word *mother*, too, wasn't quite right. Damien didn't use a name when referring to Margaret or when speaking to her unless his hand was forced, in which case he called her *Margaret*, never *Mommy*.

Margaret's thoughts were interrupted by the branch of a sapling lashing across her left eye, causing deep, sharp stinging and copious tearing. She let out a short scream of pain, which wasn't entirely a response to the physical injury. But soon she was immersed again in her own thoughts, as if she were intent on solving a problem that lacked a solution.

Sybil had a way with children that Margaret felt she would never have. It just wasn't the way she was made. Sybil had a mischievous sparkle in her eye that Damien noticed right from the outset, as did Margaret. The look in Sybil's eye seemed to say, "Stick around because what's going to happen is something you won't want to miss." Margaret had learned a great deal from Sybil about playing with Damien, consoling him, cajoling him, dreaming his future with him, as well as drawing lines that he was not allowed to cross—and this was the part that most amazed and frightened Margaret—Sybil never chastised Damien. Instead, she distracted him from what was forbidden to him with an act of imagination, which seemed to Margaret to be the irresistible music of a Pied Piper, music only children can hear, music that casts a spell over them, induces a hypnotic trance, robs them of a mind, kidnaps them.

Margaret said to herself, Enough of that. She's good with children, much better than I am. That doesn't make her a witch. Damien obeys her not because she hypnotizes him, but because he wants her to love him. Like every other child, he would do anything for his parents' love. I can't honestly say I love him. When I take him on an outing, I feel like a divorced father picking up his child for one of his every-other-weekend "visits." Do I resent Sybil? The only honest answer I can give is, A little. Should I replace her? Should I talk to her about my worries? Should I spend more time with Damien in an effort to lay claim to him? The answers to all these questions is the same: Absolutely not.

For children, Margaret thought, what's most important and engaging isn't what's happening, it's what's about to happen. You can see that at any Punch and Judy show. When the curtain opens and the puppets appear, the jaw of every child in the audience drops, not because the puppets are funny looking or wearing glittering costumes, but because the stage is set for something that is about to happen. The children don't know what it is yet; they are entranced. There is every indication that what is about to happen will be exciting—maybe funny, maybe sad, maybe scary but not too scary. Even if they've seen the same show fifteen times, they feel as if they don't know what's about to happen. Anticipation is the best part. When the something-that-is-about-to-happen has happened, all the electricity in the audience of children drains away. A puppet show that's over is always a disappointing show because its power to instill anticipation has been spent. Children don't leave a performance enjoying the memory of the happy ending or the humor or the surprises. When the show is over, it's simply time to go, time for a long drive home, time for their faces to get scrubbed hard with a washcloth to remove the residue of cotton candy.

Sybil was always the event that was about to happen. Margaret knew that she couldn't compete with Sybil, and she'd stopped trying long ago. Another branch snapped back and lashed her cheek. The sting was intense, but this time she was so deep in thought that she didn't notice the pain or the tearing. She was the father in this family, quite a good father— someone dependable, though not very exciting, someone who protects the family from the outside world, who eventually, maybe not until Damien had children of his own, would win gratitude and respect, and even admiration, but not love and warmth and affection.

What a cruel irony, she thought. She had hated her father when she was a child and still hated him, but despite herself, she'd become him in ways that made her abhor herself. When her father was at home, he overplayed the role of father. He became a perfect television father. Rose went for it hook, line, and sinker. Margaret saw through it and was not the least bit surprised or disappointed by his precipitous exit from the family. She hoped that Damien would not be as perceptive as she'd been, and would mistake form for content. She simply could not get herself to love him. How do you force love? You either feel it or you don't. You'd give up anything—no, that's not right—you'd *give* everything you have, and feel you had even more after you gave it.

Margaret's thoughts returned to Sybil, as they always seemed to do. Despite feeling upstaged by Sybil, Margaret wanted very much to protect Sybil from the profound sadness she saw in her. Sybil's laugh always finished with a slightly forced quality, as if covering something over. She was a very private person. There was only one part of her life she'd talk about—growing up in Kingston. With words, she painted a living picture of a place with lots of characters, a Bruegel-like painting in which a concatenation of minia-tures worked together to comprise a whole world, frozen in time. The house in which Sybil grew up seemed not to have an inside and an outside: Chickens, dogs, cats, mice, and a dozen barefoot children ran freely into and out of the house. The dozen children, who were brothers, sisters, and cousins to one another, were most of the time not cognizant of which of the other children were their siblings and which their cousins. It just didn't matter. What mattered were age and size and imagination and strength and daring and coordination and loyalty and trustworthiness and intelligence. It was all of those things that determined your place in this sprawl of children.

And there was one more thing that mattered, something never spoken but universally felt: The color of your skin. Light-skinned people, both children and adults, were seen as superior to the darker skinned. Sybil left it at that. Margaret needed no clarification; Damien didn't understand, but he somehow knew not to ask. The answer was in the tone of voice with which Sybil told that part of the story, which contained an unmistakable note of superiority derived from the fact that her skin was light brown.

In Sybil's childhood, school was also something that did not have a place that was strictly outside or inside the house. There was an emphasis on education in her home. The parents and aunts and uncles and grandparents all knew from their own experience that school would not prepare children to do better than they had. Sybil said that at the school she attended, most of the "coloreds" were lazy, and their parents didn't know any better, and so they dropped out, and even if they did graduate, they wouldn't have learned enough from the teachers in the school about how to read and write and add and subtract the way white children did, and they wouldn't learn enough to do anything but work as maids and dishwashers in fancy hotels, just like their mother, or become drunks, just like their father. In Sybil's family, the smartest of the older children, who were almost always the girls, taught the younger ones more about "fine" reading and writing—not learning only enough to read directions on bottles and boxes of cleaning fluids—but reading and writing the way the whites taught their children to do.

As she listened, Margaret heard self-hatred and resentment embedded in this story that made her profoundly sad for Sybil, who no doubt was one of the smart older girls who taught the young ones. Neither she nor Damien wanted to hear Sybil's response to the question, Why are you a nanny taking care of Damien when you clearly want more from life, and are capable of much more?

Margaret had trouble knowing what to make of Sybil's brand of femininity—the sexual part of it. It seemed to Margaret to be hidden away under layers and layers of her role as care-taker of the younger children in Kingston, and now Damien. Margaret knew that she did something with her sexual desires that was similar to what she supposed Sybil did, the only differ-ence being that she hid them under layers and layers of mana-gerial skill combined with uncanny, and unfeminine, business acumen. She could imagine Sybil being entertaining with a man, telling him humorous stories, but she couldn't imagine her flirting with a man. The ability to flirt, which was effort-less for Rose, was among the qualities Margaret most envied in her. She had watched Rose flirt with virtually every man with whom she had any dealings at all, even gas station attendants and men at clothing stores where she bought clothes for Erin. But most painful and mysterious of all was Rose's ability to flirt with their father—from the time she was a year old, maybe even younger. This was something Margaret had never once been able to do with him; he seemed uninterested in doing it with her. When Margaret tried to imagine what it would feel like to flirt, she could picture it in her mind, but could never feel it in her body.

That strange experience she'd had long ago—she couldn't have been more than twenty-seven, she thought, given the date of her divorce—came to her at that moment, with an intensity that took her by surprise. She could smell the stale air in the closet-like waiting room in which there was a single chair and a table with a pile of out-of-date magazines on it. When he opened the door, she saw a white-haired, lanky man dressed in a well-tailored dark gray suit, a white shirt, and a silk tie of a beautiful shade of shimmering orange that was still vivid in her mind. He introduced himself and invited her into the adjoining room. The room, smaller than she expected, was furnished with what seemed like carefully chosen pieces—to her left sat a chrome and glass writing table, facing a bank of casement windows, with handwritten pages in disarray on its surface; the desk chair, also facing outward, with its back to the room, gave an air of privacy to what occurred in the rest of the room. Immediately ahead of her were two armchairs arranged diagonally, with a black lacquered Japanese box between them, on which rested a box of tissues. And to her right, an Eames chair placed behind a mousy brown upholstered couch with a pillow at the end closest to the chair. Another box of tissues lay on the floor next to the couch. The setting was perfect and complete.

The spell was broken when Margaret heard Damien and Sybil talking as they played on the grass just in back of the house. They were punching a large striped beach ball back and forth, a game Margaret had no desire to be part of, but she didn't know how she would get past them without appearing indifferent.

# ELEVEN

One evening as she quietly left Damien's room after getting him settled in his bed for the night, Margaret was startled to find Sybil waiting for her outside the door. The two of them made their way down the hallway into the kitchen, which had a bluish hue because it was lit solely by tubes of fluorescent lights encased in long plastic cases attached to the ceiling.

Margaret's stomach tightened as she and Sybil took seats on opposite sides of the kitchen table.

"There's been something I've been putting off for a long time," Sybil began.

Margaret had lived in dread of this moment ever since she hired Sybil almost three years earlier. She knew what Sybil was going to say—that she loved Damien as if he were her own child, and that it was going to be difficult to leave the two of them, but she had decided to return to New York City. Margaret was deeply saddened to hear Sybil speak these words.

"My sister, Edna, told me that the phone company is hiring girls, including colored girls, to work the switchboards. I sent them a letter and they wrote back and said they want to talk to me. I'd like to work with people my age. I love Damien, but I get lonely for people my age and a different kind of job."

"I feel like begging you to stay, but that wouldn't be fair to you."

"I'm so sorry to do this to you and Damien. He's had more than his share of troubles. I've been waiting for a time that seemed right, but I finally realized there would never be a right time."

"Before we talk more about how long it will be until you leave, I don't want any of the planning to crowd out my telling you how grateful I am for all that you've done for Damien and me. Being a mother doesn't come naturally to me. I've watched you with Damien, and almost every time I see the two of you together, I'm surprised by what you say and how you say it. It's usually just the right thing for him." Margaret began to cry. While pushing the tears to the side of her face, she smiled sheepishly as she said, "Tears don't come naturally to me either. I feel ridiculous when I cry."

"Thank you for saying those things about me, but the things you said about yourself aren't true. There's not just one way to be with children. You have your own way, and Damien knows you love him. You made a home for him when your sister couldn't manage. He knows this is his home where he belongs, no matter what."

"I wish I could be as sure of that as you are."

Damien was stoic the morning that Margaret and Sybil told him that Sybil would be leaving to go back to New York to live with her sister, Edna. When Margaret asked Damien if he could say what he was thinking, he said, "It's okay."

On the day Sybil left, Damien acted as if nothing unusual were happening. Margaret tried to talk to him about saying goodbye to Sybil, but he seemed deaf to her. After Margaret called for a taxi to take Sybil to the train station, Sybil got down on the floor of the living room, where Damien was looking blankly at his storybook, not reading, just turning the pages. She tried to hug him, but he pulled away. Sitting on the floor next to him, she said, "My heart aches, same as yours." Damien continued to turn the pages of his book.

Margaret took time off from work to help Damien with Sybil's departure. In the days that followed, Damien remained listless. He volunteered nothing and, when Margaret asked him a question, he gave only one-word replies, if he answered at all. Often he didn't seem to hear anything. His face was expressionless. He had no appetite for food, or anything else. This continued for weeks. Margaret counted the days early on, but she eventually lost track of the number of days the two of them were going through the motions of life in that large empty house.

One night Margaret awoke in the middle of the night with a feeling that something was wrong. She immediately got out of bed and walked briskly to Damien's room, where she saw light coming from under his door. On entering the room, she was stunned to see Damien awake, lying on top of his bed dressed in his blue corduroy pants and his yellow T-shirt put on inside out, with all of the lights in the room illuminated.

"Damien, honey, what are you doing? Let me help you get back into your pajamas."

Her hands trembled as she lifted his arms and legs to remove his clothes. Margaret sat Damien on the side of his bed to get him into his pajamas. He looked straight ahead, his arms draped at his sides, his hands resting weightlessly on the bed. Margaret felt as if she were a mortician dressing a corpse, readying it for an open-coffin funeral. After getting him into his bed and pulling the sheets and blankets up to his neck, she moved the chair in which she read to him close to his bed and sat by him while he fell asleep. She remained there for the rest of the night, drifting in and out of sleep.

While listening to Damien's shallow breathing in the pale light of early dawn, the enormity of the emotional toll that Sybil's departure had taken on Damien became even more real to Margaret than it had been before. For the first time, she let herself recognize what had been apparent for some time now. Damien had lost the will to live. His body looked wasted; his eyes were sunken and as blank as a doll's eyes. She couldn't understand how she could have allowed this to go on for so long. She, too, had felt bereft, and had hoped that, like an illness, the ache and torpor that had set in would lift for both of them. As she looked at Damien's face in the gray light from the window, she saw a boy whose life, for the past three years, had been lived in a world created by Sybil. No, it was a world that *was* Sybil, a world that had the dimensions of Sybil's mind and spirit. Margaret, too, had inhabited that world, but she was not confined to that space as Damien had been. She had a life of her own at work and with Rose. As Margaret sat by Damien, a horrifying thought occurred to her. She had taken Damien out of the natural habitat of a growing child and made a zoo animal of him—in a zoo in which he was the only animal, a zoo staffed by two zookeepers. That image sent a wave of nausea through her.

When Damien opened his eyes in the morning, still lying on his back in the position that Margaret had placed him in, he turned his head in Margaret's direction and seemed to look through her.

Margaret said softly, "Damien, I know that what you're feeling about Sybil's leaving is more than you can take. You and I both loved Sybil, and we still do. She's in New York with her sister, Edna, now, but I'm still here, and you're safe with me. I don't know if you can hear me because you've gone deep into yourself, but I'll be here waiting for you when you're ready to come back out."

Margaret had hired a woman whom Sybil had found to replace her, as if Sybil could be replaced. Amy Woodruff, a black woman from Trinidad, had been doing the grocery shopping and preparing meals for Margaret and Damien—meals they didn't eat—and had made the beds and vacuumed the carpets. Margaret imagined that Amy did not know what role she played, if any, in this strange, desolate family. It must seem to Amy that she and Damien were hollowed-out people.

Margaret, one day, told Amy that she had decided not to have a nanny after all, and that she was going to take care of Damien herself. She apologized to Amy for having taken up her time, and paid her generously to tide her over until she was able to find another job.

The only person to whom Margaret could turn was Rose. But telling Rose what was happening would be to acknowledge that she had never really been accepted by Damien as his mother, and that he'd felt far more for Sybil than he had for her. And now, without Sybil, she and Damien were utterly lost. But that wasn't the worst of it. Margaret now realized that cutting Erin, Catherine, and especially Rose out of Damien's life was unforgivable. That act had not only been selfish, it was ruthless. Neither Rose nor Damien had the power to overrule her decision. Rose, by giving Damien to her, had forfeited all her rights concerning how to raise Damien, and felt so ashamed of what she'd done to Damien that she didn't feel she deserved any say in the matter, nor did she feel she had anything to offer him. Margaret had been unaware of the terrible pain she was causing both Damien and Rose. Her own ignorance—or was it willful disregard—felt deplorable to Margaret as she looked back on it. In her effort to seize by force the claim to be Damien's mother, she had demonstrated her utter inadequacy to be a mother. Damien and Rose had paid dearly for what she'd done. She knew that now.

After placing Damien in front of the television set in her bedroom and finding a channel with cartoons playing, she went to the kitchen to call Rose.

"I have to tell you something that has to be said in person," Margaret said in a highly agitated tone of voice. "Please come over as soon as you can."

"Of course, I'll come over now. I'll bring Catherine. How is Damien?"

"I'll tell you when you get here. Please hurry."

Rose knew that Margaret and Damien were having trouble managing life without Sybil, but she hadn't, until now, sensed the proportions of it.

After a few minutes, Margaret stepped out of the front door of her house where she waited, trying to discern even the slightest movement that would announce the arrival of Rose's grayish-green station wagon. She put her hand to her forehead to shield her eyes from the bright mid-morning light.

Finally, Margaret could hear the smooth rumble of a car engine winding its way up the driveway. Margaret quickly walked to the car to help Rose gather Catherine's supply of toys.

Rose carried Catherine and Margaret carried the toys as they walked over the beige gravel surrounding the front of the house.

"Thank you for coming so quickly. Let's talk in the library. Damien's watching cartoons."

As they briskly walked down the hallway to the library, the house felt to Rose as if the owners had left with the idea that they'd be returning shortly, but in fact had never come back. Catherine carried her doll in one hand and her coloring book in the other. She had grown quickly in the previous months, her head now level with her mother's hip as they walked.

The library was a large, formal room with floor-to-ceiling mahogany bookshelves lining one side and casement windows with leaded panes spread across the opposite side, above the wooden ledge and metal facing that enclosed the radiators. There was an imposing, deep fireplace with an ornate mantel at the near end of the room.

Catherine seemed familiar with the room. She lay down on the floor near one of the chairs by the fireplace, her coloring book open in front of her. Rose placed a large box of crayons next to her and sat down in the nearby chair. Rose then turned her attention to Margaret who was sitting across the coffee table from her, with her back to the casement windows.

Margaret looked pale and exhausted. Her hair looked thinner, with balding patches visible as the slanted light from the windows shone through it.

"I want to get right to the point," Margaret said, speaking rapidly. "Damien and I have been in terrible shape since Sybil left. I've been keeping from you just how bad things really are. I have made many very serious mistakes in raising Damien, which I'll tell you about later. Right now there's an emergency that has to be attended to. I think Damien is dying. Since the day Sybil left, more than a month and a half ago, he's hardly eaten or drunk anything. Once in a while he'll eat the crust of a peanut butter and jelly sandwich and some juice, but he's steadily getting thinner. There are deep, dark circles under his eyes. Losing Sybil was too much for Damien. I can't get through to him. I've taken a medical leave from work so he won't have to be alone in this house. I hired a replacement live-in for Sybil, but I let her go. It was crazy of me to think that I could hire a replacement for Sybil. I don't know what to do. That's why I asked you to come over as soon as you could." Margaret sobbed when she managed to get the last of these words out of her mouth.

Rose had never seen Margaret in such anguish. Margaret, too, had lost a good deal of weight; her yellow cotton dress hung loosely from her body. There were dark circles under her eyes, like those she'd described on Damien's face; her cheekbones protruded, and the skin that stretched over them looked thin and translucent.

Rose knelt next to Margaret's chair and held her hand. Margaret's hand felt cold, loose-skinned, and bony, like their grandmother's hands had felt in the last days of her life.

"We'll find a way to help Damien. I promise."

Margaret was silent, not believing that Rose could keep that promise.

After some time, Rose added, "Children in Damien's condition need something, and it's always the same thing. They

81

need to be loved and understood. If you give them that, they revive."

"The worst thing I've done in my life," Margaret said, "was not letting you and Damien see one another after I adopted him."

Rose tried to interrupt, but Margaret stopped her. "Don't try to tell me I'm wrong about that, or that it wasn't as serious as I make it out to be. I know how serious it was. If someone told me they were going to do that, I'd say to them, 'What the hell are you doing? You can't take a child away from his mother and not let them see each other!' I didn't know enough then to say that to myself. I worried that he would never choose me over you, if given a choice."

"The first thing we have to do," Rose said, "is get Damien to his pediatrician. Second, call the nanny you let go, apologize to her, and ask her if she'll consider returning to work here. You need help here. She can do the housekeeping and cooking while we attend to Damien. This may sound strange, but I think you have to go back to work. You need a life of your own separate from Damien."

Margaret brushed tears from her eyes.

Rose had never seen Margaret so lost. It both saddened her and frightened her. Rose felt as if she were the older sister, a feeling she'd never had before. She said to Margaret, "You don't have to be in charge of your family all by yourself. We'll do it together. We'll get through this."

Margaret, whose eyes were locked on Rose's face, nodded and said, "Okay."

## TWELVE

While Catherine was in the hospital, Margaret visited every day, bringing fresh clothes for Rose, and a book or a sweet or a magazine that she thought Catherine might like. During the week following Catherine's fall, Margaret slept at Rose's house with the boys. The three of them made strange bedfellows. Margaret was at a loss to know what to say to Damien and Erin, and they were at a loss to know what to say to her. Margaret had no idea how to relate to teenage boys, particularly Damien, given their ragged history together. As time went on, Margaret, with increasing frequency, called to say that she had to work late, so the boys should order pizza and pay for it with the money she'd left in the bowl in the front hall. One evening, when she had to work past midnight, she decided that since the boys were already asleep, it wouldn't do anybody any harm if she slept at home, just this once. In the days that followed, she began to sleep at home once in a while, and in a matter of weeks she found herself sleeping at home every night.

Once Margaret was no longer a presence in Rose's house, anarchy took hold. Dirty dishes piled up in the sink; cereal bowls half-filled with sludge lay on the breakfast table, along with the green sports pages of week-old newspapers; upstairs in the television room, empty pizza boxes were stacked on the floor, and popsicle wrappers and bowls lined with blue-green mold accumulated. Dirty laundry piled up in the corners of the boys' bedroom. Margaret, who was unnerved by the prospect of talking with Erin and Damien about doing their part while Rose was living at the hospital, responded by hiring a housekeeper to clean the house, wash the clothes, and prepare food that the boys could warm up for supper.

By the time Catherine's hospitalization moved into its sixth week, Margaret had altogether ceased visiting the boys, and instead took them to lunch each Sunday after they all visited Catherine in the hospital. Damien was painfully ill at ease while in Catherine's hospital room, not knowing what to say, still convinced that he had pushed her down the stairs.

Rose called every evening around nine to see how the boys were doing, but she was usually so tired that she could make only mechanical statements of appreciation concerning what a fine job they were doing in taking care of themselves.

During the period that he and Erin were on their own while Catherine was in the hospital, Damien felt an urgent need to take advantage of the fracture in the family to fill the holes in the story of his life. Margaret and Rose would change the topic immediately if Damien asked either of them about the parts of his life that he couldn't remember. So Erin was his only possible source of information about his past, but he knew that he had to tread very gingerly with Erin when asking him anything about the past.

One evening, after they'd devoured a large pizza and were lying on their stomachs on the floor of the TV room, Damien asked, as casually as he could, "Do you remember the day Rose gave me to Margaret?"

Erin looked at Damien with an irritated expression on his face. "What does it matter now? It's done. Forget about it."

"It's done for you, but not for me."

Erin grudgingly explained, "It's not like it happened all on one day, with some big announcement. It just sort of happened. I don't remember much. I was pretty young then. Mom pretended that nothing had changed. I remember one night, it was dinnertime, she was asleep on the couch. I don't remember what I ate, maybe cereal. Mom was in bad shape because Dad had just died. Catherine was just born, or maybe she wasn't born yet; I can't remember. Mom kind of gave up. She didn't do much of anything. That's when she went to the mental hospital, and Margaret stayed with us."

After a pause in which Erin seemed to be weighing what he was about to say, he continued, "I was afraid to ask Mom why you were at Margaret's because I was scared she'd give up with me, too, and I'd be sent away like you to Margaret's or to somewhere else, maybe worse than her house. You didn't even come home to visit. I remember Margaret saying you were sick, so I pictured you in an iron lung."

Damien wasn't surprised that Erin had pictured him that way. That story of what Erin imagined had happened to him was not far from the way Damien thought of his own life: He was a strange kid, like an iron lung kid, who never saw anything of the world outside his house. Like an iron lung kid, he was not an ordinary kid: Being told your father's been killed when you're a three-year-old isn't ordinary; being given away isn't ordinary; being raised by Margaret and Sybil, and then never seeing Sybil again, isn't ordinary; being kept away from other kids isn't ordinary; not being told you have a mother, a brother, and a sister who live only a few miles away isn't ordinary; and being given away a second time, back to the woman who gave you away the first time, isn't ordinary.

"Did you miss me when I disappeared? Did Mom miss me?"

"It's hard to explain. I don't remember that much. When you're a kid, you don't ask why something happens, at least I didn't. I just went on with the idea that you'd be back soon,

85

but 'soon' never happened. 'Soon' turned into 'a little while more,' when I asked, or something like that. You just stop asking after a while."

"Did Mom miss me?"

"I don't know."

"Did she say anything about why I was gone?"

"Look, I told you I don't know. I don't know what's going on in her head right now. Does she think about us when she's in the hospital with Catherine? I doubt it."

"What did you think when all of a sudden I was back here?"

"I was glad to have you back. Don't you remember? It had been just Mom and Catherine and me here, and Margaret once in a while. I was the only boy with two women and a girl. I was glad to have a brother."

"Margaret was around here a lot when I was gone?"

"Yeah, just like she is now. She's Mom's only friend."

"And no one asked where I was?"

"You know how things just go on when you're a small kid. You just do the things you always do."

Damien, with anger in his voice, said, "No, I don't know how you just do the things you always do. That's the problem with me. You know that. I'm not normal."

"You *are* normal."

"No, I'm not. Don't pretend you don't know that," Damien said with tears running down his face. He didn't care if Erin saw him crying.

## THIRTEEN

E rin was nothing less than revered at school. He was an intelligent boy, a handsome boy, a kind boy whom other boys looked up to. There was a sturdiness about him, an uncultivated charisma. He protected the marginal kids, not with physical force or even words, but simply by including them in what he was doing, which sometimes amounted to nothing more than lingering for a moment or two in the lavatory—that hallowed ground in a high school—simply to speak a sentence or two about nothing at all before reentering the river of students outside that place of momentary calm. He was the most popular boy in school, but didn't have a single friend, a real friend, except Damien.

Erin's stature allowed him to break a sacrosanct part of the school's unwritten social code during the time that Rose was living at the hospital with Catherine. The social code forbade a junior high school student from sitting in the half of the lunchroom reserved for high school students (physically, the two halves of the lunchroom were identical). Despite the dictates of this code, during the weeks following Catherine's fall, Erin ate lunch with Damien, who was a junior high school student at the time. Erin never explained to Damien why he did this, and Damien never asked. When they ate in the junior high school area, Erin was looked on with quiet awe. When they entered the high school half of the lunchroom, the volume of background chatter diminished, announcing something ominous. Bringing a younger brother into the high school area was unprecedented. The rules were simple, and everybody obeyed them. For Damien, walking next to Erin into the high school area was like walking on air.

One Saturday afternoon, after Margaret drove Erin and Damien home from the strange and silent lunch they'd had after visiting Catherine, the two boys rode their bikes all the way out to the Richardson River. The character of the river changed with the seasons. In spring, with the runoff from the melting snow, the river made an impressive display, uprooting trees and dragging them into the powerful current. Carved into the surface of the river were deep water-furrows that moved downstream, sucking into themselves all that was not secured. In summer, the river calmed and pulled back into its bed, its roar transformed into a lazy gurgle, taking its time as it carried small branches and green grasses as it went. Now, in January, the river—a shiny, undulating black—was quiet except for the occasional crackling of thin dead branches as they were torn from limbs trapped between protruding rocks.

Erin and Damien were half-hynotized by the undulating movement of amorphous shapes on the water surface that resembled oil slicks but were reflections of light creating different shades of black, appearing and disappearing as the river rushed past them like an infinite present endlessly sucking the future into itself. Erin was the first to wrench his way out of the trance, waking Damien as he planted one knee in the moist ground and dug both hands into the soggy earth in an effort to dislodge a rock the size of a grapefruit. Since it was in too deep to be removed by hand, he used his heel to break the earth around the rock before inserting both hands into the softened ground, like a midwife reaching into the birth canal to take hold of the head of a stubborn baby reluctant to show its face in the outside world. Damien, looking over Erin's shoulder, watched the contest with the urge to join in, but remained a spectator as if a witness to a sacred event dispensed to only one person at a time. Having unearthed the rock, Erin lifted it, carried it to the edge of the overhang, and ceremoniously let it drop. On hitting the surface of the water, it unleashed the satisfying, guttural *ga-lunk* of the river swallowing the rock, overlaid by a diaphanous shell of shattered water.

On the heels of this ceremonial commencement came a series of well-practiced preparations for the games: The collection of flat, silver-dollar-sized stones, a variety of smaller rounded rocks, and two or three very large rocks that required the two of them to carry to the edge of the overhang, as if piling depth charges on the stern of a destroyer awaiting the sighting of a submarine.

From the overhang, sidearming the flat stones meant aiming for a first skip relatively far from the bank because stones falling short of that mark invariably burrowed themselves impotently into the water, like flies stuck to flypaper. Damien's throws launched the stones further, but Erin's more educated grip, spin, and release of the stones produced far more satisfying results—a thing of beauty, really.

When they tired of throwing rocks, they sat on the familiar stone wall that divided in two the field of low grasses and leafless bushes that abutted the ledge. There were a couple of rusted metal signs nailed to trees at the edge of the field saying KEEP OUT, which had frightened them when they were younger. They talked about Margaret's new Thunderbird, a surprising choice of car for her. They agreed that she should have gotten a red one, which was a lot better looking than the black one she'd bought. Margaret was a strange and mysterious person to both boys. They didn't know exactly what sort of work she did, but they had overheard Rose and Margaret talking, and knew that she was an important person. She was famous. She was in the newspaper in articles about banks and millions of dollars. But she was not like regular people. She never made jokes. They couldn't remember her ever having laughed. She didn't have a husband and she had had Damien at her house with Sybil. Erin didn't know much about what had happened there, and Damien never talked about it.

Although Damien had not wanted anything to do with Margaret during the initial years after he returned home, he now viewed her with a mixture of respect and sadness. He was strange in a way that was similar to the way she was strange, but he wasn't as strange as her, he thought. He felt sorry for her. Anyone could see how hard it was for her to talk to anyone except Rose. Other than Rose, he knew her better than anyone else. He pictured her Thunderbird in her two-car garage, which was unlit, stank with the odor of gasoline, had big oil marks on its floor under the place where the car engine would be, and had cobwebs covering the shelves filled with old oil cans, tools, and other junk. He knew Margaret's house better than anyone except Margaret, although it had been a long time since he lived there, and he couldn't be sure whether he remembered things about the house from the time he lived there, or whether he knew about these things because of visits he and the rest of the family had later made to her house for Thanksgiving or Christmas. Margaret's house was filled with a part of his life that didn't feel like his real life; it felt like a part of his life that had been cut out of him. It didn't feel as if it was really he who had lived there. Her house was a place in which resided particular shades of light, the sounds of voices speaking in faraway rooms, and distinctive odors. They weren't located in a particular room or in the woods behind the house. They just seemed to float in the air alongside one another.

Erin broke into Damien's thoughts when he yelled back at Damien to hurry up. Damien was trailing behind by twenty feet. Erin pointed to the remains of a raccoon that the vultures had picked clean, except for the fur and its bloody lining. They talked about which kind of bike lock was the hardest for a thief to cut. A new kind of lock that was made of twisted wire cable was so tough that even a buzz saw couldn't cut through it.

"I hate the winter. When you ride your bike to school when it's raining, your pants get wet and they stink all day," Damien said.

"I saw Miss Walters in the hall today," Erin said, as naturally as he could, "and she asked me if I knew what you're going to make for the science fair."

"You should have told her I'm not making anything because I think the whole idea of a science fair is lame. People make the same dumb things every year—big drawings of the grand canyon with arrows and labels saying what each layer of stone is called, and how many millions of years old it is, and nutrition charts with pictures of food from magazines pasted under the names of the different food groups, and you can always count on some idiot shining a light through a prism so a rainbow shows up on a piece of paper that's glued to the end of a shoe box. And the kid actually thinks he's Albert Einstein for doing it."

"You have to make something."

"What are they going to do to me if I don't make anything— expel me? There's nothing I'd like better than being expelled. Why don't you tell Miss Walters, 'Ya know, Miss Walters, I think he'd rather get expelled than do a science project, and there's nothing he'd like better than being expelled.' What'd you do for your science project?"

"I forget."

"No, you don't."

"It was so dumb it's embarrassing."

"What was it? I swear to God I won't laugh."

"Just forget it, will you?'

"No, I won't forget it."

"It was a plastic model of a Saturn 5 rocket with three stages. You know how the bottom stage is ejected after it uses up its fuel and has gotten the rocket a few miles off the ground."

"Yeah."

"It was ridiculous. I glued some fishing line to the nose of the rocket with crazy glue, and ran the line over a pulley so I could pull the line and the rocket would lift up from the table a foot or two, and I made out of toothpicks something that was supposed to look like the tower next to the Saturn 5. You'd better not even smile 'cause I told you it was lame."

"Yeah, and what happened?"

"I burned some pretty big holes into the plastic at the bottom of the lowest stage, and I got some talcum powder ..."

They both began to laugh hard, so hard that Erin could get out only a few words at a time before he broke into more laughter.

"... and filled the bottom stage that could come off ... with talcum powder ..."

Tears were now rolling down both their faces.

"And I pulled the fishing line with one hand ... for lift off ..."

"Stop ... don't say any more. It hurts my ribs ... to laugh ... this hard."

"And with my other hand ... I used a fork or a spoon to tap the side ... of the thing so powder would come out of the holes ... at the bottom ..."

"All right ... I can't stand laughing ... this hard."

"... so it looked like rocket smoke ... coming out of the bottom."

Damien, rubbing the tears from his eyes, said, "That's the worst science project I've ever heard of. It's even worse than the food groups."

Erin, trying to hold back more laughter, said, "I made Mom promise not to say anything to anyone, specially you."

Damien, straightening up and holding his sides, said, "That's why I'm not going to make anything."

"Come on. I told you the truth, even though it was embarrassing. You gotta try. I'll help you think of something."

"If that's the best you could come up with for yourself, think of what you'll come up with for me."

Damien couldn't stop himself from laughing some more. "Okay, okay, I can't take it anymore. Let's talk about something else."

"No, we've got to come up with something. I promised Miss Walters."

"I read somewhere that it's not hard to make an atom bomb. You can just get a book out of the library and it tells you how to do it."

"Be serious. You could do any of the dumb projects they make every year—the Grand Canyon …"

"No, I'm not going to stoop that low."

"Okay, but think hard."

Damien exhaled hard. "I'll try to think of something, and you try to think of something, okay?"

"Okay."

Damien didn't know why he was so lucky as to have Erin as his brother. They'd know each other their whole lives. They could live in the same town and have houses right next to each other, Damien thought, not yet knowing the supreme joy the present-day gods, as did their ancient predecessors, take in the art of irony.

The winter day began darkening around five, at which point the two boys silently walked by the side of the river toward its source. They turned right just before they reached the rusty, abandoned car, made their way through the woods on the trail they'd made in the course of their many treks, crossed the paved road, and climbed the driveway of their house to the back door. Their entry, as always, was noisy as they dumped their jackets, ski caps, and back packs in a heap next to the white plastic garbage can that sat next to the back door.

* * *

Catherine finally returned home after nine weeks of physical rehabilitation. Her facial palsy had diminished greatly, but she could still not bear to look at herself in the mirror. She had regained almost all the strength she'd lost in her left arm, but her left leg was still very weak. She could now walk slowly and unsteadily with a cane for about a minute before her strength gave out.

On her return home, Damien had taken it upon himself to walk behind her with his hands placed lightly on each side of her waist as she attempted to walk with her cane for longer and longer periods of time. Catherine had been put off by his putting his hands on her waist, but given her extreme fear of falling, she didn't tell him to stop doing it. He was, after all, larger and stronger than any other person in the family. It seemed to be as important to Damien as it was to Catherine that she not return to school as "the poor crippled girl."

Catherine, after some time, could climb the stairs if assisted, usually by Damien, but the endeavor was arduous, demoralizing, and time consuming. Since her bedroom was on the second floor, and was the only place where she could fully relax, she had little choice but to climb the stairs several times a day. By evening, it was very difficult for Catherine to gather the strength necessary to ascend or descend the stairs, even with Damien's help.

One night after dinner, four or five weeks after Catherine's return home, Damien followed Catherine out of the dining room, as he did each evening, to help her up the stairs. This time, instead of placing his hands on each side of her waist, in one graceful motion, he slid his left arm behind her knees, his right arm around her upper shoulders, and lifted her from the ground as she tipped her head back to rest on his shoulder, where she momentarily settled before he carried her smoothly and gently up the stairs, and placed her feet lightly on the floor.

When Catherine felt Damien's arm behind her knees, she was stunned by this unprecedented physical contact with a boy. She had never held hands with a boy, much less been lifted off the ground and carried up a flight of stairs in his arms.

After Damien took his hands from her, and once Catherine felt steady on her feet and cane at the top of the stairs, she looked Damien in the eye, squinting as if concentrating very hard on what she was about to say. When she spoke, she enunciated each word as if it were a slap across his face. "I am not a paraplegic, and I don't want to be treated like one."

Catherine walked to her room, Damien to his room: Catherine furious, puzzled, flattered, Damien mortified.

# FOURTEEN

Margaret felt enormously relieved by the way Rose sure-handedly took charge of the disaster that had begun with Sybil's departure. Her face was still wet with tears as she walked Rose and Catherine to the door. Margaret leaned down and kissed Catherine on the top of her head. Now, in late morning, the sunlight was nearing its full intensity, bleaching the color from everything it touched. After closing the door, Margaret returned to the library and collapsed into the chair in which she'd been sitting while talking with Rose about Damien's despair, and her own. Leaning back, she deeply inhaled the stillness and silence of the room. Before Rose left Margaret's house that morning, Margaret had asked her to promise that if Damien didn't begin to show improvement, Rose would take Damien to live with her, permanently. Rose promised she would.

Margaret sat with Damien on her bed that night as she read him his favorite bedtime stories, in which he showed not the slightest interest. Even though it was only seven-thirty, they were both exhausted. Margaret got Damien into his pajamas, helped him get under the bed sheets of her bed, and climbed into bed herself, where, for the first time, she lay next to Damien. He had confirmed her worst fears about herself. She didn't feel like a woman, much less a mother, when she was with him. She had hoped to feel protective of him, and proud of him, and happy with him in a way a mother does, but only on rare occasions had she felt any of those emotions.

When Margaret awoke early the next morning, Damien was already awake, staring blankly at the ceiling. She said as cheerily as she could manage, "Damien, let's get up and see what you'd like for breakfast." He made no reply. Margaret got out of bed and tried to lift Damien to a sitting position in bed, but his head fell back as if it were the head of a floppy doll. At this point, Margaret said through gritted teeth, "Damien, I know that you're upset about Sybil's leaving. I can understand how hard that is for you. It's hard for me, too. She was very important to both of us, but she's gone and you and I are going to have to make the best of it. Giving up is not a choice for either of us. We both have our jobs in life. Yours is to be a boy who is growing up and will soon be in school. My job is to be the best mother I can be to you. I know I'm not so good at that, but I try very hard. All I'm asking of you is that you try, too."

Margaret then straightened up to a sitting position in bed. She hadn't realized that her face had been only a foot from Damien's face as she was speaking to him.

"Now," she continued, "I will expect you to get out of bed and let me help you get dressed."

He didn't move. Margaret paused to gather herself. She felt infused by the impulse to yell at him, to drag him out of bed, even to hit him. So she left the room before she did any of these things. She walked to the kitchen and called Rose.

"I don't have it in me to give Damien what he needs," Margaret said. "I've just finished lecturing him, and holding myself back from hitting him. I know that we haven't spelled out the specifics of how to reintroduce you to him, or how to tell him that you're going to take him back to live with you, but I think you should take Damien today."

Rose said, "Calm down. I'll come over in a few hours, right after I get Erin off to school."

Margaret, unable to let Rose put the phone down, continued to talk. "I let Damien sleep in my bed last night. Dr. Taylor, the pediatrician, told me to do that. I think that was the right thing to do, but I don't know. I doubt everything I do—I really don't know how to handle children. I feel so relieved that he'll finally have you as his mother again. Should I talk to him about the fact that he'll be going back to live with you?"

"You and I will figure out what to do when I get there."

Now less frantic, Margaret returned to her room and sat at the foot of her bed. She said to Damien, "It's not a good idea for you to lie in bed like this, so we're going to go to the living room. We'll have something to eat while we watch cartoons on TV." She stood and walked to the side of the bed, held out her hand, and took his hand gently into hers. He slid off the side of the bed feet first and stood next to her, his hand still in hers. They walked slowly to the living room where Margaret helped Damien climb up on the couch, where he sat looking at the blank television screen. Margaret wrapped a blanket around him and turned on the television. She went to the kitchen to prepare a breakfast that she knew neither of them would eat. Nothing felt real to her except her profound feeling of failure.

Margaret opened the living room curtains to look out at the street as she waited for Rose. The sound of the cartoons grated on Margaret, but she did not let Damien out of her sight for more than a few minutes at a time for fear he would do something destructive.

Margaret recognized the sound of Rose's car as its tires crunched the gravel. She hurried to the door to help Rose bring in Catherine, with all of her accoutrements. With a great deal of commotion, Rose entered the foyer carrying Catherine and an orange nylon sack. Damien, still sitting on the living room couch, could see Rose as she came in the front door. Rose's attention was so tightly focused on Catherine and Margaret that she didn't see Damien looking at her from the living room, as if he were seeing an image from a dream that he'd forgotten until that moment.

After greeting Rose and Catherine, Margaret went back to the living room. She tucked an afghan around Damien, who was now sitting up on the couch, his feet outstretched in front of him. He seemed much smaller to her than she had expected as she touched his back, and shoulders, and arms.

"Are you all right there?" Margaret asked, not expecting a reply.

Damien looked her directly in the eye and nodded in a way that seemed to her to indicate that he knew something important was happening.

"I'll be in the library, so if you need me, I'll be there."

When Margaret entered the library, Catherine was asleep in Rose's arms with her head tucked into the hollow of Rose's left elbow. Margaret quietly shut the door behind her. She said she was sorry that she had not taken more time to see if Rose could help her manage the situation. The two sisters talked about how to tell Damien that he was going to be living with Rose and his brother and sister. They believed that Damien, in his current state, would not resist anything they instructed him to do, but they also felt that he would be aware of the magnitude of the change that was taking place. They spoke for nearly an hour before Margaret returned to the living room, where Damien was sitting on the couch just as she had left him.

His large brown eyes were fixed on hers as she sat down on the couch next to him.

"Damien, why don't we go into the kitchen, where you and I and Rose can sit together and talk?" She was painfully aware that this was the first time in years that she had used Rose's name while talking with Damien.

Margaret stood and helped Damien off the couch. He padded behind her in his pajamas and socks. On entering the kitchen, he climbed onto his usual chair. Rose sat on the chair to his right and placed Catherine at her feet in the middle of a bevy of stuffed animals and dolls. Catherine fussed a little; it wasn't clear whether she would play quietly or insist that attention be paid to her. Margaret took the seat on the other side of Damien at the circular kitchen table.

Margaret, trying to catch Damien's gaze, said, "I want you to know I love you and want you to feel happy and safe."

She paused, waiting for some sign of understanding, but none was forthcoming.

"What we're going to tell you might be hard to understand. You'll have lots of questions. It is a confusing thing that we're all in the middle of. Do you understand so far?"

After a long silence, Damien, looking down at the table, said quietly, with a hint of anger, "Understand what?"

Margaret was stunned by Damien's response. Since the day Sybil left, this was the most direct and substantive thing he'd said.

"You're right. I haven't told you what I'm going to talk to you about, have I?" She paused, looking to Rose for help, before saying, "I guess the place to start is the story of how you came to live with me. I'll let Rose tell you."

Rose was caught off guard because she had expected to be listening to Margaret talk for quite a while.

Rose, clearly flustered, said, "Damien, I don't know if you can remember any of this, but before you lived with Margaret, you lived with me and your older brother, Erin, and with Catherine, here, who was just a baby. This thing I'm about to say is a big thing. Even though you've been living with Margaret, I'm your Mommy."

"You are?" Damien said as he lifted his head and stared at Rose.

"Yes, I am."

There was loud silence in the room. In the space of a single sentence, the previous order of things had been shattered, and a new order had yet to be revealed.

"You must be wondering why you've been living with Margaret and not with me."

Damien was now looking at Rose, but gave no sign he'd been wondering anything of the sort.

"So I'll tell you. I couldn't take care of you in the way you deserved when you were very small because I was so sad about the fact that your father had just died. I asked Margaret if she would be your Mommy because I wasn't able to be a good Mommy to you."

There was still no indication that Damien understood a word of what Rose was saying. She began to feel that she was talking to him in a foreign language, but she wanted to say what had to be said, even if he didn't understand much of it.

"It made me very sad not to have you with me, but I knew that you were with Margaret, who could love you and take care of you better than I could. I've already said much too much for you to take in all at once. Do you understand any of what I've said?"

"No."

Rose repeated what she'd said, this time trying to divide it up into very small bits.

When she finished, Damien, asked, "Who are you?"

"I'm your Mommy."

"No, you're not."

"It will take time for you to understand what I've already said, but there's another very big thing I'm going to tell you. You've been very, very sad since Sybil left. Margaret and I have decided that you will be happier if you come live with me and your little sister, Catherine, and with Erin, who is a big boy who wants to have you back because he really misses having you to play with. Is that any clearer?"

"No."

"It's all too much at one time. The most important thing to know is that I'm your Mommy."

Appearing utterly confused, he asked, "What's a Mommy?"

"A Mommy is the person who loves you and takes care of you."

"Sybil's my Mommy."

"I know you love Sybil and she loves you, and that she took good care of you. I can't explain what a Mommy is now because it's too complicated, but I promise you that I will answer that question. I won't forget you asked it."

"Who are you?" Damien asked, looking straight at Rose.

"I'm here because I'm your Mommy and I'm going to take you home with me and Catherine."

"No, you're not."

"I am because that is what's best for you, and because I want to be your Mommy and love you and take care of you every minute of the day and night."

Damien's face exploded into tears. He paused only to get his breath before the next flood of fat tears came rolling from his eyes. Rose pushed her chair back and stood up. She picked Damien up from his chair, wrapped her arms around him, and held him tightly to her, his wet cheeks pressed against hers. He didn't resist. He was much heavier than she'd expected. She clumsily made her way to the living room couch where she lay Damien down with his head on her lap. She stroked his hair and sang to him as he fell asleep. He slept for three-quarters of an hour while Margaret played quietly with Catherine in the kitchen.

When Damien woke up, he rubbed his eyes with his fists, but didn't try to pull away from Rose. Rose stood up, her hand still on Damien's shoulder. She looked at Margaret to signal that she was going to bring Damien out to her car, and that Margaret should bring Catherine. Once they were settled in Rose's car—Catherine in her car seat, Damien harnessed into his seat belt, with Rose between them—Margaret started the car and drove slowly to Rose's house, as if she were driving a hearse.

## FIFTEEN

E rin was surprised to see a boy in the kitchen with his mother and Catherine when he returned home from school that day in early June. Rose explained as best she could that Damien, whom Erin remembered as a very young child, was now going to be living with them again. Erin didn't really care about the details of why Damien was there. All that mattered to him was that he finally had a brother. The girly things that his mother and Catherine liked were boring and annoying to him. Erin asked his mother if Damien was going to be staying forever. When Rose said he was, he beamed with excitement. Erin's enthusiasm caused Damien to pull back, but he soon became entranced by this older boy who was so full of a feeling that he had never before encountered. It was a good feeling, a feeling he could feel in his body that was like laughter in his chest.

Before his mother finished her explanation of what was happening, Erin grabbed Damien's arm and pulled him off his chair, into the front hall, and up the stairs. Before Damien knew what was happening to him, he found himself in a room with two beds separated by a small table, two windows above the beds, a closet to his left, and a dresser in the middle of the wall opposite the beds. "That's your bed," Erin said, pointing to the bed farther from the door, "and this one's mine."

Realizing that Damien had not yet spoken a single word, Erin asked, "Do you know what I'm talking about?"

"Yeah."

"You get it that I'm your brother?"

Damien said, "Yeah," even though he didn't really know what a brother was or what he had to do to be a brother to this boy who was much older than he was.

Things seemed to move very quickly in this house. At Margaret's, everything was planned ahead of time. There were no surprises. In this house, almost everything was a surprise—most of all, Erin bursting upon the scene.

Damien felt as if he had awoken, or maybe he was still dreaming, and found himself in a different world—a world in which he was a visitor, and he didn't know how long he would be allowed to stay, no matter what anyone said. He wondered, Why was there no one like Sybil in Rose's house? Maybe there is and he hadn't met her yet. Rose kept saying she was sad that his father, who was also Catherine's and Erin's father, had died, but even though he knew that a father was a man, he didn't know what the man did to make him a father. He'd never really understood it in stories and cartoons.

He was fascinated and puzzled by Catherine's girlishness. She was pretty. Neither Margaret nor Sybil was pretty. Rose was pretty. Everything of Catherine's was either pink or purple. She was delicate, light—as if there were just air inside her. She always had a doll with her. He couldn't understand that; he had seen dolls in packages at toy stores where they looked like rock-hard, miniature dead babies, which gave him the creeps.

Bedtime, that first night at Rose's house, was frightening for Damien. He had had a growing feeling of dread as it got dark outside and he could feel bedtime approaching. Catherine had her own room, and Rose put her to bed while he and

Erin watched television. He could hear Rose reading bedtime stories to Catherine. He wished Margaret were there to read stories to him. He didn't know where Margaret was now. Was she alone in her house? He missed Sybil terribly and tried not to think of her, but she came to mind anyway—many times every day.

Damien had seen boys as big as Erin at playgrounds, but none had ever shown any interest in talking to him, much less playing with him. At the end of the television program, as a police show began, Rose told them it was time for bed. Damien's stomach tightened. Rose helped Damien wash his face and hands and brush his teeth. Once they were in their beds, she gave Erin a kiss on his forehead, and then gave him a kiss too.

After Rose left and the lights were out, Erin said, "Damien."

Damien was so surprised that it took him a few seconds to utter the word, "Yeah?"

Damien didn't know what he was supposed to do when Erin spoke to him from his bed in the faded light. He hardly knew Erin, but he already trusted him. Erin didn't make fun of him or Catherine, and hadn't laughed at him when he asked questions that everyone else knew the answers to. Damien had watched everything that Erin did that day very carefully because he wanted to do things exactly the way Erin did them.

"You've been living at Margaret's house, right?"

"Yeah."

"Were you sick all the time when you were there?"

"No, I wasn't sick. Just a cold or stomach ache once in a while."

"And you're going to live here from now on?"

"I think so, but I'm not sure."

"Do you want to live here?"

"I don't know ... I think so."

"That's cool. Catherine's a girl, and she's okay, but I want a brother."

"What's a brother?"

"You really don't know?"

"They told me, but I forget what they said you have to do to be a brother."

Erin didn't feel like explaining what a brother is. He'd been curious about who this person called Sybil was, so he asked, "Who's Sybil?"

"She was my Mommy, but she left."

"What do you mean, she left?"

"Sybil said that she wanted to live with her sister who lives in the Bronx, so she left."

"I don't get who Sybil is."

"I don't know. She played with me and cooked and used the vacuum cleaner. I think she was my Mommy."

"What do you mean you 'think'?"

"I don't know."

Erin was stunned by how much Damien didn't know. It seemed to him that Damien had been kept in Margaret's house from the time he was hardly more than a baby, and they—Margaret and someone named Sybil—hadn't taught him anything. Erin had only a vague memory of Damien as a little kid and didn't remember much about him, other than the fact that he used to cry a lot at night. Erin felt sorry for Damien when he asked questions like "What's a brother?" He didn't know how to answer questions like that because when he was young, he had never had to have anyone explain to him what a sister or a brother was. You don't have to have someone explain something like that. You just know.

Erin, beginning to catch on to why Damien didn't know what these words meant, said, "You don't know what happened to you, do you?"

"What do you mean?"

"You don't know why you were living with Margaret and why you're coming to live with us now, do you?"

"No … they explained it, but I can't remember. Do you know?"

"Not really, only that it was too hard for Mom to take care of all three of us after Dad died."

"Who's Dad?"

"I knew you were going to ask that. Dad died just before Catherine was born."

"What did he die of?"

"He was riding a motorcycle."

"Yeah, I know what a motorcycle is, so you don't have to tell me."

"He was hit by a truck that didn't stop at a stop sign and he died. So that's why he's not here in our family."

"Do you remember him?"

"Yeah, but I can't tell which parts of what I remember are things I actually remember, and which things I was told about. I know I liked him a lot. One thing I definitely remember was sitting with him on a cement wall. He was peeling an orange with a jack knife. When he got all the peel off, he tore the orange in half and gave half to me, and kept half for himself. A woman policeman came to the house here and told Mom he was dead. I was here when she came and told her. You were, too, I guess, but I don't remember you being there."

Damien didn't understand very much of what Erin said, but he could hear that Erin missed his father, maybe the way he missed Sybil. It seemed Erin had been talking to himself mostly.

The two boys were silent for a long time as they fell asleep. The light from the windows over their beds had darkened and made the dressers, desk, and door nearly invisible. A blacker darkness seemed to gather in the corners of the room, which scared Damien.

# SIXTEEN

In late August, the humidity was beginning to abate and the formerly lush green leaves of the oaks and maples seemed dry and tired, readying themselves for the burst of color that announced their own death and the beginning of fall. There were a few days when the air was filled with white fluff carrying the seeds of the cottonwoods. Damien, now at Rose's house for almost two months, was unrestrained in his rapture for Erin. He followed his older brother around the house with his eyes drinking up his every gesture.

Having a brother, for Erin, was an entirely different thing from having a friend. Erin had what others would call friends, but he found little pleasure in spending time with them. He sat with them in the lunchroom and talked with them for a while after school, but he rarely felt glad to see them. Erin was well coordinated and had a natural talent for sports, but he felt bored playing the same games day after day—baseball in the spring and summer, touch football in the autumn, and ice hockey on the frozen ponds in the winter. Erin was a kind and very likable boy. His friends made allowances for him, and accepted the fact that he had his own way of doing things.

He saw Damien as a very cute little guy, but he was keenly aware that Damien was a boy who would be considered odd, and would be picked on by other kids at school if he didn't learn how to act normal. Erin took it upon himself to teach Damien about the real world. At first, it was difficult for Erin to discern what kind of boy Damien was, what came naturally to him. Erin taught him how to throw and catch a tennis ball, how to ride a bike, how to ask Rose for money and walk to town together to buy candy. Erin was endlessly patient with his younger brother, rarely showing frustration in response to Damien's ignorance of the most basic things in the life of a boy. Damien didn't even know how to swim or who Babe Ruth was. Erin occasionally couldn't stop himself from saying out loud, "What did you do while you were living at Margaret's?" Damien didn't have an answer to the question. It hadn't seemed strange or boring to him at the time. You had to know Sybil to understand, and Erin would never meet her, so he'd never understand.

What gave Damien the greatest pleasure was going to the movies with Erin, where they'd eat popcorn from the extra-large container that they propped between them. The first time Erin saw Damien overflow with excitement was while they watched *Rocky*. Erin liked the movie, but even more he enjoyed watching Damien out of the corner of his eye. Damien was mesmerized by the story, the fights, the music; he leaned forward in his seat, not wanting to miss anything anyone said or a single blow dealt out by Rocky. He winced each time a punch landed squarely on Rocky's face. Damien's face fell when Rocky was thrown out of the gym by Mickey, the gym manager, for letting himself go to pot as a boxer. Mickey was tough on Rocky, but he was the only one to see his potential, and eventually to love him as he would a son.

As they were walking up the aisle of the movie theater afterward, Erin knew, before Damien said a word, that Damien imagined himself to be Rocky and Erin to be Mickey. Erin was the only one who saw the potential in Rocky, whom everyone else saw as a misfit. Damien, although younger than Erin, was taller, broader-shouldered, and larger-framed, which made their *Rocky* roles all the more real and captivating for Damien. As they pushed open the front door of the movie theater and felt the blast of mid-afternoon August heat, Damien couldn't get the words out of his mouth fast enough. "It didn't matter that Rocky lost the championship fight—it was good enough for him to get there, wasn't it?" Erin had never seen Damien so excited. He was acting like a normal kid. Damien tried to talk like Rocky and told Erin to talk like Mickey. Erin said to Damien, "You're a lowlife, you're out o' shape, you don't know nuttin' 'bout boxin'. If you wanna 'mount to anyting, you gotta listen to me, ya got dat?"

"Yeah, okay," Damien replied somberly, trying to echo Rocky's lack of belief in himself.

"Forget I said anyting. Ya know so goddamn much. Be a loser for the rest o' your life if ya want. Get outta here! I don't wanna look at ya."

Damien, not completely able to separate Mickey from Erin in his mind, said pleadingly, "Nah, I'll train right. You'll see."

"It's too late for ya. I tink I'd be wastin' my time."

"Just give me a chance. I'll show you."

"You're built big and you act tough, but you don't know da first ting 'bout boxing. Boxing ain't fighting. Any thug can fight, but you gotta know what you're doin' if you wanna box. Ya gotta dance in da ring, 'float like a butterfly, sting like a bee.' You ever hear that before?"

Damien, not knowing if it was Erin or Mickey asking the question, said meekly, "No."

"Ya' never heard of Muhammad Ali?"

"No."

"Where da hell you been, kid? You don't know nuttin'."

Erin knew immediately that he had hit a nerve when he spoke those words. Damien loosened the tight grip he'd had on Erin's eyes and let his gaze drift.

"Come on, kid. If you're gonna get knocked down so easy, you're never gonna make it. You wanna make it or don't ya?"

"I wanna make it."

"You gotta get ready for the next fight 'cause if ya lose twice in a row, you're washed up, you're back in the gutter where you started."

"I know that."

"You gotta start trainin' now—not tomorrow, not next week, now. You in or not?"

"Yeah, I'm in," Damien said, hardly able to contain himself.

"See that telephone pole at the street corner up there, with the big white thing near the top? Let's see what you can do. Run up and back. I wanna see ya fly."

Damien took off, but he lumbered along as if he were carrying dead weight on his back. He had never once tried to run as fast as he could. Damien was big, but he could feel as he ran that he was neither fast nor agile.

As he crossed the makeshift finish line that Erin had made with a few sticks across the sidewalk, Damien was gasping for air and dripping with sweat.

"You're outta shape. I seen guys like you come and go. If you wanna 'mount to anyting, it's gonna take work, a lotta work. I don't know if ya got it in ya to be a boxer."

Again unsure whether Erin was speaking as himself or as Mickey, Damien said, "Yeah, I do. I'm slow, but I've never run that long before. If I work at it, I can do better. You'll see."

"You're damned right you're slow. Boxing is all in the legs, not the arms. Before you set one foot in da ring, you gotta become a runner."

"You tell me what to do and I'll do it," Damien said, still not sure if Erin was speaking for himself.

By the time they got home, it was dinnertime. At the table, Damien was quiet. He was afraid that the training Erin had talked about was just playacting that didn't really mean anything to Erin. When they were in bed and the lights were out,

Erin said, "No talkin' tonight. Ya gotta rest. Tomorrow's da beginning of training. We'll see what you're made of."

Damien didn't say a word, but he couldn't sleep. He was too excited to sleep. He could hear the music playing in the movie as Rocky worked out in the gym wearing his black boxing shorts—all sweaty, no shirt, with a white towel draped around his neck. He could see Rocky running in place, lifting his knees waist high again and again. Rocky pounded the long leather punching bag: Bam, bam, bam, bam, bam. After at least a hundred punches, Rocky climbed up through the ropes into the ring where he put on his sparring headgear and mouth guard. He bounced on his toes while throwing compact punches into the air in front of him as he impatiently waited for his sparring partner to climb into the ring.

Now imagining his first real fight, against a second-rate opponent, Damien saw Erin standing in Rocky's corner of the ring—Rocky sitting on his stool, his eyes fixed on his opponent as he listened to Mickey tell him how to handle the first round. "Remember, you're a boxer, not a fighter. Let him chase you 'round da ring, tire himself out punchin' at air. When he ain't expectin' nuttin' from ya, you hit him with an upper cut to the chin and then a cannonball to the gut. He'll lean to ya, and you land a strong right to the head. Ya got that?"

Damien slept lightly for most of the night, looking at the illuminated clock on the dresser across the room every half hour or so.

Standing next to Damien's bed, with Damien's back to him, Erin gripped him by his upturned left shoulder and shook him hard. Damien was startled, but after a few seconds understood what was happening. It was only six-thirty on Sunday morning. Nobody else was awake. They walked out the front door, not saying a word. The air was already sapped of the coolness of the night air. Gnats were buzzing around their heads. The sun was hanging low in the cloudless, pale blue sky.

Erin led the way to the ridge overlooking the floor of the valley where dark green fields of soybean stretched outward, as if trying to reach the foot of the hills that were half hidden in morning haze. They walked on the dirt road that ran along the top of the ridge. The road was only wide enough for a single car or piece of farm machinery. The two boys walked quickly along the crest of the ridge for a quarter mile or so before Erin stopped, turned to Damien, and said, "Let's see what we're startin' wit. Jog the road we just walked. Don't worry 'bout speed, we're lookin for endurance. This is a marathon, not a sprint. Whatever ya do, don't stop runnin'."

Damien didn't know what a marathon or a sprint was, but he lumbered down the road like a slow-moving freight train, running slower and slower as he went, trying with every ounce of energy he had not to stop moving. His arms, for the most part, were slunk to his side, but occasionally he lifted his forearms in an attempt to look like Rocky, but when he did, he looked more like a chicken beating its wings as it jumped a few feet to get some feed.

When he finally got back to where Erin was standing, he bent down, hands on his knees, out of breath, his T-shirt soaked with sweat.

"That's okay for day one, but it's nuttin' ta brag about."

It was never entirely clear to either boy whether they were speaking for themselves or for the characters they were imitating. The workouts were real. Both boys took them seriously. Erin pushed Damien hard. When school resumed in September, they walked home briskly, changed their clothes, and walked to the ridge or some other place that Erin thought would be right for the training he had in mind for that afternoon. Erin was much happier spending his time with Damien than hanging out with school friends. Damien had no school friends, and he cherished every minute with Erin.

As Erin watched Damien train, his heart went out to this boy, big for his age, with large round cheeks and deep dark eyes—a clueless innocent. He didn't know anything about how the world really works. Rose knew that the two boys were imitating something they'd seen at the movies, but she didn't ask any questions for fear of interfering with something she felt was good for both her sons. She washed Damien's sweat-soaked clothes and overheard bits of conversation between the brothers that they thought were sufficiently encoded as to keep their story line a secret. For Rose, as she watched Erin and Damien together, Erin was the innocent—he really believed he could give Damien all that he'd never had from their father or anyone else. It was just like Erin to become the father he himself had had only briefly, she thought. Such a sweet boy. It pained Rose to recognize that while she loved Erin deeply, she didn't love Damien, or loved him in a very different way. Her heart went out to him, and she felt terribly guilty about what she'd done to him. She thought he probably couldn't remember a lot of what had happened, but not a second of it was lost to her.

In the world of the Rocky game, Erin and Damien created something that both of them badly needed. They kept the game secret in order not to have it spoiled by anyone. Their own feelings about it changed, sometimes from hour to hour. They argued, they yelled at one another, they fought, they'd walk off by themselves, but they always came back. There was a constancy to the Rocky game: They were tied to one another for reasons that they did not have names for—not because of the limits of their vocabulary, but because the names simply didn't exist. It felt as if this were something no two other people had ever had. Surprising to both of them were the intensity of the feelings the game evoked and the tenacity with which they protected it. It would remain an important part of their lives for years—in truth, for the rest of their lives. It would be one of the closest relationships either of them would ever have.

The bond between Damien and Erin was both an introduction to life with other people in the world, and a barrier to it. Damien learned to talk with the other boys at school in a way that was a reasonable facsimile of the ways the other boys talked to one another. School, for Damien, was not a place in which to grow up with other boys, and later with girls; it was a place in which to learn about what could be done with words and numbers, both of which interested him greatly. Nevertheless, all day as he sat in class, Damien looked forward to walking home with Erin.

## SEVENTEEN

Only after Margaret settled into the smaller of the two armchairs in his office did she have a chance to study his face: Hazel eyes, a close-cut white beard, bushy eyebrows, probably in his late sixties, maybe seventy—a kind face, she thought. He nodded in her direction.

"A psychiatrist friend gave me your name. He said that you're the most highly regarded psychiatrist in Chicago."

"I'm sorry," he said in a thick French accent.

"Why?"

"I'd hoped it would be a larger area than that."

Margaret smiled, but was wary of his humor. She didn't like it when people were witty because it was difficult for her to read the intent beneath it.

"Where should we start?"

"Do you want the truth?"

"We could try that."

"To get some help divorcing my husband."

"I doubt that."

"Doubt what?"

"That that's why you're here."

"You just met me, you know nothing about me or my marriage, and you presume to tell me that that's not why I'm here."

119

"You know very well that you didn't come here to get help divorcing your husband. I can tell right away that you're an intelligent woman who knows the mechanics of getting a divorce, and you're not someone who's unable to take care of herself in a struggle, so why not try to tell me the truth about why you're here."

"The truth is I don't know."

"That sounds more like the truth to me, too."

"I didn't want to marry in the first place."

"Allow me to interrupt. Please try to leave your husband out of this. You have good reason for wanting to be here, and it's not him. He's just a distraction."

Margaret was taken aback by his forcefulness.

"I feel more lonely in the house when he's there than when he's not, and please don't interrupt me to call me a liar again. I've never wanted a husband or children. My sister, Rose—the pretty one, the girly one, the maternal one—she's good with men and good with children. I've been puzzled by this difference between us all my life, and felt bad about what's missing in me, but I've never wanted to change places with her. Every boy and every man who has laid eyes on her has wanted to have sex with her—not just a one-night stand, but to marry her, adore her, and spend their lives with her. No one would want that with me, and I don't blame them, I wouldn't want it with them either."

"I would marry you, but my wife would kill me if I did."

Margaret laughed. It was more than a nervous laugh, it was a deep laugh. He actually seemed to like her, she thought, but she couldn't be sure. Was he flirting with her? She had never known how to respond to flirting. Rose had tried to teach her by playing the role of a boy trying to flirt with her, but she was hopeless at it.

"I didn't expect you to have a sense of humor."

"Thank you, you're very kind," he said.

"No, no one has ever accused me of being kind. I'm pragmatic, not kind. You interrupted me."

"I'm sorry, please go on."

"It's not easy for me to talk, so when I'm doing it, don't interrupt me."

"You were saying that Rose is the one everyone wants to marry, and they'd be foolish to choose you."

"That's right. And I'd be foolish to choose them. Marriage doesn't suit me; it just doesn't. I'm not attracted to women either, if that's what you're thinking. As self-centered as it sounds, I like my own company. I don't even like pets. They're nothing but a nuisance as far as I can tell. I like puttering in my house with classical music playing. I know I sound like an old woman, but I don't feel old. I've already filed for divorce, by the way. He's being very decent about it, actually. No squabbles over money or property. We don't hate each other, we just don't want to be married to each other. I know you're saying to yourself, everything is good, no trouble with the divorce, she's looking forward to living on her own again with her classical music playing, so why is she here? I'm not an impulsive woman—you must have figured that out by now. I've thought for a long time—probably for years, maybe since I was a teenager—that I wanted to see a shrink. I'd never admit that to anyone, except maybe Rose, but I've never said it to her. As a teenager it was because I felt bad about not being like other girls and their endless chatter about 'cute' boys. In college and graduate school, I no longer wanted to be like other girls. I liked being good at what I was doing, I liked being smart—not because it made me better than anyone else—simply because I found the world and my own mind to be interesting. I had my brief feminist jaunt—reading Simone de Beauvoir and Isak Dinesen, whom I liked, and Gloria Steinem, Germaine Greer, Betty Friedan, whom I didn't like—too political for me. I don't like books that try to convince; I like books that are convincing because the book works, and the author trusts the reader to do their part of the work. I may sound like a snob, but I really don't care what I sound like."

"What do you care about?"

"I care about feeling good about the work I do and the way I do it. I'm meticulously honest in my work; I work in the investment division of a bank. Being dishonest would land me in court or in jail, but that's not the reason I'm honest. What satisfaction is there in winning a game in which you've been cheating? Anyone can win if they cheat. I know I haven't answered your question, or is it mine, about why I'm here. I think I'm getting there, so don't rush me. I was not my father's favorite. Guess who it was … and I'll give you a clue: It wasn't my mother. Did I care?: Yes. Do I care now?: As far as I can tell, no. Winning that game is like winning a game you don't want to win. Your prize is a man you want nothing to do with. I know you're saying to yourself: Little does she know, she longs for her father's love, and she won't accept a substitute for the real thing, so she'll never be attracted to any man. Am I close?"

"No. You'll know when you're close."

"So give me a clue."

"Even if I had a clue to give you, it wouldn't do you a bit of good to hear it from me."

"So what's your job here?"

"How would I know? You'll have to teach me that."

"I thought it was only in cartoons and Woody Allen movies that psychiatrists use couches."

"There are a few of us left who do."

"Do you want me to lie on the couch?"

"If you want to."

"I don't know if I want to."

"I think you do know."

"It would feel like pillow talk, wouldn't it?"

"How would I know? We haven't tried it."

"I didn't come here to talk about lying on your couch."

"Maybe you did, but I don't think that's what's most pressing now."

"So what is most pressing now?"

"You're asking the wrong person."

"Isn't there anything that's your job here?"

"Yes, I'm waiting to hear you tell me what it is. I'm not playing word games with you, I'm telling you the truth. Try not to reply right away, and see what happens."

Toward the end of the session, he asked, "Would you like to talk again?"

Margaret was surprised that he'd be open to seeing her again after the way she'd treated him.

"Why not?" Margaret said, surprised to hear the words come from her mouth.

# EIGHTEEN

It had been an unusually cold autumn and early winter, with the first heavy snow in October, and by November the temperature rarely rose above forty degrees. For months on end, the sky was gunmetal gray in the early morning, and seemed to grow only slightly brighter as the day progressed before collapsing back into sooty darkness in the late afternoon.

As Damien waited for Erin after school, he paced back and forth near the bicycle stand atop the hill that overlooked the weathered brick high school building. Damien stopped to look at the bicycle that was attached to the stand by a rusty chain. The bike was a beat-up, black Schwinn that reminded him of the one he'd had when Erin taught him how to ride a bike a few months after he returned to Rose's house. For Damien, where he had lived at that time was "Rose's house," not "his house." But now he thought of it as his house, most of the time.

His mind drifted to his life with Margaret and Sybil. As he pictured the house, it had no doors. He wondered where Sybil was living now. It was hard to imagine because Sybil didn't feel real to him; it was as if she had come into this world from nowhere and returned to nowhere when she left. Sometimes he felt she was a ghost who had haunted him, and no one else had ever seen her, not even Margaret.

The wind was picking up now and sent a chill through Damien's body. From his elevated lookout, he saw students pouring out of the high school building in a steady gush. The girls were bundled in thick parkas, scarves, gloves, earmuffs, and various forms of woolen ski hats. They looked like grown women compared with the junior high school girls. They also seemed older than the high school boys who were walking in packs alongside the girls. It wasn't just the curves of the bodies of the high school girls that made them seem older; it was the knowing look on their faces. They were in charge, and they knew what was going on. They looked like they knew all about sex. The boys didn't have that look. They looked green.

Damien spotted Erin coming through the doors. He looked up to the top of the hill and waved a gloved hand at Damien.

At this time of year, the streets were too icy to ride their bikes, so they walked. They made an odd couple. Erin, blond and slender; Damien, olive-skinned, tall, and large-framed, but not fat.

"Mr. Lerner was really cool today," Damien said, bursting to tell Erin what had happened. "He asked two kids to come to the front of the class and playact being a slave owner and his slave before the Civil War. And he told the kid who was playing the slave owner to order the slave to do something. Did Mr. Lerner do that when you had him?"

"No, not with slaves, but with other things."

"So the kid playing the slave owner said, 'Get me my book from my desk.' And the kid playing the slave went over to the desk, got the book, and brought it back, and handed it to him. Mr. Lerner said that the scene the two kids had acted missed the most important part of slavery. He asked if anyone in the class had had the same feeling he did as they watched the kids act it out. A lot of kids said that they felt it wasn't acted right. But when he asked them what was wrong, none of them could say what it was. I thought I knew why it wasn't right, but I didn't raise my hand."

"Why not?"

"You know why."

"I don't."

"I've told you a hundred times."

"What?"

"For the hundred and first time, I'm afraid no words will come out of my mouth."

"You're a smart kid."

"Forget it."

"No. I won't forget it. What's the worst thing that could happen?"

"Just let me tell you what happened."

"Okay, go ahead."

"You know Mr. Lerner. He likes to make things all dramatic. He looked around the room, looking for someone who got it. Then he said that the kids who felt there was something wrong probably didn't have the words to put the feeling into. He said the way the two kids had acted it just seemed to him like someone ordering someone else around. You know the way he talks.

"Everyone looked at him all confused. They thought he hadn't said anything more than what he'd said before. You see what he was getting at?"

"No."

Damien was grinning now. He had waited all day to tell Erin the story, but he wanted to make the moment last.

Erin was silent for a few seconds. "Tell me again what Mr. Lerner said."

"He said that when the two kids acted the scene, it was wrong because it was just one person ordering someone else around."

"Isn't that what slave owners did to slaves, order them around?"

Damien laughed a big belly laugh—not a mocking laugh, but the laughter of a boy who feels life doesn't get any better than this.

"You have to listen to every word that Mr. Lerner said! He said the scene was wrong because it was just someone bossing someone else around. His point was that there wouldn't be two 'someones' in a realistic scene of a slave owner and a slave. In a scene that really understands slavery, there's only one person, one 'someone,' only one human being, and that's the slave owner. Do you get it now?"

"Sort of."

"The slave isn't 'someone,' he isn't a person, he's no one, he's a possession the same as any other possession, like a car or a watch or anything else. Mr. Lerner asked the kid playing the slave owner to act the scene again, and Mr. Lerner played the part of the slave. So when the scene began, Mr. Lerner just stood there looking at the floor. When the kid playing the slave owner ordered him to get the book from his desk, Mr. Lerner didn't move right away. He just kept looking down for a little while, and then walked to the kid's desk in a kind of daze, always looking at the floor, and then he picked up the book and walked slowly back to where he'd been standing in front of the slave owner, not too close. You expected he'd just hand the book to the slave owner, but he stood there with the book in his hand by his side, and then it seemed like the slave might be disobeying or refusing to go through with it, but then he lifted his hand slowly, not to give the book to the owner, but to put it there in front of him so the slave owner could take it or not take it, or do anything else he wanted to do with it. The slave had made himself into a kind of table with a book on it. It was spooky. It was like he was dead, but could move around."

"You got that before Mr. Lerner explained why he was acting it that way?"

"Yeah, not exactly in the way he explained it, but I knew it was wrong to have the slave behave like an employee. To be owned by someone hollows you out. You're already dead. That much I got."

128

Erin said, "And you didn't say anything. Why not?"

"I was too scared. Anyway, I haven't even told you what happened. Even after Mr. Lerner played the slave in the way he did, no one got what he meant when he said that the scene was wrong because there was someone ordering someone else around. Mike Kapoc, who's got a really big mouth that he's flapping all the time, said he didn't get it.

"Mr. Lerner asked him to listen carefully to each word as he explained how he thought about the scene. Mr. Lerner said what I just told you about his reasons for acting the part the way he did. I could tell that Kapoc still didn't get it, even though he said he did.

"This girl said that she thought the slave owner would have whipped the slave because he wasn't doing things fast enough. The slave owner would use any excuse to whip the slave. Mr. Lerner said that slaves were a cheap form of labor, much cheaper than buying farm machinery, so the slave owner isn't going to damage a valuable possession any more than he'd intentionally bash a piece of machinery, unless he was crazy, and some of the slave owners were crazy, but most of them weren't—they just thought that slaves were the cheapest way to run their farms.

"Mr. Lerner said a slave would never look a slave owner in the eye. He said that looking someone in the eye means you're someone. Privates in the army look a sergeant in the eye when the sergeant is giving them orders. Teachers and students do that, too, or at least they should. Mr. Lerner said we're his equals, even though we have different roles. He said not all teachers in this school treat students as equals, but he didn't name any of them. Did he say things like that when you had him?"

"Yeah, he was famous for that. He's the only teacher who would talk about the fact that there are bad teachers. Even though he never mentioned anyone by name, you had a pretty good idea who he was talking about."

"After some different kids acted out other scenes of slaves and slave owners, Mr. Lerner asked what we thought a slave owner imagined it would feel like to be a slave. Different kids said that a good slave owner would feel sorry for his slave, and other kids said he wouldn't give a shit—they didn't use that word—about what the slave was feeling. Mr. Lerner said that every person is different, and so he couldn't say what all slave owners felt, but he guessed that most of them never asked themselves that question, any more than we ask ourselves what a chair feels like when we sit on it or when we knock it over. And then he said he wondered how many of us tried to imagine what it's like to be a black kid in our school that has twelve hundred white kids and about thirty black kids in it. No one said anything after he said that.

"At the end of the class he told us to try to imagine what it would feel like to be no one—not a nobody, but no one. He didn't want us to say anything now, but we should really think about it, not just brush it off."

Erin and Damien were so absorbed in what they were talking about that they were oblivious to the familiar terrain on which they were making their way home. They had, without noticing what they were doing, left the school parking lot and walked west, past the apartment buildings with their faded green awnings on which were stenciled in cracked white paint the street numbers and occasionally the name of the building. Some of the names—Pinnacle House, The Emperor Hotel, The Regency—were names for apartment buildings that had seen better days. As they walked, the neighborhoods changed from residential to commercial and the apartment buildings gave way to cavernous warehouses, some of which were being used as body shops in which sparks flew from welding torches like white and orange fireworks; corner markets and liquor stores were scattered here and there. Outside the stores, men talked quietly, occasionally laughing, all drinking from liquor bottles wrapped in brown paper bags: The men, part of the stores, and the stores, part of the men; once in a while they'd cross paths with a gang of high school boys roaming their territory, looking for a fight with anyone who dared look at them.

The end of the commercial district was marked by three huge conical concrete blocks that looked like the forms a child might make on a beach with a pail filled with wet sand, turned upside down. Beyond the cones, a dirt path sloped steeply into a gully, across which loomed the tall arched entry to the tunnel that ran beneath the railroad tracks. As you got near to the mouth of the tunnel, dull gray daylight became visible at the far end.

Every detail of the physical surround of their walk home had become so familiar as to be virtually invisible to Erin and Damien, but if even one detail were altered, both boys would have been immediately alert to it. Neither boy wanted anything to change. If they could have frozen time that afternoon, they would have, and would have gladly lived in that moment forever.

## NINETEEN

On that late August morning when Erin was getting ready to leave, he said he didn't want anyone going with him to the train station. Rose had made a mushroom omelet, which sat untouched in a fry pan on the stove. Damien remained in the bedroom that was now his alone, while Catherine and Rose gathered last-minute items that they thought Erin might need for the train trip.

After he knocked on the door to the bedroom he had shared with Damien, Erin thought he heard a muffled voice, but knocked again in case he was wrong. This time he heard Damien's grumbly voice saying, "Come in."

The room was dark and thick with the smell of sweaty shoes and clothes that lay on the floor under the deeply scratched wooden desk. Damien lay face down on his bed, his hands buried under his pillow.

"Damien, it's not so bad. We can talk on the phone and I'll come home for vacations, and there are lots of long vacation breaks, and you can come visit me."

"It won't be the same at all," Damien said into the pillow. "I'll be here with Rose and Catherine, and you'll be there in a new place, with new people. I don't have a place here, or anywhere else, so don't act as if I do."

"You're a senior this year. In a year, you could be there at the university with me, if you want."

"You can say you'll want me there, but you don't know how you'll feel a year from now. You'll be different then."

"I'll be the same asshole I am now."

Damien couldn't hold back a smile. Erin sat down on the bed next to Damien and put his hand on his back.

"I promise you I'm going to be the same asshole I am now when you join me next year. I don't promise things I don't mean. Have I ever promised anything and not kept my word?"

Damien nodded, his face still pressed into the pillow.

"What do you mean, I've broken a promise?"

"You probably don't remember, but I do," Damien said, lifting his head a few inches, but still looking down. "After I got back here from Margaret's house, you told me that I would be just as much a member of this family as you and Catherine were. I believed you, but it never happened. I've never felt that."

"I don't remember promising that. Give me a break, I was just a little kid when I said that."

"Sure I can give you a break, but this is the same kind of promise. You're claiming to be able to predict the future, and you can't."

"It's not the same thing as back then," Erin said. "I thought I could predict how we all were going to be. I shouldn't have promised that. But this time I'm telling you what I really know for sure. You're my best friend. And we've been best friends almost our whole lives. That doesn't wash off."

Damien lifted his head a little more, and then slowly turned and looked deeply into Erin's face, holding him in his gaze, gathering as much of him into himself as he could.

Erin's voice was choked with tears as he tried to get the words out, "It'll be fine, I know it will." Tears rolled down Erin's face.

Rose called up to Erin to rush him along.

After Erin left the room, Damien pulled the top sheet and blanket over his head. The ache in his chest persisted as his mind drifted. Sounds and images and feelings from that awful afternoon, now a year or two ago, were still very much alive in him. Because the roads were icy in the morning, he and Erin had walked to school. On the way home, they'd made their way down the steep hill leading to the tunnel. It was spring and the path was muddy. In the tunnel below the railroad tracks, stagnant pools of water gave off a horrible stench. The bricks on the walls and rounded ceiling were covered with dark, wet moss. Big drops of liquid congealed and then fell from the ceiling, making dull splats as they hit the black pools of water on the ground.

Erin was the first to hear the footsteps and forced laughter of high school thugs behind them. Erin told Damien not to look back and not to run, but to be ready if he heard them closing in. There was no need to say another word to signal to Damien that they were now living an episode from their childhood game. They had never rehearsed this kind of situation, but they both immediately knew how they would play it.

They could tell from the sound of the voices and footsteps behind them that there weren't many of them, five or six at most, which was a little disappointing. Both Damien and Erin felt a surge of excitement coursing through their bodies as the footsteps of the gang quickened. They could hear the voice of the gang leader, Jimmy Hetch, a senior who was periodically suspended from school for throwing a kid against the lockers, or sticking someone's head into the toilet, or smoking pot behind the gym (though no one could prove it was pot because he swallowed the joint before it could be taken from him). Damien and Erin turned and looked briefly at the thugs—three with dark hoodies pulled up over their heads, two in sweats with shaved heads and blue tattoos that looked like snakes crawling up their necks.

135

In the space of a few seconds, the gang had surrounded them. Three of them leapt on Damien and pinned him to the wall of the tunnel, while Hetch grabbed Erin and twisted his arm behind his back.

"You're not the hot-shit, pretty boy you think you are when you're out here in the real world, are you, you fucking Mick? You're nothing but a faggot, you and your overgrown ape of a faggot brother over there. You think you can do whatever you fucking want?"

Hetch threw Erin in the direction of Lascalzo, his lieutenant. Erin stumbled, almost falling to the ground. Lascalzo, who had the face of a pit bull, then grabbed Erin's arm and jerked him upright. He wrapped his arms around Erin from behind and squeezed his ribcage, forcing all the air out of Erin's lungs, while Hetch pushed his face into Erin's so close that Erin could feel the warm moisture of Hetch's foul-smelling breath spread across his face. Lascalzo released Erin and shoved him to Hetch, who had stepped back a few paces. Hetch caught him in his extended arms, turned him around, and pushed him away while sticking out his foot. Erin fought to keep his balance, but fell chest first onto the slime-coated floor of the tunnel.

"Are you high on something, faggot boy? No? Then why can't you stand on your own two feet, you fucking dick?"

Damien, not able to watch what was happening any longer, shook off the three who'd been restraining him and flew at Lascalzo, who appeared paralyzed as he waited for the collision of bodies that knocked him sharply to the ground. Damien then turned to Hetch, walked a few strides toward him, and wrapped his hands around his neck as Hetch reached clumsily for the knife in his pocket. Damien, without uttering a word, lifted Hetch a half foot from the ground. While looking him straight in the eye, Damien carried him by the neck across the mud and pools of water to the wall, where he released him and let him drop.

In character, Damien said to Hetch, "If you ever again lay a finger on my brother, I'll kill you. Ya' got that?"

Hetch was silent.

Damien, in a booming voice, repeated, "*Ya' got that*?"

Hetch paused before nodding.

With their eyes evading Damien's stare, the three who had restrained Damien walked toward Hetch, who was slowly getting to his feet on the other side of the tunnel. Hetch looked at Damien as threateningly as he could manage under the circumstances.

Erin stood and gathered himself. His hands and face and the front of his jacket and pants were coated with a thin layer of mud. He and Damien walked next to one another in silence.

After a minute or two, Erin said with imitation swagger in his voice, "I guess we showed 'em who's boss."

It was true that they had won the fight, but the whole thing had a stale and tawdry feel to it as they entered into the gray light of the afternoon.

Even now, as Damien lay in bed with his head under the covers of his bed, that episode of their Rocky story left him feeling ill—a mixture of shame and sadness. Damien could still smell the foul odor of the tunnel, could see the look on Erin's mud-stained face, and feel the slimy filth under his feet as he carried Hetch to the wall. It was rare that he allowed himself to think about that afternoon. What upset him most was the look in Erin's eyes as Lascalzo held Erin, while Hetch breathed into his face in a way that was close to spitting on him. Erin hadn't looked frightened or angry; he looked humiliated. But not just any kind of humiliation—it was the indignity of being physically and emotionally violated. No, *raped* is the word, he thought. This wasn't supposed to happen. Damien hated himself for letting it go on for the sake of playing out, in the real world, a scene they'd imagined so many times as kids. *He* had allowed it to happen by not responding immediately, and instead waiting for the right moment in the hackneyed script he had in his head. He and Erin had many times taken roles in scenes in which Rocky fights off enemies who threaten Mickey, but the reality of it had been different. The manhandling had been real, the denigration had been real, the emasculation had been real. Damien remembered watching Erin wash his face and hands after they got home and use a washcloth to get as much mud off his clothes as he could before putting them in the hamper. He hadn't wanted Rose to know what had happened to him.

Damien was jarred by the sound of the front door slamming shut behind Catherine and Rose as they returned to the house after seeing Erin off.

\* \* \*

In the initial days after Erin's departure, Damien was desolate. Colors were almost entirely indistinguishable: Reds, greens, and yellows appeared to be the same dull shade of gray. Life was of value only if Erin were there to talk to about it. Why go to the river if Erin weren't there to hear the water make its biggest gulping sound yet when he dropped a small boulder into it from the overhang? Why go bike riding if Erin weren't there to hear him yell out, "Did you see that?"

Damien compliantly went to school each day, though he couldn't concentrate. It seemed odd to him when others complained or celebrated or argued or laughed together. What was the point to any of it? On returning home after school, he went directly to his room and slept a dreamless sleep until he was called for dinner.

"Any word from Erin?" Catherine asked Rose as she carried a plate in each hand to the table.

"No, you have to be patient. He's been at school three weeks, and he's called every Sunday," Rose said. "He's getting settled in a place where he doesn't know a soul."

"Don't act like you have no idea who Erin is," Catherine spat back. "You know that by now he has twenty boys, and twice as many girls, vying for his attention."

Catherine and Damien sat on one side of the kitchen table, Rose on the other.

Catherine, looking at her plate, said, "Welcome to the land of the Keanes. What you see here is the remains of a family. Rose, the mother, who is puzzled by life; Damien, who has lifetime visitor status; and Catherine the gimp, a girl who was born looking normal and acting normal, but look at her now—her body and her mind are twisted. Oh, and there's Erin, the ghost at the table, a perfect boy, but then again, there are no perfect people, so we all wonder if he's human."

"That's enough, Catherine. You think it's funny, but I don't," Rose said, failing in her attempt to catch Catherine's eyes to convey to her that she was making things even harder for Damien, who missed Erin more than she and Catherine could know.

Damien turned to Rose, and for the first time since Erin had left, made a request. "Can I have the car tomorrow afternoon? I'll do the grocery shopping if you want."

"Of course, you can, but be careful how you drive. You're young to be driving."

"Seventeen isn't young to be driving," Catherine interjected. "You can get your driver's license at sixteen if you want to."

"It's hard to remember what happened when Erin began driving," Rose said, not talking to anyone in particular.

Catherine, again narrating: "Rose, the mother, doesn't live in the past or the present or the future, she lives in a world without time. Time and age don't exist for her. People are here, then they disappear, then some come back, others don't."

"Catherine, I'll have no more of that," Rose said with anger and fear in her voice. "You have to learn to be careful with

139

your cruelty. It's a powerful thing that can strike so deep it will never be forgotten."

"We've all done unforgivable things, haven't we?"

"Stop, just stop. Talk like that isn't good for anyone."

Catherine threw her napkin down on the table as if she were about to leave, but she didn't leave.

"You both have to stop," Damien said. "Catherine, you have no right to speak for me."

"Then speak for yourself."

"I'm fine."

"Who do you think you're kidding?"

"I'm here, aren't I?"

"Bullshit, you're not here in this family. You can't even call her Mom."

Rose turned to Catherine and said, "What kind of heartless game are you playing?"

"This isn't a game, this is life, which as you may have noticed is heartless. You can't change facts. They just sit there staring back at you."

"Stop it, Catherine."

"No, I won't stop it. You know what I'm saying is true. Do you want to know how I know it's true?"

"You're being horrible to both Damien and me. I know you think I've been a terrible mother, but what has Damien done to make you take it out on him?"

"I'm only speaking the truth. It's about time this family had a small taste of the truth. I can't stand the lying anymore."

"You don't know what you're talking about, Catherine. You were a baby when Damien went to live with Margaret— that's what you're talking about, aren't you? You have no idea what was happening then, and you have no right to talk about it."

Catherine turned to Damien and asked, "Do you want to know the truth about what happened to you?"

Damien said, "I don't trust either of you to be able to tell the truth, so I'd appreciate your leaving me out of whatever this is you're doing to each other."

Rose and Catherine fell silent. The three finished eating in a matter of minutes. They briskly cleared the table, washed and dried the dishes, and swept the floor. Once Damien and Catherine left to go to their rooms, Rose made herself a cup of tea, sat down at her place at the kitchen table, and disappeared into herself.

## TWENTY

Rose, standing at the chopping block quartering a large chicken she'd bought at the new A & P, was deep in thought. She missed Erin terribly. He was a very sweet boy, a very smart boy, and a very handsome boy. When he was little, and even now, she imagined that every woman who saw him with her wished that he were her son. She had been afraid that if she had a boy, she would be unable to love him because boys seemed to her to be a different species from girls, a species she didn't understand and for the most part didn't like. She didn't understand why boys were as loud as they were, forever racing around, throwing things at one another, burning leaves all afternoon, punching each other in real fights, and the rest of it. It was no wonder that when boys grew up, they behaved as they did: So quick to get drunk, treating girls as things, denying they have feelings, and rarely being interested in talking about anything except sports. They have sex with any female who consents, and with some who don't.

She recalled that, to her surprise and great relief, Erin had not been that way. From the very first moment she laid eyes on him in the delivery room, he seemed to be looking around, delighted by what he saw, and waiting for the party to begin. He loved her and loved life. He nursed well, which was probably the happiest experience of her life, she thought. She loved him with every fiber of herself. What an extraordinary feeling that is. And as he grew, he didn't become hardened or inward; he wore his feelings on his sleeve.

A particularly vivid image of Erin came to Rose's mind. On the first airline flight Erin had taken—it must have been to Brian's mother's funeral—they had been served airline food that was barely edible, but she'd been famished and ate it all. As clearly as if it were a photographic image, she could picture Erin's distraught five-year-old face, with his brow furrowed and eyelids tented, as he asked her if she would mind exchanging their trays because he had left virtually untouched all the food on his tray, even the dessert, and "didn't want to hurt the chef's feelings." Standing there in the kitchen, Rose wept quietly as she remembered that sweet, sweet boy Erin had been, and still was.

Catherine opened the door to the fridge to see what vegetable her mother would want her to prepare for dinner. She preferred to figure it out herself rather than ask her mother. She didn't like to ask her for anything.

Rose told herself that it was normal for teenage girls to be angry at their mothers, but nonetheless she felt lonely in her own house. Now that Erin was gone, she was the mother in a new family composed of herself and Damien, whom she had increasingly grown to love despite their early troubles and despite the intense guilt she carried, and Catherine, who seemed to see her as nothing but a mental health hazard. Catherine had become the kind of girl she'd seen at school when she was growing up: A girl who was artsy and very smart, and who looked down on other girls. She could still feel what it felt like to be invisible—or worse—in the eyes of that kind of girl.

Rose had been thrilled when Catherine asked her to teach her how to sew and to use the sewing machine. She looked forward all day to the hours after dinner when she and

144

Catherine worked together pleating a skirt, sewing a lining into a jacket, changing the buttons on a blouse, installing a side zipper on a pair of pants. But once she learned how to sew and mend, how to use the sewing machine and make clothes from patterns, Catherine seemed to have no more use for her. Rose could see in Catherine's face the feeling that her mother was hopeless in her lack of sense of style, and even more so in her ignorance of what was new in the fashion world. Catherine would be ashamed to be seen in public with such a woman. But that's the way it always is with children, both boys and girls, isn't it? They use you up and throw you away, not knowing that you've given your life to them. You're like a yolk sac the chick consumes while inside the shell before cracking it open and walking away.

Catherine could tell that her mother was so lost in thought that she wasn't even aware of her presence in the room. She wondered if Rose was becoming *dotty*, a word she'd read in George Eliot and Dickens—a word that seemed just right for her mother. She'd always been reclusive—different from the mothers of any of the girls she knew. Maybe losing Erin, her favorite, had pushed her over the edge.

Rose blamed herself for Catherine's limp. The bones in Catherine's weakened left leg had not grown as much as those in her right leg, so she had to wear medical-looking orthopedic shoes with a higher heel on the left foot, and she still had to use a cane; probably she always would. Rose thought that if only she had been organized enough to keep the house tidy, toys wouldn't have accumulated on the landing, and Catherine might not have tripped over them, if that's what had caused her to fall. Rose made an effort to interrupt her ruminations about the fall by reminding herself that the neurologists at St. George's Hospital had told her that even though Catherine's EEG showed normal brain waves, it was possible that Catherine had had a brief seizure, and the seizure had caused her to lose her balance and fall.

145

Damien was upstairs, lying on his bed, looking up at the web of cracks in the ceiling plaster. From the time he was very young, he made up stories about the figures he saw in the tangle of cracks above him, almost as if he were looking at the stars in the night sky. Some of the stories he'd told himself had been terrifying to him when he was younger, and they still were a little frightening—the scariest of which was the shape of Humpty Dumpty, sitting on the wall about to fall and be shattered into a million pieces that couldn't be put together again. There were amoeba-like creatures silently swallowing other creatures, and heads with open mouths biting the backs of the necks of other heads.

Damien silently rehearsed again and again what he would say to Erin the next time they talked, which might be a month from now or a year from now, who knew? It had been two and a half months that Erin had been at school. His phone calls had diminished to one every few weeks, and when he finally did call, it felt as if he were merely checking off a duty on his list of obligations. Erin said he could not receive calls because the freshman dorm rooms didn't have phones, and the only phones he could use were the pay phones in the basement of the building. Damien didn't believe it.

As he practiced what he was going to say, he didn't want to sound pathetic, but he did want to tell Erin in no uncertain terms that he was a liar. Erin was not treating him as his best friend. He practiced telling Erin that in all the time he'd been away, he hadn't made a single call to speak to him alone, at a time when the two of them could talk freely, the way they used to. He yearned to say to Erin, "You gave me your word, but your word isn't worth shit."

But Damien knew he wouldn't say that to Erin. It would sound as if he were begging Erin to keep his promise. It had only taken Erin a few weeks to change into a different person— a person who had no family.

Wherever Rose's thoughts began, they ended up in the same place: She lacked the sort of solidity that Margaret had. At one time, she had been prettier than Margaret, or so people said. She didn't feel it any more. A girl's prettiness doesn't last. She'd once heard someone say—and it had stuck with her ever since—that beauty is a gift not given, but lent. Rose recalled the way her father made her feel like an angel. She'd been thrilled to hear the crunch of the tires of his car on the pebbles in the driveway. How she had loved being Daddy's girl, and how devastated she'd been when he disappeared and disowned her and the rest of the family. His departure seemed to her to be the most important dividing line in her life: "B. D." and "A. D.," before his departure and after his departure. It depressed her to recall that, as a teenager, she'd been loose with boys. She remembered with terrible clarity the afternoon in front of the school—it must have been during the autumn or winter because she remembered the pale blue ski parka she was wearing—when Laurie Franker, whom she'd thought was a friend, called her a slut in front of a group of girls. That word stung. She could still feel it. And the sting transformed itself into the feeling that she smelled bad, had a bad sexual odor, and no matter how thoroughly she bathed, she couldn't get rid of the foul smell. It was no wonder that everyone kept their distance from her after that.

It came as a complete surprise to her that a boy she happened to be sitting next to on a bus, while returning to university after Christmas break, seemed to like talking with her. For the first time in a very a long time, she felt pretty. Brian Keane was a handsome boy who made her laugh. He was a junior at the same campus of the state university where Rose was a sophomore and Margaret a senior. She liked his County Wicklow accent that she'd heard in the voices of her aunts and uncles and cousins on her mother's side of the family, who all lived in Ireland. She fell in love with him before she knew much of anything about him. When she arrived at the campus, she was bursting to tell Margaret about Brian. Rose remembered her disappointment when Margaret cautioned her not to be impulsive and to find out if he drank heavily, as most Irish men did, before getting too involved with him.

Brian was serious about his studies, more so than Rose was. His dream was to become an architect. He had taken all the required courses, but said that he would have to work to save money to pay the tuition of the state university school of architecture. During the winter term, they spent every minute together. Rose recalled how she had delayed having sex with Brian because she still believed that there was a foul odor coming from her. She also believed he'd be able to tell that she'd been loose with boys. She had tried to tell herself that she was a virgin in a more important sense: He was the first boy she had ever fallen in love with, and the sex they would have would be the first *real* sex she'd ever had. The other times she'd had sex didn't count for anything. But she couldn't quite get herself to believe it.

Rose eventually agreed to have sex with Brian. He was disappointed that Rose wasn't passionate during sex, and wondered if he was doing something wrong. She eventually told him that she had had sex in high school with two boys she didn't love, and she felt ashamed of that. He told her he was sorry that she felt ashamed. There was no need to be. She recalled crying and putting her arms around his neck and loving him all the more for having said that. She thought that those early years with Brian had been the best years of her life.

Catherine, too, was alone in the kitchen despite her mother's presence. Catherine had felt sorry for Damien when he appeared at the kitchen table as they were getting ready to have lunch that day so long ago, when he was brought back from Margaret's house. For her, this didn't mark his "return" home because he had never been there in the first place. She had only overheard her mother and Margaret mention his name, but she hadn't known whom they were talking about. The only thing that had bothered her when Damien showed up was the change in Erin that resulted. There was no room for a girl in the games he dreamt up for Damien. It was as if she didn't exist for the two of them. She hadn't *gained* a brother when Damien arrived, she'd *lost* one.

Catherine was also thinking about how she hadn't known what to make of Damien's behavior when she returned home from her rehabilitation after the fall. He was very possessive of her. Strangest of all was his sweeping her into her arms to carry her up the stairs. It was as if something had come over him, and he was behaving like a romantic hero in a movie. She'd never experienced anything like the sensation of being carried in that way. Never once, she realized, had she felt her father's touch, though she'd imagined it many times. He was dead by the time she was born. As Damien was carrying her, she was so stunned that she was unable to speak. He seemed as surprised as she was to have her in his arms. Before he did that strange thing, along with his odd insistence on helping her walk, it had felt to her as if they had been invisible to each other in the shadow that Erin had cast. Catherine had kept her distance from Damien for a long time after the incident, maybe for longer than he deserved.

"Catherine, are the string beans ready? The chicken will be ready in a few minutes. Please rinse the beans and put them in the pot of boiling water on the stove."

She thinks I don't know how to cook string beans. Unbelievable!

# TWENTY-ONE

The walk from the dormitory to the restaurant on the south edge of the campus seemed endless to Rose on that dry, cold day in late February. Margaret was a senior majoring in economics, Rose a sophomore, not sure what to major in. The sky was a cloudless, deep blue, crisscrossed with powdery trails of jet stream that looked as if Zeus were drawing with chalk on the surface of a dome. The snow that blanketed the expansive lawn in front of the library and administration building reflected the sunlight as if refusing to take it into itself and hurling it back to its source. Margaret and Rose made their way down the steep street that ran along the edge of snow-covered lawn, keeping their eyes fixed on the gritty, black, pock-marked road.

Rose had worn shiny black pumps, with a higher heel than she was used to, in an effort to look stylish and mature for her father. With each step she took, there was the distinct possibility of falling. As they stepped through the outer doors of the inn, they found themselves in a small, crowded foyer. Rose and Margaret involuntarily took hold of one another in order not to bump into anyone else while their eyes were adjusting to the dim interior light. Margaret disliked this instinctive embrace because it shrieked female weakness and mutual dependence.

On passing through the restaurant's inner set of doors, Rose scanned the dark pseudorustic room, humming with table talk, for a man sitting alone at a table for three or four. Her eyes met those of her father. He was rising to his feet, motioning her to join him at his table by the leaded glass windows. He looked much older than Rose had remembered. She had expected that he would look exactly the same as he had when she last saw him. His hair was thin and silvery gray, leaving exposed much of his shiny pink scalp. The skin on his face was loose, and his eyes were narrowed, his upper eyelids unwilling or unable to fully open. Finding herself in the middle of the room several paces ahead of Margaret, Rose stood still in order to get a better look at her father. Margaret bumped into her, nearly knocking her over. Margaret muttered under her breath, "What are you doing? Don't just stand there gawking. You're getting in everyone's way."

The greetings they gave one another were awkward. None of them could decide whether to hug, shake hands, or simply take a seat. A fatherly hug or kiss on the cheek was out of the question.

Margaret, wasting no time on pleasantries, looked sternly at her father and said, "Should we call you Daddy, or Dad, or Frank?"

Sidestepping Margaret's initial punch, Frank said, "I'm so glad that the two of you were willing to meet me here. I don't deserve another chance, and I'm grateful that you both were willing to give me one anyway."

Getting right down to business, Margaret fired back, "Tell us why you left."

"During the past few days, I've been trying to come up with small twists of the truth—sudden illness and long hospitalization, taking care of a relative, letters that I wrote to each of you that your mother destroyed, and even less believable stories than those."

Margaret interrupted, "You sound like you're giving a speech you've practiced in front of a mirror all morning. Why don't you just say what happened?"

"What happened was that I left both of you and your mother on an impulse. I hadn't planned it. I just did it, and I'm still not sure how I could have done such a thing."

Even before her father arrived at the end of his sentence, Rose cringed and hoped that Margaret wouldn't lash out at him again before he regained his balance.

"You're a slippery customer, aren't you?" Margaret said. "You make it seem like telling the truth is an extraordinary feat that you're about to perform, and then you follow that build-up with one of the biggest clichés going: 'I did it on impulse.' No reason, just impulse. If that's all you know, we might as well end the conversation here and enjoy our lunch. The problem with your maneuver, Frank, is that it fails to account for seven years during which you failed to make a single phone call, write a single letter—a postcard would have been nice—or meet us as we got out of school, so you could tell us what had happened to you, and why your two children, twelve and fourteen years old, had not been sufficiently important to you to make it worth your time to stick around and take part in raising them."

"What can I say other than 'You're right, and I'm sorry'?"

"I can't tell you how relieved I am to hear that you're sorry, Frank."

As Rose listened, she couldn't tell whether she felt sorrier for Margaret or for her father.

"What do you want me to say?"

"I don't want you to say anything. I don't need anything from you."

"Let me tell you what happened when I left. You can do with it what you will. Your mother and I were having a very hard time together. She didn't like me working as much as I was. I think she thought that I was seeing other women. In a way she was right, I was seeing other women, but I wasn't having affairs with any of them. I swear to you, I was faithful to your mother—but she wouldn't believe me. I hope both of you will."

"Why would she ever suspect such a thing from a man like you?"

"I enjoyed talking to women, I still do. Rosie, you remember when I'd take you with me while I did errands on Saturday mornings, and we'd stop to talk to Florence, the secretary at the insurance agency in town. Remember how she'd give you rubber stamps and ink pads and you'd make designs on sheets of paper that you spread all over her desk? We had a good time. You remember, don't you, Rosie?"

Rose nodded.

"I liked chatting with Florence and she liked chatting with me, but there wasn't anything more to it than that. I'm not very smart, but it would be a terrible idea for a man to bring his eleven-year-old daughter with him when he talked with a woman he was having an affair with."

He paused, seeming to feel he had said something salient in his own defense.

"The fact that I felt appreciated by other women doesn't justify leaving the three of you in the way I did. If I wanted out, I should have filed for divorce and set up alimony, child support, visiting privileges, and the rest of it."

Margaret, not about to allow Frank to slip a lie into his story, said, "But you did file for divorce once you were in hiding."

"What gives you that idea? I've never filed for divorce. Your mother and I are still married in the eyes of the law."

"She told us she'd been served with divorce papers," Margaret said defensively, sensing she was on slippery ground and regretting she'd given her father the opportunity to play the victim.

"That's not true, but it doesn't matter. I didn't plan on deserting you. I stopped by the agency late one afternoon to chat with Florence for a little while before going home that evening. She and I had this game of imagining how we'd start over—move someplace where no one knew us, without any of the baggage from the past."

Margaret turned to Rose and asked, "Were you the suitcase and I the steamer trunk, or was it the other way around?"

Ignoring Margaret's remark, Frank went on, "I imagined I was getting a second chance in life—a chance to find a place to live and a job, as if I was young again. The truth is, I was trying not to think or feel anything in order not to be paralyzed by guilt about what I was doing. Neither Florence nor I wanted to be married to one another, or even have an affair, because that would have led us back to the very obligations we were trying to escape. I can't justify my selfish decision. I knew that the two of you needed a father, and I treasured being your father. But continuing to be your father meant living in a continual fight with your mother. So I chose the easy way out."

"You just cashed in the seven lousy Scrabble pieces you were holding for seven new ones."

"I was cowardly, and I've continued to be cowardly each day for the past seven years, as I've pretended the two of you don't exist. There's no apology I can make that can begin to set right the damage my selfishness has caused you both."

Margaret said with fatigue in her voice, "Frank, I have to tell you, I'm beginning to get bored with your 'My name is Frank, I'm a deadbeat dad' speech."

"All I hope to be able to do is explain to the two of you what happened, so you'll have something real to react to instead of having to rely on your imagination. It all boils down to the fact that I was a coward and thought only of myself."

For the first time since Margaret and Rose had sat down at the table across from their father, there was silence. Margaret felt the futility of saying anything to her father; Frank hadn't foreseen the intensity of Margaret's bitterness; and Rose felt like a child sitting outside her parents' bedroom, listening to them argue, wishing they'd stop and make up.

Frank broke the silence by saying in a voice more sorrowful than defensive, "A few weeks ago, I decided to get in touch with both of you because I knew that you both were at the state university here, and so I could write to you without taking the chance that your mother would see the letter. You've both been here a long time. I don't know why I waited so long. I never stopped supporting the family financially, including money for college, and I will continue to support both of you and your mother no matter what happens."

Rose, who had not said a word the entire time, said, "Daddy, I thought you loved me more than anything."

"I did, and I still do, Rosie."

"So how could you have left me?" Rose asked as tears rolled from her eyes.

"I'm so sorry that I did, Rosie. I promise you I'll do everything in my power to try to make it up to you, if you let me. You don't have to forgive me, because what I did was unforgivable, but I hope you'll let me back into your life."

And so went the reunion of father and daughters. Margaret never again had more than a civil relationship with her father; Rose resumed her adoration of him as if nothing had happened to interrupt it. Frank died of cancer before he had the chance to give Rose away at her wedding.

# TWENTY-TWO

An Indian summer stretched deeply into October the year Erin left for college. Damien walked in the woods along the bank of the river, where he and Erin had spent so many hours. The leaves of the maples, birches, tulip trees, and beeches that lined both sides of the river wore their colors as if competing with one another for a prize. The intense crimson and ochres, the bright yellows, the deep burgundies changed into deeper, darker colors as clouds blocked the sun now and again. The display of color, for Damien, was just a reminder that he was alone, that Erin wasn't there to see all this with him.

The first frost came in late October and turned the leaves brown, and then, as if overnight, stripped the trees bare. The naked branches etched black lines into the sky. When Erin returned home for Thanksgiving that first year, he spoke in the high-pitched voice he used when he was trying to impress someone or hide something. Damien felt relieved to have him leave. Having him home was worse than being alone.

In late winter, Catherine returned to school for the first time since her fall down the stairs. Rose drove her. Damien walked or rode his bike, preferring to have the time to himself. The cold air against his face while riding his bike to school helped him enter a state of pure sensation, free of thoughts of any kind.

Damien, Catherine, and Rose said little to one another at home. Damien hid in his room, studying while listening to music on his Walkman; Catherine spent the afternoons and evenings in her room, measuring and cutting fabric, sewing by hand and on the sewing machine; Rose sat at her place at the kitchen table, lost in thought, drinking tea and occasionally bourbon after the children were asleep. Catherine's return to school made for a change Damien had not expected. She was not the spoiled brat she was at home, endlessly criticizing Rose for her lack of brains, ambition, talent, artistry, and on and on. As he watched her from a distance talking with other girls, he saw a girl who was very different from the one he'd seen at home. He saw an odd girl, and to his surprise, a very pretty girl, despite the fact that she limped, used a cane, and wore those orthopedic shoes.

Though Damien had heard Catherine say to Rose that the other girls stayed away from her so that the stigma of her limp and cane and her witch's shoes would not rub off on them, Damien could see that this was not the case at all, and that Catherine knew it.

Damien developed an ability to watch Catherine out of the corner of his eye. He had to keep his distance as he watched her because his height and bulk made it impossible for him to be inconspicuous. Damien was impressed by the fact that, despite Catherine's unapologetic strangeness—or maybe because of it—most of the girls in her grade, and even older girls, admired her from afar. Damien thought that one girl, probably unaware of it herself, walked with a slight limp that seemed to be an imitation of Catherine's, as if it were the latest thing in fashion. He imagined that the girls who revered Catherine saw in her something that was new to them, something about her that made her more intriguing than any girl they'd ever met. Perhaps they saw a way of being feminine that was different from

158

anything they'd imagined, different from their friends' and older sisters' ways of being feminine, and certainly different from their mothers' ways.

For Damien, what was most striking about Catherine—and this took him quite a while to put into words for himself—was that she was mysterious, unfathomable, and that made her at once alluring and forbidding. But he felt that there was one thing she lacked: softness. She was so fiercely independent that she made herself unapproachable. You could watch her, be impressed by her, want to be like her, feel proud that she would talk to you and seemed to think well of you, but you could never be her friend.

As the winter gave way to early spring, Catherine decided to walk to school instead of being driven by Rose because she was so angry at her mother that she didn't want to be beholden to her in any way, much less be seen in public with her. Because Catherine and Damien were now both walking to and from school—the patches of ice on the sidewalks and roads made it too dangerous to ride a bike—walking together felt to each of them inescapable.

The pain that flared in Catherine's hip whenever she walked more than a couple of blocks made it necessary for the two of them to walk slowly and rest on public benches along the way. They used the bridge over the railroad tracks, which made the route longer than the one Damien and Erin had taken. At first, they said very little to one another. They gave the appearance, Damien thought, of a big brother dutifully helping his gimpy sister to and from school. Their silence made the walk unpleasant for both of them, so one afternoon when Damien couldn't stand the stalemate any longer, he decided to try to strike up a conversation with her, despite the fact that she was moody and might say something cutting. The best he could come up with was, "What are you reading now?"

Catherine replied acerbically, "I hate it when someone starts a conversation with a question. If you want to talk about

159

books, why not say something like, 'I just finished a book I liked,' and then say something about the book, or the author, or anything."

Damien hadn't anticipated anything so scathing as this. For what? Because he had the guts to break the silence? Screw her. He didn't know what she read—probably *Jane Eyre*; girls love *Jane Eyre*. And no doubt Catherine, with all her pretensions, had read all of Jane Austen.

Putting her snipe aside, he decided to try again. Anything was better than the silence. He said, as if she hadn't been condescending to him, "Actually, I don't read that much. I start a lot of books and then get bored and stop reading. I can give you a long list of books that have bored me to death. Most of the books they assign in school make me want to scream with boredom—*The Red Badge of Courage*, all of Shakespeare, all of Faulkner, all of Ibsen's plays, *Moby Dick*, everything that Jane Austen ever wrote, *The Sun Also Rises*. Would you like me to go on?"

Catherine had to smile. She asked, "Is there any book you've read that you've liked? I mean, really enjoyed? And I promise I won't ask you why you liked it."

"Yeah, there has been one, actually more than one. Once in a while, I look forward to continuing to read a book I had to stop reading because I had to do something else. I know they don't rank up there with Shakespeare, but I liked them and was sorry to have them end. I liked *1984*. It's the only book I've read that has made me so scared that I kept the lights on all night for weeks after I read a scene in it—the scene where they figure out what the thing is that most terrifies a person, and then they do it to them. Have you read *1984*?"

"No, I haven't," Catherine lied.

"The thing this guy is most scared of is rats, so they make a cage that they put over his head that has a starving rat on one side of a little gate that they'll raise and let it eat his face off if

160

he won't give in to believing the propaganda they're feeding him."

"I don't have a favorite book now," Catherine said. "For a long time—until pretty recently, really—I have to admit I liked books for girls. Yes, *Jane Eyre*, the Brontë sisters, Jane Austen. I read to live someone else's life for a while, any life other than my own. But when the story is over, I leave that life. If you asked me what happened in a book I read yesterday, I couldn't tell you. The only one that comes to mind that I really liked is *A Death in the Family*. I love that book. It's about how a family, especially the two children in it, react to the death of their father."

They went on to talking about other things, but Catherine interrupted herself mid-sentence to say, "I was lying."

"About what?"

"You remember I said I read to live another person's life, instead of my own, for a little while. That's true, but what's truer is that I read because I want to find someone else who knows what it's like to live a life without a father, with a spaced-out mother, no friends, and a dead piece of brain that makes it impossible to get around without a cane and witches' shoes. There you have it. The story of my life. You know it all now."

Damien had been afraid of Catherine most of the time he'd known her. She could rip someone to shreds in a few seconds if she felt like it. He'd seen her do it to their mother many times, to Erin once, and to him that once when he carried her up the stairs. She could have done it to him today if she'd wanted to.

# TWENTY-THREE

When they arrived home, Catherine said she'd look through her bookshelf to see if she could find the book about the family. Agee was the author, she thought. She walked up the stairs, holding tightly onto the banister. Damien hesitantly followed her into her room. He felt self-conscious, finding himself in the midst of Catherine's very feminine things—her robin's-egg-blue bureau, her hairbrushes, barrettes, bobby pins, and hand lotion. Her bed was no longer just a bed—it was a place where people kissed and touched and had sex. She had to know that inviting him into her room would have the effect that it was having. It was her room so she was in charge, which was the way she liked to have it.

Catherine moved her desk chair over to the dark-stained wooden bookshelf and sat down in front of the bowed shelves to read the names on the book spines. While she was scanning the titles, Damien sneaked a closer look at her room. There was a strange-looking table in the middle of it, on which there was a sewing machine, lots of scraps of fabric, and small, clear plastic packages in which there were buttons, zippers, sequins, and things he didn't recognize. No underwear was visible, to his relief and disappointment.

Removing a book from the shelf and handing it back over her shoulder, she said, "See what you think."

"Where'd you get all that stuff on the table next to the sewing machine?"

"At the fabric store."

Not knowing how to phrase the question, he asked, "What do you do with all that stuff?"

"I use it to make clothes."

He fleetingly recalled the sensations in his penis he'd felt in response to Catherine's girlishness when he first returned home after his years with Margaret. The words Rose and Catherine had used for Catherine's girl-things, especially the word *leotards*, had felt like code for something dark and forbidden, and incredibly exciting.

"How can you make clothes out of that?"

Catherine, for the first time, wasn't able to hide her self-consciousness. She sputtered a little and said, "I'll explain what I do, but you won't be interested in it. On second thought, I'll spare you talk about fabrics and dress patterns."

Damien stood there silently, looking at her in a way that conveyed the feeling, Stop all the hemming and hawing and tell me how you make clothes.

"All right," she said, as if Damien had talked her into it. "I buy remnants at fabric stores, which are pieces left from a bolt of fabric that are too small for anyone to use to make a whole dress or blouse or curtain or anything else. I also buy old clothes at thrift stores, and I make something from a combination of this and that. You see, I told you—this doesn't mean anything to you. No boy would be interested."

"What have you made?" Damien asked nervously, because speaking about Catherine's clothing was equivalent to talking about her naked body.

"You've seen them every day for at least a year, like what I'm wearing now."

Damien felt very uneasy about Catherine's inviting him to look at her body.

"I'm sorry I haven't noticed ..." he blurted out.

"Don't apologize. Girls notice everything other girls are wearing, boys don't notice anything except for really cheap outfits."

"You make us sound like Neanderthals."

"Yeah, I do."

"So what about the clothes you're wearing now?" Damien asked, not quite believing that he'd spoken the words he heard coming from his mouth.

"I made this skirt by sewing together cotton prints. They're supposed to look a little, not a lot, like a wave that curls at the top, and then unfurls like a wave breaking. It doesn't really matter if you see the waves, it's the total effect that matters, a feeling of movement. If it works, it looks interesting, it looks a little unusual, but not like you're trying too hard. It has to look natural—no big deal. Had enough?" For Damien, and maybe for Catherine, every word she said referred to sex—not directly but it was there, everywhere.

"No, all this is new to me. I like to learn about things I've seen all my life, but have been invisible to me."

"I'll show you a little more," she said. His face turned bright red. Was it possible that she was completely unaware she sounded like a stripper when she said those words?

Catherine went to her closet and took out a few blouses, skirts, and pants on hangers. She carefully laid them on top of one another on the bed, and took the top piece off of its hanger.

Jesus God, she's a cock teaser, he yelled in his head. What other explanation can there be?

"I bought these jeans at a second-hand clothing store. These were expensive jeans when they were first sold. You don't get those lines in inexpensive jeans. I dyed them to give them just a little hint of burgundy. That makes them look as if shadows are running through them. It makes you look like you're not trying. I lined them with lime green satin, and I've made small tears in the denim so the lime green shows through, just a bit—so little that you're not sure it's there. That's it. Show's over." She added, "You've never seen me wear most of this stuff because I never have, and never will wear it."

All the talk about "seeing through" the jeans and "not wearing" most of it was driving Damien crazy. What he feared most was getting an erection and ejaculating.

"Does that bother you, to make clothes and not wear them?" He tried to get these words out as nonchalantly as possible, but as he heard the words, they sounded as nonchalant as a fire alarm: You don't wear your clothes! You're completely naked.

"I don't mind making things that only I see. I couldn't wear jeans to school with tears in them and with lime green satin showing through. I couldn't carry it off, limping along like an old lady. The witch's shoes drive the last nail into the coffin."

"Those shoes don't make you look like an old lady or a witch. No one notices them," Damien said, examining each word he uttered, not knowing how the sentence would end.

An awkward silence began that Damien filled by saying something as tepid as possible. "I've never taken anything I do as seriously as you take what you do."

"You and Erin took very seriously what the two of you did together."

Damien, a little calmer now, replied, "That's true. I took very seriously the training and the story we built up around it. I don't know if you know this, but Erin invented that game for me as a way to make a place for me when I came back here after living at Margaret's. It sounds stupid to talk about this with anyone but Erin. He made up a game where I was Rocky, the underdog boxer, and he was my trainer. Making up that game, and keeping it going for so long, was … I don't know what to call it … good-hearted, big-hearted … I don't know."

"Of course I knew about that game and the movie. How could I have missed it? The two of you were best friends. Sewing is simpler than what the two of you did."

"They're two different kinds of things."

"I think you're missing the point."

"What's the point?"

"I'm too embarrassed to say, and please don't push me to say it because I won't."

"Okay."

Catherine's saying that she was embarrassed was surprising. Of course, he imagined that what she was embarrassed about was something sexual. He and Erin had never talked about sex, or even joked about it.

Damien's legs were getting tired. He'd been standing the entire time they'd been talking. There had been no place for him to sit. Catherine was sitting on the only chair in the room, and he wasn't about to sit on her bed or at the sewing table. Right from the beginning, he had firmly in mind that he was going to be the first to say he should leave her room. He wasn't about to put himself in the position of being evicted from her room. He came up with the corny line, "I hear Rose calling us to help with supper."

Catherine said, "Yeah, I heard her, too."

## TWENTY-FOUR

Catherine took the bus to town Saturday mornings. The buses came at forty-five minute intervals, but there was no printed schedule.

Damien, now fully in love with Catherine, and not knowing how she felt about him, longed to spend the day with her on Saturdays. He had rehearsed a scene in his mind, and when he was sure no one could hear him, he spoke his lines aloud. "Would you like me to drive you to town so you don't ... so you don't *what*? ... so you don't tire yourself out ..." Or, "Ya' want a ride into town? I'm going anyway." He couldn't get any version of it to sound natural.

For weeks, he tried to find the right moment, but just as that moment seemed to be arriving, something happened to spoil it.

One warm but overcast Saturday morning in late May, Damien saw an opening and seized it. Catherine was already outside, cane in hand, slowly, carefully making her way down the wet, slate steps between the house and the street. Damien opened the front door and called to Catherine, "It looks like it might rain. Why don't I give you a ride into town? Rose won't be needing the car this morning."

Catherine said, "Thanks. I wasn't looking forward to waiting for the bus this morning."

"Let me get the keys. We'll be off in a minute." He hated himself for having used the canned phrase, "We'll be off in a minute." He sounded like Mr. Rogers. Dashing back into the house, he grabbed the keys from the table in the front hall where Rose always left them. He hadn't asked Rose if he could use the car, but he couldn't risk losing this opportunity.

The traffic slowed as car after car stopped to let pedestrians cross the main street, which bisected the town. Damien, frustrated by the steady flow of pedestrians, made a sharp turn to the left, down a side street. After a few minutes, they were on a two-lane highway heading west, past the used car dealerships, the fast food restaurants, the Walmart, the lumber yards, and finally out into the farmland, where some of the fields were worked by the few remaining chicken farmers and dirt farmers. Most of the land was divided into parcels by barbed wire fences. Catherine didn't object to Damien's dispensing with the charade of driving her to town.

Neither of them knew what to say. Nevertheless, it was thrilling for Damien to be sitting next to Catherine. He loved her girlishness. She was a girly girl. He loved everything about her. Even though he was driving, he could see her face, mostly looking forward but occasionally out of the side window at the open fields and billboards. He took in every detail of the shape of her face, her thick dark eyelashes, the delicate upward turn of her nose, the blonde peach fuzz over her upper lip and cheeks, the way the wind blew her hair over her face and eyes, and she, in a gesture only a girl could make, took the lock of hair the wind had blown over her eyes, and pushed it back and tucked it behind her ear as if it were going to stay there—with complete indifference to the transience of the solution to the problem. Maybe it wasn't a problem, but a simple sign to herself that she was a girl, and that was quite a wonderful thing to be. He couldn't think of an equivalent un-self-conscious movement that he and other boys made. Boys don't notice that they're boys because they can't really believe that there's anything else to be, he thought. Boys are in a state of constant movement. Girls move less and notice more, catching every inflection of voice and movement of the person they're scrutinizing.

Catherine was the most beautiful thing he had seen in his life. Catherine's beauty wasn't perfect—it was better than perfect, because each imperfection was more exciting than the perfect beauty of girls and women in the movies, and on television, and in magazines. The timbre of Catherine's voice had lost some of its highest register, which was replaced by newly minted lower, slightly hoarse tones, like those of female jazz singers he'd heard on the jazz radio station. He suspected that Rose was probably very pretty when she was young; she was still pretty. He'd seen her use her femininity to coax, cajole, enchant a favor from men in stores or at the gas station once in a while.

Once they turned onto the two-lane road heading south, they both rolled down their windows and allowed the warm air to wash across their faces. After a while, Catherine rolled up her window, which was a signal to Damien to roll his up. There was a sudden quiet in the car that felt to both of them as if pressure were building and an explosion was imminent. He hoped Catherine wouldn't spoil the mood with clever, cynical banter. She didn't. He had rehearsed this moment in his head countless times, but the few lines that he could remember were useless to him now.

Succumbing to the pressure to say something, he said, "It's gotten much warmer, even since the time we left the house. Ten degrees or so." He hated himself for talking about the weather, but hated himself far more for talking about the temperature rising, which Catherine would hear as his pathetic attempt to woo her.

"It has. It's turned into a beautiful day."

171

"What are your reading now?" he asked, again throttling himself for the cliché.

"I'm reading Updike's *Rabbit, Run* ..."

Damien interrupted her, saying, "Don't bother with that inane question. I don't care what book you're reading."

Neither of them knew what to say to that abruption, which clearly signaled the beginning of something else that neither of them was willing to be the first to introduce.

Damien took the next right he could. It was a straight dirt road lined on both sides by green iron stakes with the upper six inches of each painted white, carrying three horizontal lines of barbed wire. The car kicked up a cloud of dust that hung in the air behind them as they drove. After about a half mile, the road came to an end in front of an abandoned farmhouse. Some fifty yards to its left, a Gambrel barn with a rusting metal roof stood huddled against a grain silo.

Damien stopped the car in front of the farmhouse and asked Catherine if she wanted to stretch her legs. Catherine had thrown her cane onto the back seat as she'd gotten into the car at home. As Damien half-turned to reach into the back seat to get the cane, Catherine, at the same moment, turned in his direction to say something. They found that their faces were only inches apart. Damien moved those few inches closer to her face and kissed her on her lips. It was by no means a peck. He pressed his lips softly into hers, and felt her lips pressing back, shaping themselves to his. A shudder went through him. He felt her warm breath caress his upper lip. She opened her mouth slightly so their tongues touched. Damien was astounded. He had not known such a sensation existed. Where had she learned to do such a wondrous thing? This question gave way immediately to the voluptuousness of the kiss.

After a long while, Catherine very slowly removed her lips from his and pulled her head back, at first keeping her eyes closed, and then opening them without letting her eyes move from his. She then turned her head and looked forward in an unfocused way.

It seemed to Damien that he'd waited his whole life for that moment. He was in love with Catherine and had been, in different ways, for a long time, long before he had a name for his feelings. He knew that many people would find what they'd just done appalling, but at that moment, he didn't care. It didn't feel like a brother and sister kissing. He had never for a minute in his whole life felt that she was his sister. He had never even felt that the two of them were members of the same family. He didn't feel that he was Rose's son, or even her adopted son; he felt like a foundling who had been taken in and treated "just like" a member of the family. These fleeting thoughts didn't detract from what was happening at the moment. He felt nothing but the languid, sensuous, wildly exciting kiss.

## TWENTY-FIVE

Rose's health had not been good for quite some time. It seemed that she had never recovered from Erin's departure almost a year earlier, but in truth, that was only part of the problem. Margaret was fully engrossed with her new job and worked until late at night, sometimes forgetting to call Rose to say she wouldn't be dropping by on the way home from work. Rose would say to herself, or to anyone else who happened to be around, that she didn't have the energy to do anything, and that she hated the house in which she was now living in the outskirts of Chicago. "My life was in that house that Brian and I made our own, the house where I raised my children. This house is just a stage setting. Nobody lives here. I certainly don't live here and I don't want to die here."

Margaret had been offered a high-level post in a private international bank that was headquartered in Chicago and Geneva. When she was offered the promotion, Margaret told Rose that she was going to move to Chicago, and that she'd make all the arrangements for Rose and Catherine. Catherine would be the only one of the children living at home in the fall, when the move was to take place. Damien would be attending a university in Chicago. Rose had no choice but to make the move. She could not live without Margaret. It was also true that Margaret could not live without Rose, but Margaret lived in the outside world while Rose lived only in her internal world, which was portable.

Margaret sold the houses in which she and Rose had lived in central Illinois, and bought a house for each of them in a suburb a half-hour by train from Chicago. Only a matter of weeks after the move, Damien began his freshman year at the university, and Catherine began her junior year in an exclusive private high school. Catherine said that it was a waste of money sending her to a school for rich kids, but Margaret insisted.

The move had depleted Rose greatly. At Margaret's urging, Rose saw a doctor for her fatigue, which had been steadily increasing. The internist ordered a number of tests, the results of which were unremarkable. The doctor thought that the problem was depression and prescribed something that Rose never took. He said that he wanted her to consult with the gynecologist in his group practice, "Just to be thorough."

After a great deal more prodding from Margaret, Rose went to see the gynecologist, who ordered an MRI. When she returned to the gynecologist's office, he told her that she had a mass in her left breast, two centimeters in diameter. Rose took the news with indifference. The doctor said that he'd schedule a biopsy. When Margaret called to ask what the doctor had said, Rose told Margaret that there was a tumor in her breast that was going to be biopsied, and she didn't want to hear another word about it.

At breakfast on the Sunday before the biopsy, Rose told Catherine that she'd be in the hospital for some routine tests the following day, would stay in the hospital overnight, and return home on Tuesday. She assured Catherine that there was nothing to worry about. Sensing that Rose didn't want to talk with her about what was actually happening, Catherine later called Margaret to find out what was going on.

Rose insisted on going by herself to speak with the gynecologist about the results of the biopsy. She forbade Margaret from even driving her to the appointment. She said that Margaret could meet her at her house after the appointment if she wanted to find out what had happened. Margaret kept to herself her anger about Rose's controlling behavior. After all, what affected Rose affected Margaret at least as much.

Once Rose had made tea and the two of them were seated at the kitchen table of Rose's house, Margaret said, "So tell me what happened."

"He said they found cancer in the lump, but it's not the worst type."

"What did he say they're going to do about it?"

Rose, who had been looking into her teacup, lifted her head and looked Margaret directly in the eye as she said, "They won't be doing anything I don't tell them to do. He told me to meet with a breast surgeon and an oncologist to discuss what treatment I should receive, but I've done as much as I'm going to do about this. I'm not going to let them butcher me or poison me or irradiate me and turn me into a neon sign. That's all there is to it. I hope you'll respect my decision about this."

Margaret was dumbstruck. She knew Rose would be stubborn about cancer treatment, but she hadn't expected her to forbid any discussion of it. Margaret tried to hold back her tears, but couldn't.

"Now stop crying. I asked you not to meddle, and your crying is a way of meddling. Just go along with me on this, won't you? The doctor said it was a slow-growing type."

Catherine knew that her mother wouldn't tell her the truth about the results of the biopsy, and she suspected that Rose would swear Margaret to secrecy, so she eavesdropped on the conversation between Margaret and her mother. After listening for about a half hour, Catherine made her way to her room as quietly as she could. She phoned Damien, but he wasn't in his apartment. She left a message on his answering machine, saying that there was something urgent she wanted to talk to him about. She told him not to call her. She would continue to try to reach him. Finally, he picked up, and she blurted out, "Mom has breast cancer. The biopsy confirmed that, but she's refusing to get any treatment for it."

"Why not?"

"You know her. Nothing she does makes any sense."

"What does Margaret say?"

"There's nothing she can say. She just cried. I've never heard Margaret cry."

"I don't blame Rose, really," Damien said.

"How can you say that?"

"Maybe she doesn't feel like holding on to the life she has." After a long pause, Damien added, "Living is hard work, and I think Rose no longer feels that she has any reason to do all that work."

As tears rolled down her cheeks, Catherine was reminded once again that she and Damien didn't really have the same mother. She had been a different person for each of them.

Rose stood by her decision not to undergo cancer treatment, which pained Margaret more deeply than had any other event in her life: More so than her failure to win her father's love; more so than her failure to become a feminine girl and a feminine woman; more so than the failure of her marriage; more so than the failure of her attempt to be a mother. All those failures had not left her alone in the world—she always had Rose, but now Rose had decided to leave her utterly by herself.

# TWENTY-SIX

L ate one afternoon, toward the end of the spring semester of his junior year, Damien was dozing at his desk in his Chicago apartment when the ringing of the phone startled him. On picking up the phone, he was surprised to hear Rose's voice. It was now two and a half years since she'd been diagnosed with breast cancer. Each time the phone rang, the thought would go through his head that it was a call from Margaret telling him that if he wanted to see Rose one last time, he had to come now.

Rose asked Damien if he'd mind coming by the house because she had something she wanted to say, and it had to be said in person. There was urgency in Rose's voice, so Damien told her that he'd be right over, if that was all right with her.

When Rose opened the front door of her house, she looked old and somewhat lost. They sat down in the kitchen, which was the only room in this house that Rose felt she had made her own. The same red-and-white-checkered oilcloth that had covered the kitchen table when he was growing up in "the old house" now covered the same kitchen table in the new one. While slowly and methodically serving the tea, Rose seemed to be readying herself to tell Damien something that was very difficult to say.

"There's something you need to know. Maybe you've already guessed it, but even if you have, I want to tell you myself and fill in parts that you couldn't possibly know about. I want you to know certain things about yourself; otherwise you won't know who you are. I'm about to tell you something I've never told anyone, not even Margaret, because it's no one else's business but yours and mine. I've waited until you got old enough to understand what I'm going to say, but I don't want to put off telling you for so long that I die or lose my memory."

Damien's heart sank as he heard Rose speak these words in the hoarse voice with which she'd begun speaking about a year ago. He expected to hear further reasons to feel unwanted.

"Before you were born, Brian and I were having a lot of trouble in our marriage. Things got much worse when Erin was born. Brian couldn't or wouldn't accept the changes that occur between a man and wife after they have a baby. The lives of the two people change; their whole world changes. He couldn't accept those changes. He couldn't accept the fact that he was no longer free to do whatever he wanted to do, whenever he wanted to do it. Brian got angrier and angrier with me, as if I had done something terrible to him by having a baby. We had wanted a child, a son in particular. Erin wasn't an accident. He seemed to think that I had it in my power to return us to the life we had before Erin was born, but obviously I didn't. He began drinking heavily with his friends at bars and seeing other women. A lot of Irish men, here and in Ireland, seem to feel it's their right to remain children their entire lives. I tried to talk to him, and I even got the priest at our church to try to talk to him, but he'd have nothing of it."

Damien's sinking feeling became fear, a child's fear, as Rose spoke.

"I felt very lonely and did something very stupid. When I took Erin out for a walk in his stroller the first summer after he was born—he was born in September, so he was a little less than a year old—we'd always stop for a cold drink at a restaurant near the park that had outdoor tables. The waiter, who was a very kind and outgoing person, always brought a little something extra for Erin—a small cup of ice cream or a sliver of cake or a cookie. The waiter was tall and European-looking. He dressed and carried himself differently from other people—his father was French and his mother was from Italy, where he grew up. He spoke with a lovely Italian accent. We enjoyed talking with one another, and I fell in love with him. Unfortunately, I got pregnant. I didn't tell him I was pregnant, but I told him that I had to stop seeing him because I was married. He was heartbroken. I was heartbroken, too. He was a good and generous man, so he didn't put pressure on me to do anything other than what I thought was right. He moved away soon after that. I don't know where he settled.

"It's hard for me to tell you about this because a child shouldn't have to hear such things from his mother, but there's no other way to tell you what you should know about who you are. When I got pregnant, I wasn't sure whether the father was the Italian man or Brian. I hoped it was Brian, but when you were born, both Brian and I knew immediately that he wasn't your father. Your complexion and hair color were much darker than anyone else's in either of our families. Brian was furious, and I thought he was going to hit me and leave me, but he didn't do either. He spent almost all of his time at bars drinking. I think he stayed because he loved Erin too much to leave.

"Things between Brian and me calmed down during the year after you were born, and we decided to make a new start in our marriage by having another child that was both of ours. We never had a chance to see what would happen because Brian died in the motorcycle accident while I was pregnant with Catherine."

Damien, who had been looking intently into Rose's eyes, interrupted her to say, "I have a different father from Catherine

181

and Erin? Is that what you're saying?" The color had drained from his face.

Rose nodded.

"Is that why you gave me to Margaret? Because I wasn't really a part of the family?"

"No, that's not right. I was about to tell you that the four of us—you, Erin, Brian, and I—made a very good family together after Brian and I forgave each other for our infidelities. You've seen photographs—like the ones on the living room table and on the mantelpiece of the old house—of the four of us standing in front of the first car we had. We made a good family."

"You said you wanted me to know what really happened, so please don't make up still another story. Can you honestly say that Brian treated me as his son?"

Rose was silent for a long time. Damien refused to release his gaze from her eyes. Rose bent forward, the fingers of both hands knitted together tightly on the table.

She finally said, "No, I don't think that there was ever a time when Brian treated you as his son."

"Did *you* feel that I was a member of the family?"

"No, not a member of the family I had with Brian, but I did feel that you were my son—my son and Alberto's son, my son with the man I was in love with. Of course, I had to hide that from Brian."

"So when Brian was present, you acted as if you didn't really consider me your child."

"I'm trying to tell you the truth, but the truth can't be told under cross-examination. I never in my heart forgot that you were my son, but I knew that if I were to dote over you when Brian was in the house, it would make things worse for you."

"And worse for you, too?"

"Yes, and worse for me, too."

"So, after Brian died, you were left with three children, no job, and your parents were dead."

"Yes, that's right. But Margaret was always there to help me when I needed help. She was very successful at her work at the bank—and she supported us financially, as she's done ever since Brian died."

Rose paused, gathering her strength.

"There is one thing more that you should hear from me and not from someone else. Before you went to live at Margaret's house, she said that if you came to live with her and she was to raise you, as I was asking her to do, she wanted to be certain that I wouldn't change my mind one day. She said she never wanted to have to choose between you and me once she came to love you. She said that adopting you was the only way she could feel certain that that wouldn't happen, and I agreed to the adoption. I don't want to make this sound as if any of this was Margaret's fault. It was a terrible thing I did to you."

Damien, speaking slowly and deliberately, his voice constricted by the anger he was attempting to hold back, said, "So my going to live with Margaret was not a temporary measure. You gave me to her, and intended never to allow me to return home. Margaret was to be my mother. Who were you supposed to be? My aunt? Who were Erin and Catherine supposed to be? My cousins?"

Rose paused to think. After a long while, she said, "I'm ashamed to say I never asked myself that question."

"Tell me the truth about why you gave me to Margaret."

"You have to understand that I didn't know at the time why I did what I did. I thought I understood, but I didn't. I know more now than I did then, but I don't think there's enough time left in my life for me ever to understand why I did such a stupid and horrible thing."

More sadly than angrily, Damien said, "Why was it me you chose to give away?"

Rose looked exhausted. "You deserve an answer to that question, but I'm not sure I can give it to you. Not because I'm holding back, but because I don't really know. What I can tell you is that Catherine was a baby, and Margaret doesn't know anything about taking care of a baby. It's just not in her nature. I couldn't have borne giving Catherine away when she was an infant. I can't explain it to you, I just couldn't have done it. And Erin not only takes care of himself, he takes care of everyone else, too. If I'm honest with myself, it was because he was a help and a comfort to me that I chose to keep Erin with me. It was a selfish decision, one that wasn't good for Erin, but I wasn't thinking of Erin at the time. I was thinking only about how to survive without breaking down mentally. It would not be true to say that I decided to give you up—I wasn't able to decide anything at the time. I just did what I felt I had to do. I was desperate. I didn't feel I had a choice."

"But you did choose."

"I did choose. And I'm sorry that I made the choice I did."

"Why didn't you ask Margaret to help you out rather than give me away to her and have her adopt me? You could have hired a nanny. Margaret would have gladly paid for that."

"I've asked myself that question more times than I can count, and I've never been able to answer it. That's what I should have done, and it's what Margaret should have told me to do, but we just didn't have enough sense to see that. You deserved much better than I was able to give you. You are a wonderful boy, a kind and intelligent boy, and I'm very proud of you. I hope you know that."

The sound of those words echoed in the room for what felt like a very long time.

Damien wished that Rose had said she loved him instead of saying she was proud of him, and that she had used the word *son* instead of *boy*, but she hadn't, and he knew he would just have to accept that.

Rose's face was pallid. Damien noticed a tremor in her right hand. Only then did he realize that Rose had been tightly clasping her hands together to hide the tremor, and that she now lacked the strength to continue to subdue the movement.

"I know you're tired, but I have one more question."

"Yes, please ask it."

"What's my father's name?"

Rose was surprised by how hard it was for her to say the words, "Alberto Moretti."

"So my name should be Damien Moretti."

"That's a beautiful name."

"Does he know he has a son?"

"No, I never told him."

"Have you said all that you wanted me to know?"

"There's so much I've been waiting to tell you, and I'm afraid I may not have said some important things you have a right to know, but I can't remember what they are now."

They said goodbye, and Damien left the house while Rose remained at the kitchen table.

# TWENTY-SEVEN

Geoffrey Barnes, the Spellman Professor of English, now in his late sixties, first met Damien when he was a freshman in his seminar on the mid-twentieth-century novel. Barnes was a regular contributor to the *New York Review of Books*, the *Times Literary Supplement*, and the *London Review of Books*. He was known as a prickly character at the university, widely respected by some of his colleagues and deeply loathed by others. Among his students, Barnes always had a favorite, and Damien in his junior year was the "chosen one." But being the favorite did not mean being fawned over.

One cold, windy Chicago afternoon, in the early winter of his senior year, Damien made his way across campus to meet with Barnes during his office hours, only to find that Barnes was already out the front door of the late nineteenth-century brick building that housed the English department. As Damien's path and Barnes's crossed, Barnes, slowing his pace, asked, "Are you expecting to meet with me?"

Damien, turning to walk with Barnes, said, "I was hoping to."

"About what?"

"The structure of the first chapter of my honors thesis."

Barnes peeled off to the left, saying under his breath, "Oh, is that all?"

Later the same week, Damien received in his campus mailbox a sloppily scrawled note from Barnes asking him to set up a meeting with him with the department secretary.

When Damien arrived at the massive oak door to Barnes's office—one of a series of almost identical doors on both sides of the long monastic hallway—he found it ajar. Damien knocked. When Barnes saw Damien's face meekly peering into the office, he said in a gruff, beleaguered voice, "Don't just stand there, come in, come in. Take a seat." There was only one seat, a shiny black, spindle-backed wooden chair positioned directly in front of Barnes's desk. Damien waited for Barnes to begin.

Leaning back in his chair, Barnes seemed to be taking a final look at Damien to be sure that the person he had in his mind was the same person as the one sitting in front of him. He finally said, "There's a job that the editorial board of *Interludes* would like to offer you. You know *Interludes*, don't you? Or has the old rag completely gone out of existence for your generation?"

"Of course, I know *Interludes*."

"That's good to hear."

Barnes softened his voice like a salesman taking the customer into his confidence about the most select of his products— a product in short supply, and in high demand—which he will make available to the customer because the customer is an unusually discerning man. "*Interludes* used to be a good literary and social commentary magazine, a very good one. But it has been neglected and is currently in wretched shape. The people running it now don't care if they bore the reader to death with articles that lack both intelligence and imagination. For some reason, I care what happens to it. There's almost no money in it for those running it now because they've let circulation fall to a level that's about the same as that of my grandson's school newspaper. A group of us—McKee, Sigward, Marks, Gustafson, Levine, Goldsmith, and Shapiro—are committed to returning *Interludes* to its former stature, and to make it a cutting-edge voice in today's literary dialogue. A group of us see you as having one of the finest critical minds that has come along in a long time, I mean among our students."

Damien blushed, hating his body for refusing to allow him any privacy.

"Let me get to the point. We'd like to have you join *Interludes* as the assistant managing editor. It's a part-time job, but not simply a secretarial or administrative job. As a member of the editorial board, you will have a voice in the direction the magazine is taking and you will be a reviewer of submissions. There will be some copyediting and the like."

Barnes went on to tell Damien that the reconceived *Interludes* was intended for a broad readership. In each issue, there would be book reviews of recently published books, as well as of books that for one reason or another had not yet been given the place they deserve in the Western canon. Also featured in the magazine would be interviews with authors as well as essays on the impact of current cultural shifts and cultural traumas.

He explained that, while the editorial board was composed almost entirely of university professors, *Interludes* was privately owned and depended for its survival on revenue raised from subscriptions and donations. The "new" *Interludes* was being supported by a large contribution from a philanthropist, a long-time "friend" of the humanities departments of the university. The incoming board of the magazine wanted to make it a more daring, more politically informed, and controversial version of the old *Saturday Review*. "If it fails in becoming that, we're all better off spending our time doing something else."

Barnes ended by saying that the newly formed editorial board had appointed him the editor-in-chief. Looking over his horn-rimmed glasses that had slid down to the end of his nose, Barnes waited for Damien's reply. Damien, without a moment's hesitation, accepted the job.

Barnes had understated the degree to which the magazine was currently in a shambles. The publisher had given notice to the board of trustees of *Interludes* that the magazine would be shut down if, in the next fiscal year, it was unable to demonstrate that it was financially solvent. The infighting and finger-pointing among the former editorial board had made it practically impossible to conduct the business of the magazine. Damien would receive only a nominal salary until the magazine was firmly in the black.

The entirety of the former editorial board had been asked to resign, which they did gladly, with the exception of Sam Winters, the managing editor. He was the only person who knew how a magazine actually works in the real world, but he was in his mid-seventies and planned to retire in the not-too-distant future. It was more than a youthful perspective that Barnes was expecting from Damien. Barnes was asking him, without saying it directly, to learn from Winters how to manage the magazine, and to learn it quickly, before Winters retired. In a matter of weeks, Damien would find that the "part-time job" required far more time and work than he'd been led to believe.

In the late afternoon of the Friday following Damien's meeting with Barnes, a group of eight—most of the editorial board and a member of the board of trustees—assembled in one of the reception rooms of the English department to share a glass of sherry in honor of Damien's acceptance of the position. The board—which was divided evenly by gender—seemed to Damien genuinely pleased to have him join them in the effort to revitalize *Interludes*. He wasn't sure why they were so welcoming, much less having a meeting in his honor. Catherine, then a sophomore at a school of design in Chicago, would of course not be present at the occasion.

Damien was astounded by the tenor of the editorial board meetings that were held monthly, on Wednesday evenings, at the home of one or another board member. The board members seemed to genuinely enjoy the meetings. The rivalries and turf battles that Damien had expected seemed to play only a minor role. He saw a side of Barnes at the meetings that both stunned and amazed him. Barnes had a winning charm and charisma. The board member closest to Damien's age was a professor of sociology, about twenty-five years Damien's senior. In each monthly meeting, board members presented succinct critiques of articles that three editorial readers—usually academics and other writers with expertise in the subject matter of the article—believed were exceptional contributions. If there was a consensus among the board members that the article had unusual merit, it was left to Barnes to make the final decision.

The board, both its male and female members, took an instant liking to Damien. They liked the way he brought to the meetings originality of thought wrapped in genuine humility. His youthful ways served as an elixir for this group of people whose ideas were rarely surprising to one another. The group did not try to stick strictly to the business at hand; illnesses of parents, spouses, children, and the board members themselves were spoken about in an emotionally truthful way, as were divorces and other sources of pain. Damien was open about the strange circumstances of his own early life with Margaret and Sybil, but in his rendering of his past he had no siblings, and both of his parents had died in an auto accident when he was seventeen.

After several months, Damien was asked to present to the editorial board the reviews of an article on the question of whether there was a meaningful "progression" in American literature in the work of Isaac Bashevis Singer, Saul Bellow, and Philip Roth. Damien worked extremely hard on this, his first report to the board, and received an appreciative response. The female members of the board took Damien as their surrogate son, and the male members took him as their surrogate kid brother. Damien left each of the board meetings feeling very fortunate to be part of this group, the first group in which he held a place that was his own, a family in which he was wanted.

*Interludes* made great strides in regaining national attention during Damien's first year at the magazine. Of particular interest to its readers was a series of well-conducted interviews with E. L. Doctorow, Norman Rush, Annie McDermott, and John Updike.

Damien did everything he could to keep out of public view, in part by putting his name at the bottom of the magazine's masthead among a group of administrative assistants. The fact that his surname was different from Catherine's, and from that of the rest of his family except Margaret, helped disguise his identity. He took some comfort in the idea that nobody he had ever known, including Mr. Lerner, was likely to subscribe to this magazine or even peruse it at a bookstore that carried it. Nevertheless, Damien realized that putting his name in the masthead, regardless of how well buried it was, exposed him to a large audience, and it took only one person to recognize his name and to begin wondering about what had become of Catherine or Erin or him. Jealousy would be a sufficient motive for trying to bring him down. Who the hell did he think he was, someone from his past might ask. As he put to bed each issue of *Interludes*, he felt as if he were pulling the trigger of a revolver aimed at his head in a game of Russian roulette.

As the months passed, Damien's fear grew increasingly intense, at a pace equal to the joy he felt while participating in the meetings of the editorial board and in the lunches with individual members of the board to which he was invited. Perhaps the person who took most pleasure in having Damien on the board was Barnes. He asked Damien to sit in the chair to his right, claiming that he had trouble hearing the specific tonal range of Damien's voice, but it was obvious to everyone that this was a ruse. He just liked having Damien by his side.

Damien developed severe migraine headaches, for which none of the medications the doctors prescribed did more than blunt the agony a bit. The piercing, aching pain in the right side of his skull felt as if a pair of pliers were taking hold of the optic nerve of his right eye and tearing it from his skull. On one occasion, after twelve hours of unremitting torture, Catherine called a cab and took Damien to the emergency room of Michael Reese Hospital, where he was given an injection of morphine. The doctor who attended to Damien—a tall, thin, balding man in his forties, wearing wire-rim glasses—said to him and Catherine that, given the fact the migraines were now occurring less than two weeks apart, and that they seemed not to be responsive to the medications currently available, the most effective treatment for his headaches was preventative, which meant reducing the strain in his life. He also recommended that Damien consult his internist because his blood pressure was dangerously high. Later that night, Damien, in tears, said to Catherine as they lay in bed in the dark, "The source of the pressure—*Interludes*—is the most important thing in my life, other than you. I can't leave *Interludes*, I just can't."

Catherine knew, and Damien tried not to know, that *Interludes* wasn't the real source of the pressure; it was Damien's fear that their relationship would be discovered. Catherine chose not to confront Damien about his self-deception because she knew that he was doing everything humanly possible to keep two loves alive—the love of his home at *Interludes* and the love he felt for her.

Despite the intensity of the torment wrought by this dilemma, Catherine was able to cheer Damien, sometimes in surprising ways. For reasons neither of them could understand—not that it mattered—there was a form of charade they played that could be counted on, more reliably than anything else, to relieve Damien of the pounding, relentless internal pressure he lived with. In the charade, Catherine played the role of a mute French girl. Damien would ask her in French for directions to a museum or a Metro station and Catherine, as the mute girl, would wildly try to communicate the answer to the question by pantomime. Damien would howl with laughter at her emphatic nodding when he understood what she was trying to communicate, and her ferociously shaking her head and her disgusted facial expressions when he wasn't able to understand. Catherine, too, loved these moments. She deeply desired to soothe Damien. The joy they felt in playing this game, and the belly laughs they had in response to the absurdity of it, brought a form of relief that lasted longer and reached more deeply into both of them than any other way they had of dealing with Damien's internal torment.

Although Damien could talk with Catherine about the demon living inside him, he felt that it would be hurtful to Catherine to speak of the intensity of his devotion to—maybe the word for it was his love for—Barnes and several other members of the editorial board, two of whom were women in their fifties and sixties. The women were a good deal older than his mother, and yet he found them beautiful and sexy. He felt that he must be very warped psychologically, a freak, really, to be having these feelings for women older than his mother. They weren't a replacement for Catherine. He found her beautiful, and she was his closest friend—in fact his only friend—and she was the person whose opinion he most valued because she was not only intelligent; she was also very perceptive and wise about the most important things. Catherine was very calm when things went wrong—a missing passport, a lost wallet, an overflowing toilet. He was the hysterical one, not her. Catherine was not only the person he loved; she also felt like a part of him. Their sexual relationship was passionate despite or—he sometimes thought—because of its secret, forbidden nature. To lose her was unthinkable, and yet he knew he was risking exposure of their relationship by becoming less secretive as he came to know and like, and maybe even love, the people with whom he worked at *Interludes*.

By the end of the first year of "*Interludes* reborn," as the members of the board liked to call it, the magazine was in the black—barely so, but nonetheless an achievement that the

194

publisher recognized by sending the board three bottles of good champagne.

Also at the end of the first year of "*Interludes* reborn," Sam Winters, the long-time managing editor, announced his retirement. Damien, now having graduated from the university, was hired as managing editor, even though the job no longer included business management, which was to be handled by a newly hired woman with experience in the business of publishing. Nonetheless, Damien's workload increased significantly, which added to the physical battering he was taking. He was now having severe migraine headaches even more frequently, which incapacitated him while they were occurring, and left him physically and emotionally depleted for days afterward.

Damien proved himself an equal to the other board members, not only in reviewing articles submitted to *Interludes*, but also in writing book review essays, which the magazine published under his own name. During the third year of his tenure at the magazine, Barnes called him into his office. On arriving, Barnes, with a sweeping movement of his arm, motioned Damien to the black spindle-backed chair in front of his desk. He said, "We have an agreement for an interview that I'd like to have you conduct, but you should know that it's a touchy situation." Barnes paused. "Philip Roth has accepted our invitation to be interviewed, but he's a very narcissistic man, even more so than I am, so he may feel insulted by having a man just a year or two out of college conduct the interview. I will give him your name if you want to do the interview, but I will not send your CV to him. To do that would be an apology for you. So, what I'm saying is that I'd like to have you do the interview, but you should know that he may respond to what you ask, or what you say, as an insult to …"

Damien interrupted, "I'll take my chances with him."

Having read all of Roth's novels while writing his honors thesis and reviewing the article submitted to *Interludes* on Singer, Bellow, and Roth, Damien felt prepared to conduct the interview with Roth without behaving like a young acolyte. The interview was conducted in a small library in the English department. Two brown, deeply creased and well worn leather armchairs were placed in the center of the room, with a coffee table between them on which were placed a pitcher of water, two glasses, and a cassette tape recorder.

Roth was an imposing figure—a trim man with an enormous pate and two stretches of long, thick, salt-and-pepper hair running the length of the sides of his head. Most prominent of his features, for Damien, were his hauntingly dark eyes, accentuated by semi-circles below them, and a five-o'clock shadow that seemed to be a permanent feature regardless of the time of day.

Damien's initial self-consciousness was dispelled by the animation and energy that were generated as he and Roth talked and thought with one another about the subject both of them loved most, reading and writing literature. Damien was taken by surprise when Roth, the moment Damien pressed the stop button of the tape recorder, stood up and, without uttering a word, left the room. As Damien sat alone in the room after Roth left, he had the odd experience of not being able to remember much of the content of the hour-and-a-half interview. What stayed with him was the feeling he'd had at certain moments of the interview in which Roth seemed to convey, in the way he spoke, that he found Damien an intelligent and exciting person to talk with. Roth sat forward in his chair a number of times in the course of the conversation—it felt more like a conversation than an interview. He came most to life while discussing the role of Jewish writers in twentieth-century American literature, moving his large hands as he spoke, as if conducting the music of the words he was speaking. Most important to Damien was his impression that Roth appreciated his ear for good writing as they discussed the passages from *Herzog* that Damien read aloud.

A few days after the interview, Damien asked the department secretary to schedule an appointment for him with Professor Barnes. When he and Barnes sat down in Barnes's office, as they'd done so often in the past—first when Damien was an undergraduate, then the assistant managing editor, and finally the managing editor and a full participant in the life of the magazine—he felt sure that Barnes expected him to be looking for fatherly praise for his Roth interview.

Instead, Damien began by saying in one sentence the whole of what he was there to say. He was afraid that if he didn't get these words out right away, he might lose the courage to say them: "I feel terrible about doing this to you and to *Interludes*, but I have to leave." Barnes's face dropped in a way that Damien had never before seen from him.

Damien continued, "Being part of the board of *Interludes* has been the most important experience of my life. I'm not exaggerating when I say that. I can't tell you how much it has meant to me to have you mentor me ... *mentor* is the wrong word ... I'll tell you the truth. You've been more of a father to me than my own father was, and I will always think of you that way."

"I don't understand. Why are you leaving?"

"I'm leaving because of my health. For the past four years, I've been having terrible migraines and my blood pressure is out of control, and they don't have any medications that help. I wish I could stay, but the doctors tell me it will kill me to stay." All of this was true.

Barnes was speechless, which was a first in Damien's experience with him. After a while, Barnes said, "Isn't there anything they can do about these medical conditions? I can ask my doctor for the names of specialists in migraines and hypertension."

"Thank you for your offer, but I have seen specialists at the Mayo Clinic, and they have had nothing to offer except stress-reduction techniques, like breathing exercises, which haven't helped."

"Have you tried seeing a psychiatrist?"

"I have, and the medications they've prescribed haven't helped, nor has talking about the problem ... I'm so sorry to do this to you and the magazine after all that you and the members of the board have done for me."

"How do you want to do it?"

"I'll do it in whatever way you think best," Damien said, knowing that he was causing Barnes enormous pain. Damien wished he could tell Barnes the real reason he was leaving, which he now could accurately name. To tell Barnes the truth would spoil what he and Barnes had had together. Damien would forever be, in Barnes's mind, the sick kid who was having sex with his sister, the kid who had burdened him with a secret that he had no wish to hear, and yet he was stuck with it.

Barnes and Damien sat silently as they absorbed what Damien had said. Damien was feeling a familiar ache that began in the pit of his stomach and ran up through his chest into his head, and settled, throbbing, behind his eyes. How could he have done this to himself? He had not only done it to himself, he had done it to Barnes, and to the members of the board who had grown to like him and appreciate his literary talents. A stronger person could have stayed, he thought, but he was not such a person.

Barnes finally broke the silence when he asked, "Is there anything I can do?"

"I wish there were."

"We'll find another managing editor, but no one will replace you." This was not the way Barnes ordinarily spoke. Both of them could feel that.

Damien stammered as he said, "No one will replace you either. I can't tell you how much I appreciate all you've done for me ... how important you've been to me." Damien worried that he'd said too much—people don't talk like this in academia—but he wouldn't take it back if he could.

Barnes leaned back and brushed the fingers of both hands through his thinning hair.

* * *

In the initial meeting of the editorial board, Barnes announced Damien's departure. He said that Damien was leaving for medical reasons. The announcement was not met with the customary toasts to the person leaving, thanking him or her for all they'd done and wishing them well in their next undertaking. Instead, it felt as if a pall hung over the room. Some of the board members looked at Damien in dismay; some looked at him angrily; others were stunned, not knowing what to feel, but the ones who had grown to love him, particularly Geoffrey Barnes, felt profoundly sad—for themselves, but even more for Damien. They sensed that "medical reasons" was a disguised way of saying that something terrible was happening in Damien's life, so awful that it had become necessary for him to leave a place and the people he loved, and they would probably never know what it was.

Damien felt that the truth of what was happening was unspeakably tawdry. Out of cowardice, he was moving to Ohio, a state where he had no ties, no prospects for becoming the person he had begun to be while on the board of *Interludes*. He had chosen to move there because it had no laws against incest. He felt that this was not a love story in which the hero gives up everything for his beloved. It was the story of a man— or was he a boy—who felt unwilling and unable to leave the woman—that word, too, was hard to say—he loved, even though he wasn't sure what the word *love* meant. He thought he loved Catherine. He knew he could not live without her and that he would give up anything to be with her. That has to be love, he thought—his willingness to give up a job, a home, a group of people who were enormously important to him in order to have a life with her, a life that would not be lived in a

199

place where their relationship was an ugly crime. That was the truth, but it wasn't a truth he could tell the board.

The board meeting ended late. Damien said his goodbyes and then walked home in the thick, cold mist of that winter night. His mind was empty of thought and feeling as he walked several miles from the suburban home where the board had met to his apartment on the south side of Chicago. He was in a daze as he put one foot in front of the other, crossed streets at crosswalks, stepped around puddles of water. The city disappeared as the place where he'd lived; he felt himself disappearing as the person he'd been and the person he thought he was becoming. Everything had changed. He didn't live anywhere; he wasn't anybody.

Damien mechanically unlocked the front door of his apartment building and walked the five flights to the unit he'd been renting. Once inside, he walked to his bedroom, took off his clothes, got into bed, and pulled the covers over him. The phone rang, but he didn't answer it. It rang again, and he unplugged it from the wall.

# TWENTY-EIGHT

Damien didn't move from his bed for two days, except to urinate. Neither did he eat or answer the phone. His not answering his phone did not worry Catherine because Damien didn't answer his phone when he was concentrating on his work, or in the grip of a migraine, or simply wanted to think something over before talking to her. She knew that the board meeting was going to be very difficult for him, and so it was understandable that he'd want to try to take it in on his own for a while.

After three days of not being able to contact Damien by phone, Catherine, mid-morning, anxiously walked the ten blocks from her apartment to his, through a squalid part of the city she wouldn't ordinarily cross on her own. Out of breath after climbing the five flights of steep steps, she knocked on the door to Damien's apartment and received no answer. After knocking loudly several times, she used her key to open the door.

The air in the apartment was still, with an acrid odor. Catherine's knees felt wobbly as she walked through the living room, looking for clues that might tell her what had happened to Damien, increasingly afraid that she might find him dead in blood-stained bathwater or hanging from a door frame. She braced herself as she opened the door to his bedroom, where she saw him lying absolutely still in bed on his stomach. She quickly crossed the room and shook him gently. Getting no response, she shook him as hard as she could and punched his shoulder with as much force as she could gather as she stood unsteadily at the side of his bed. Groggily, he pulled his elbows up, as if preparing to do a push-up, and turned to face her, his eyes sealed shut like those of a newborn.

"Please go away," he mumbled.

"Are you all right?"

"Yes, I'm okay, I just want to be by myself."

"What's happened?"

"Nothing."

"I refuse to play this game with you. Tell me what happened at the board meeting."

"I said, 'Please go away.'"

"Please grow up. Something has happened to you, and if it's happened to you, it's happened to me, so I want to know what it is. Look, get out of bed and we'll sit in the living room and talk like adults. We're not children any longer, if you haven't noticed."

"Don't talk down to me."

"Get out of bed. I don't want to talk in this dark smelly room." Catherine pulled up the blinds to let in the sharp morning light.

"Don't do that. You're blinding me."

"Good."

Damien dragged himself in his T-shirt and boxer shorts into the living room, where Catherine was already sitting on the slipcovered, pale green couch. He sat next to her and put his head on her shoulder, like a young boy with his mother—not that Damien had ever done that with Rose, Margaret, or Sybil.

"All right, tell me what happened."

"Nothing bad happened at the board meeting. Barnes announced my quitting for medical reasons. No one got angry, telling me I'm an ungrateful brat for leaving them in the lurch. They were stunned and nobody said much of anything for a while, and then someone said they'd miss me and that I'd done a good job, and a few others said they were sad, and two of the women, Janice and Elaine, cried. I thanked them for everything, and then they went on with the meeting. Barnes had already asked me to continue to do the administrative work by phone and fax and be the assistant to my replacement for a year or so. He told everyone that, and they were pleased to hear it. There's no official title for this job, so my name won't appear in the masthead, and that's a relief. Barnes also invited me to contribute book review essays and social commentary essays."

"You haven't told me that before. Isn't that good that you'll continue to be a part of *Interludes* after we move?"

"It is," he said in a compliant way.

"Don't do that. Don't denigrate a genuine gesture of respect from Barnes. He's been wonderful to you, and he doesn't want to end the connection with you."

"That's true, but I don't feel it. Other than the two of us— our little family of two—I've never had a family like the one I've had there, and it hurts to go. I keep asking myself why I'm leaving. I say to myself, You know why you're leaving. The secret. But why can't I just keep a secret? That's what I don't know."

"You don't have to know. That's who you are."

"I don't like who I am."

"Well, I like who you are. I know that you're doing this for the two of us. I know how much you're giving up. It's insane that our secret has to be a secret, but we've decided it does."

"Do you think we're being cowards or paranoid?" Damien asked.

"You know the law in Illinois. What we're doing can be punished with twenty-five years in prison. Does that sound paranoid? We've talked this over and we've decided we don't want to be waiting for the knock on the door by 'the authorities.'"

"I know, I know."

"I'm giving up my apprenticeship with Jeanne. It hasn't meant to me what your work and the people you work with have meant to you. We're both leaving something for nothing. No, that's not true. We're leaving something for something else that matters more to us."

* * *

Damien and Catherine made their exit from Chicago with as little drama as possible. Each of them politely endured "good-bye dinners," where they invented jobs that they "just couldn't turn down" in Cleveland.

Very early one clear Saturday morning in June, hired men loaded Catherine's furniture and boxes of books and clothes into a rental truck, and then drove to Damien's apartment to load his things. In the early afternoon, Damien climbed into the cab of the rental truck, where Catherine was already seated in the passenger seat. He took a route through the city to the interstate that avoided landmarks that held any meaning for him. Once on the interstate, both he and Catherine felt a great weight lifted from them. They rolled down their windows and let the warm air wash over them as they had many years earlier, that morning of their first drive together into the central Illinois farmland.

On arriving in Cleveland, they presented themselves to a real estate agent as brother and sister looking for apartments in the same building. After a day of looking at a series of apartments, ranging from luxurious places with a doorman to houses divided into several units occupied by people in their thirties and forties who looked permanently stoned, they settled on two apartments in the same building. It was located in an industrial area of Cleveland not unlike the one that Damien and Erin had walked through on their way to and from school, an area where flashes of blue light from blowtorches jumped from garages, and the smell of melting steel wafted through the air, where groups of men talked and stood unsteadily outside corner grocery and liquor stores, where drugs were sold in doorways by kids wearing hoodies. It was a building where they could sense that no one would ask questions, no one would offer their name, favors would not be asked—it was perfect for Damien and Catherine.

And yet, what occurred inside their apartments during their first few weeks was far from perfect. They wept with homesickness. They longed for the clandestine, but very rich and intimate life they'd had in Chicago. They also longed for homes that each of them had had on their own, not shared with the other. For Damien, it was the home that the members of the board of *Interludes* had made for him. He was the young man whom they were helping grow into the mature man they saw in him, and they took delight in doing it. There were no rivalries among his "parents," and everyone knew that he and Barnes had a tie to one another that was the anchor of Damien's place in the family. They told Damien that he had changed Barnes, that Barnes had become a softer, kinder, more open and likeable man as a result of his relationship with Damien.

Catherine's homesickness, her longing, was for the home that she and Rose (whom she sometimes still called Mommy) had made with one another when she was a little girl, a home that despite Erin's presence, was a very feminine home in which they had sewn clothes for her dolls, washed their hair, changed their diapers, and to whom they sang as they went to sleep in their cribs. Catherine could remember her mother beaming with joy as she and Catherine held hands as they walked in the park. One day in particular stood out. Catherine remembered wearing a new, marine-blue pinafore over a soft white blouse with ivory buttons. She had hoped that day that she would never grow up. She never wanted to have to give up these walks with her mother.

The world in which Catherine and Damien lived in Cleveland had shrunk to the size of Catherine's apartment. Damien furnished his studio apartment as if it were a monk's cell with only a mattress, a desk, and a chair. He rarely slept in that apartment. The name tag he slid into the slot on the badly tarnished bronze mailbox allocated to him was illegible, but the first few letters were enough for the mail man to indentify where to put his mail—not that there ever was any, except mail bundled and forwarded by Margaret (who was told not to give anyone their Cleveland address). A couple of months after the move, Damien told Catherine that he'd received a letter from Barnes, forwarded by Margaret, asking him to open a small office in which to do his work for *Interludes* and to conduct interviews with authors. His Roth interview, he was told, raised the bar for the magazine's author interviews.

Damien called the real estate agent who had helped find the apartments in which they were living. She was no longer with the agency, so they referred him to Denise Crane, another agent in the company. Damien felt shy and awkward with her, which brought to his attention the depth of his withdrawal from the outside world. She was the first person other than Catherine with whom he had spoken in months, with the exception of Rose and Margaret, with whom he'd had brief, perfunctory exchanges. Everything about Denise was crisp—her short hair plastered in place by hair spray, her ironed and starched blouse and skirt, her almost new, midnight-blue 1996 Buick Skylark. She showed him half a dozen places in the space of a single morning, and he signed a lease that same afternoon.

* * *

By mid-November, Catherine and Damien had settled into a routine. They spent their evenings together in Catherine's apartment after they each returned from work—Damien from his small office, and Catherine from her job as an apprentice to a clothing designer. Despite the fact that they were living in what they called "a safe state," and their surnames were different, Damien was never satisfied that he had successfully hidden his and Catherine's identities. His fears of being "uncovered" steadily increased. No reassurances on Catherine's part made any difference. In fact, her efforts to calm him angered him rather than soothed him. He reluctantly acceded to her request that he move into her apartment and give up his own. She felt that he hid there, and that it was time for the two of them to live as a couple. She told him she didn't want to be his sister, she wanted to be his wife. He understood, and with great trepidation, moved into her apartment.

Margaret supported Catherine and Damien financially as she had always supported Rose and her household. The fact that they did not have to earn a living increased their isolation during their first several months in Cleveland. With no one else to talk to, they had only their own thoughts with which to gauge the truth. Over the course of time, conversation had become superfluous because they thought they knew each other's thoughts. They'd endured their loneliness separately and completely.

# TWENTY-NINE

Alice squirmed in her chair between Catherine's and Damien's at Rose's funeral service. Rose had lived for sixteen years after her breast cancer was diagnosed. After almost twenty-five years of having children at home, Rose had felt not only lonely, but useless after Catherine moved into an apartment near the school of design in Chicago. Being a grandmother to Alice for four years had given her what she called "a second chance that I don't deserve." Her health had been relatively good until the cancer spread in the last few months of her life. Although she didn't like to leave her "new house" in the Chicago suburbs, she frequently took the train or drove with Margaret to visit Catherine, Damien, and Alice. She adored Alice and Alice adored her. Alice seemed to bring out Rose's youthful fascination with the magic she found in virtually everything she and Alice discovered together, whether it be a personality they invented for a doll, or a story they made up about two springer spaniels they'd seen at the park, or the flight to the stars Alice took on the swings. Alice helped Rose come to know that even though she had made terrible mistakes in raising Damien, that sad experience was not the totality of who she was as a mother. Alice had been crushed when she was told that Rose had died and that they would never again be able to spend time together. She'd become easily frustrated and angered when she didn't get her way, which was unusual for her.

Catherine leaned over and whispered in Alice's ear, "This is only going to last a little bit longer. Come sit on Mommy's lap."

Alice's shiny chestnut brown hair, which Catherine liked to keep long, had a natural wave in it like her mother's and grandmother's. Alice was a very pretty, very endearing little girl, who, like Catherine, was a "girly girl." She paraded around the apartment wearing the dresses her mother made for her. Her face, with its delicate features that seemed to frame her rosebud lips, had a definite resemblance to Catherine's face, and her light olive skin just as definitely resembled Damien's. Alice had a winsome sparkle in her eye that seemed to invite others to be co-conspirators with her in some sort of mischief she invented. She was tall for a four year old, and had had a mind of her own seemingly from the day she was born. When, at two and a half, she had accidentally knocked over a standing cardboard figure in a store, Damien, as he was righting it, had said, "Don't worry, it doesn't matter." Alice looked him straight in the eye and said, "It matters to me."

Alice, who was sitting between her parents, slid off her plush, cushioned, folding chair in the dimly lit "Going Home Suite" of Duggan's Funeral Home, and turned to put both hands on Catherine's right knee. She looked up at her mother to see what was taking her so long to lift her onto her lap. Using Catherine's knee as she might use a protruding stone on the face of a cliff, Alice tried, without success, to hoist herself up onto her mother's lap. Catherine leaned forward to help her up. Alice didn't stop to find a comfortable spot on which to sit; instead, she refused to bend her knees and stood with one foot on each of her mother's nylon-covered knees. With Catherine's hands holding on to both sides of her waist, Alice turned to get a better look at what was happening up front.

There were only a few people whom Alice did not recognize in the small room of the funeral home. Her father had slid over to the chair she had just vacated. On the other side of her mother were Uncle Erin, whom she'd only seen once or twice before, and Aunt Margaret. The dark green curtain behind the man who was talking on the stage was just like the one in the movie theater she'd been to. Alice had been frightened by the sight of her mother and father crying after Aunt Margaret called to say that Gramma Rose had died. She had never seen her father cry, and she was afraid that he was angry at her for bothering him at such a sad time, or maybe he was blaming her for Gramma Rose's death, even though she didn't know how she could have caused it.

Once Alice was convinced that there was nothing much to see up front, she turned around on her mother's lap and tried to slide back down onto the floor. Catherine pulled her back up, turned her around, and pressed her down onto her lap. Alice began whining loudly. Damien leaned over and, putting his hands under Alice's arms, lifted her onto his lap.

Damien whispered over Alice's shoulder into her ear, "If you just sit here for a very few more minutes, this will be over, and then you and Daddy will get something to eat. When we get back to Aunt Margaret's house, Daddy will take you to play on the swings in the park near her house. How would you like that?"

"I want to go now."

"We can't go now, but it won't be too much longer."

Finally, the man speaking at the front of the room finished talking, and invited everyone to go into another room to have something to eat. Catherine and Damien exchanged a glance of relief. Catherine's eyes were red from crying, and her eyelids were puffy.

There were only about five or six guests in attendance other than the immediate family, all neighbors of Rose in Chicago. None of Margaret's colleagues from the bank had been told

211

of Rose's death. The move to Chicago had allowed Margaret a fresh start in that she kept from everyone outside the family her failure to be a mother to Damien. Her colleagues in the central Illinois bank had been discreet, as far as she could tell, about what little they knew about the failed adoption. To her new colleagues in Chicago she said only that she had a younger sister.

For some years, Catherine had felt that Margaret had been deeply hurt by Rose's decision not to accept cancer treatment. She thought that Rose's stubbornness must have felt to Margaret like a statement that she didn't love Margaret as much as Margaret loved her. Margaret would have accepted cancer treatment, more for Rose's sake than her own, Catherine thought.

Rose had moved into Margaret's house for the final months of her life. She rejected hospice care, saying she hated doctors and nurses, and just wanted to be left to die in peace. Rose was fifty-seven when she died. Catherine had to smile when Margaret told her what Rose had said about hospice care. She liked the vitality Rose had managed to sustain until the day she died. For Catherine, her mother's single-minded devotion to her, and protection of her, during the long months of her hospitalization after her fall had been Rose's finest hours. That person was the woman her mother really was.

When Catherine realized that she had been standing in front of her seat, lost in thought, for quite some time, she looked around for Alice and Damien. The room, scented with a cloyingly sweet perfume, was empty except for two women lingering at the doorway.

On entering the reception room, Catherine was blinded by the glare of light coming through the three tall windows to her left, which filled one end of the long rectangular room. She reflexively put all her weight on the handle of her bleached white cane to keep from falling. As she regained some of her vision, she found shelter from the assault of light in a corner, next to the windows. She lowered herself onto one of the cushioned folding chairs. As she caught her breath, the room, as it emerged from behind translucent orange and yellow spirals, had the feel of a motel lobby.

Catherine, from her corner, surveyed the small group of mourners as if from a great distance. The thin buzz of conversation was like white noise that carried her into half-sleep. Catherine had always imagined, though she was never certain of it, that as hard as her mother had worked to disguise it, Rose had only one child whom she loved from the core of her being, and that was Erin. Only after Damien told her about Rose's confession of the circumstances of his birth, and hers, did she finally understand how Erin had come to inhabit his particular place in the family. She vividly recalled the evening in her apartment in Chicago when Damien returned from his talk with Rose. As Damien recounted Rose's confession, Catherine's father, whom she had never met, became permanently transformed in her mind. No longer did she picture him as the dashing young man for whose love she had longed her whole life. He became, in that moment of discovery, a rather petty, self-engrossed figure who had not only exchanged betrayals with her mother, but had conspired with her to conceive a baby—any baby would do—to repair the damage that the two of them had done to one another. Catherine's very existence in that new light was a mere byproduct of a battle that had nothing to do with her.

Catherine remembered feeling, as Damien talked with her about what Rose had said, that the story of his conception was even bleaker than the circumstances of her own. Not only was he a mistake, he was an affront to the man whom all his life he'd thought was his father. And at that moment at Rose's funeral, sitting in the corner next to the windows, she said to herself, "Erin, poor Erin." To be the only child to have been wanted must have placed a heavy burden of guilt on him. Catherine had never before thought of Erin as "poor Erin."

Catherine's thoughts continued to float as she sat by herself. Damien was the only person in her life who had been capable of making her feel fully and genuinely loved. It had been a first love, an immature love for both of them, but their immaturity hadn't made their love any less real or any less intense. She wondered where Damien, the least loved member of the family, had acquired the ability to love her so deeply. He probably came by it as a result of being loved by Erin, she thought. Very early in the course of the years that Erin was trying to help Damien learn how to live a normal life—Catherine remembered this part of things clearly—Erin began to love him, and Damien began to love Erin. It was unusual for Catherine to allow herself to think about her childhood because it was too sad to dwell on, and because she was afraid that if she dwelt on it too long, she would be pulled under by it.

The loud metallic clatter of a serving tray falling to the floor roused Catherine from her waking sleep. The room was too large, and there was much too much food on the long table in the center of the room for the small number of guests who were thinly scattered around the room. The one person whom Catherine worried about was Margaret. Rose had not only been Margaret's sister, she had been Margaret's closest friend, and probably the only friend she had ever had. Margaret looked desolate. Catherine thought that she would be dead in less than a year.

Margaret looked lost as she stood by herself in the middle of the room. As Catherine approached her, Margaret gathered herself quickly and allowed Catherine to embrace her, which was an awkward gesture for both of them because of the cane Catherine held in her left hand. Margaret's dress was wrinkled, as if taken from storage; her mascara lay in vertical black streaks down her pale white, doughy cheeks like clowns' paint.

"I feel sad about losing Mom, but to tell you the truth, I feel sadder that you've lost her."

214

"That's kind of you to say. I suppose it's true. I miss her terribly. I don't know what to say." Margaret covered her face as she sobbed. Catherine let her cane drop to the floor and put her arms around Margaret. She was surprised by how small Margaret felt. She was as small as Rose. Margaret had always seemed much bigger to Catherine than her mother.

When Margaret noticed that a guest was trying to catch her eye to say goodbye, she said to Catherine, "Would you excuse me for a few minutes, I have to deal with some of the formalities of funerals." She picked up Catherine's cane from the floor and handed it to her before attending to the couple.

Catherine felt strangely unable to keep her balance after Margaret left. A young man, a member of the staff of the funeral home, noticed that Catherine was unsteady on her feet, as if the ground beneath her were moving. She had caught his attention earlier—such a pretty woman, he thought, whose beauty wasn't diminished by the elevated heel on one of her black orthopedic shoes or by the cane she used. He found her the most interesting and the most mysterious of the guests. He hurried over to her and asked if she'd like some assistance. She looked at him, but seemed unable to reply. She then said, "Yes, please help me to a chair." Standing to her left, he quietly asked her to hook her left arm through his and grip his arm tightly. When she had done so, he said, "When you take a step with your left leg, put as much of your weight on my arm as you can, and when you take a step with your right leg, put as much weight on your cane as you can. I'll be right here with you. I won't let you fall."

Catherine didn't understand how this young man could be so sure that he could prevent her from falling, but she believed him nonetheless, and felt comforted by his quiet confidence. She was also pleased that he was not patronizing. After all, she wasn't an old lady, she was only thirty-two. She liked the softness of his voice and his brown doe's eyes. She wondered how a boy with such confidence and such kindness could find himself working in a funeral home. He looked to be about twenty-four or twenty-five. Perhaps he was a son in the family business. He seemed cut out for the business of life, not for the business of death.

They slowly walked to one of the folding chairs near the windows where Catherine had been sitting earlier. Once they were in front of one of the chairs, he helped her turn and lower herself slowly onto the cushioned seat. Her face was cold with perspiration, and her legs were trembling. The young man went to the table to get her a glass of water. He asked if there was anything else he could get her. She said, "You've been very kind. I mean that, it's not just a figure of speech. I'd just like to sit here for a few minutes."

Being seated again felt luxurious to Catherine. She could feel her breathing and her heartbeat gradually slow and become stronger. She noticed that she was holding a glass of water in her right hand, balanced on her thigh, that she'd forgotten was there. Carefully leaning forward and to her right, she placed the glass on the carpet. Catherine leaned back and shut her eyes. She let herself sink into a state of calm that filled her body. She was deeply saddened not only by the brevity of Rose's life, but also by how underappreciated she'd been.

# THIRTY

As Catherine sat in the corner of the funeral reception hall, more as a reliving than a remembering, she smelled the scent of pine needles in the air on that gusty, mid-April evening as she and Damien walked down the hill from where they had parked their car to Margaret's house in Chicago. The afternoon rain had left a mist in the air and a thin coating of moisture on the sidewalk. The pale orange three-quarter moon moved in and out from behind fast-moving cloud banks, like a lost child peering through a milling crowd in search of his mother. Margaret was waiting anxiously at her front door, atop the red slate staircase that rose from the street.

Catherine had called the previous evening to arrange a time to talk. Damien was a junior at university in Chicago, and Catherine a freshman at the school of design. They were seeking sound and practical advice from Margaret, not comfort. You don't go to Margaret for comfort.

The decision to turn to Margaret came more naturally to Catherine than to Damien. Catherine had never experienced Margaret as a warm person, but from the time she was very small, she had looked up to Margaret as a woman who had a solidity to her—more than a solidity, a dignity about her—that her mother lacked. Margaret could use her mind in a way that was crisp and efficient, but at the same time, wise and humane.

Damien, of course, knew Margaret in a way that Catherine never would. His life had been in her hands for more than two years—hers and Sybil's. From what he could remember of that experience, he knew that she had no maternal instinct, not a clue about what it means to be a mother. But far more disturbing to Damien was the fact that she never really loved him, even though she'd tried, he thought. He imagined that Margaret would be able to help them manage the immediate problem they were facing, but he did not expect her to be able to offer any assistance with the much larger dilemma they were contending with.

Margaret seemed ill at ease as she greeted them.

"Damien, Catherine, please come in."

Standing in the large atrium just inside the front door, Catherine took the lead. "As I said when I called you, we'd like to talk with you about something important."

Margaret, in her awkward way, said, "Where should we talk? Although I never use the living room, it would be a good place to talk, I think. Your mother and I have always talked in the kitchen of her house—both the old house and now the new one. This house still seems like someone else's, even though I've been living here for almost three years. I'm sorry for babbling on like this. Let's go talk in the living room."

The living room was a large room, windows at one end, fireplace at the other, a cathedral ceiling with two large dark-stained beams. A beige couch sat in front of the fireplace, with an armchair at right angles to the couch at each end. Damien and Catherine sat on the couch, and Margaret on one of the armchairs.

Catherine, looking down at the pale blue and white oriental carpet, as if studying its pattern, said, "I don't have words to express to you how embarrassed I am to be telling you why we've come here tonight."

Margaret said, "There's no need to be embarrassed with me. I've done far worse things in my life than either of you will ever do in yours."

Margaret was quite certain from the moment that she received Catherine's call last evening that they were going to tell her that Catherine was pregnant and Damien was the father. She felt neither shocked by that idea, nor judgmental about it. She was deeply saddened by it, and felt somehow responsible for it.

Catherine, calmed by the accepting tone of Margaret's voice, but still unable to look Margaret in the eye, said, "I'm pregnant."

"And Damien is the father," Margaret said, completing the thought.

"Yes," Catherine said, astounded and relieved that Margaret knew without having to be told.

"I'm glad you both felt you could come to me about this, that you're entrusting me with something so important."

Margaret moved in her chair slightly so she could better hold both Catherine and Damien in her gaze at the same time.

"I don't want to pry, but I have to understand the situation in order to know how best to advise you. As your aunt, I should know this, but I want to be sure: You're both over eighteen, aren't you?

"Yes," they said in unison.

"We're nineteen and twenty-one," Catherine added.

"And what would the two of you like to do about the pregnancy?"

"We want to terminate it," Catherine said.

"Both of you?" Margaret said, turning to Damien.

Damien said, "Yes."

"Catherine, do you know how far along you are in the pregnancy?"

"About two months, I think, judging from when my last period occurred and from the pharmacy pregnancy tests."

"Mercifully, abortion is legal now in every state, so it can be done by skilled doctors in a good hospital. Some states make it more difficult than others by requiring interviews and waiting periods, but that's not the case now in Illinois or Ohio, or most other states. Catherine, you will have to tell the obstetrician that you don't know who the father is because there are laws in Illinois against relations between a brother and sister, and even between a brother and half-sister."

It became evident to Catherine and Damien that Margaret had not only surmised the reason why Catherine had called, she had also thoroughly researched the laws concerning statutory rape, abortion, and incest.

Damien was caught off guard by the fact that Margaret knew that Brian was not his father, which meant that he and Catherine were not brother and sister, but half-brother and sister. Rose had assured him that that was something she would keep strictly between the two them, but he was free to tell anyone he chose. He had told Catherine, but nobody else. He then abruptly stopped himself from blaming Rose for breaking her promise when it occurred to him that, when he was born, it must have been just as obvious to Margaret as it was to Rose and Brian that he was not Brian's son.

"What are the laws against relations between a brother and half-sister?" Catherine asked, her voice tremulous.

Margaret hesitated before answering Catherine's question. She didn't want to frighten her or Damien, or make them feel that they had done something horrific, but she also wanted them to know the facts concerning the laws dealing with their relationship.

"I apologize if this feels intrusive," Margaret said in her distinctive matter-of-fact way, "but our discussion will only be of use to you if we are all honest with one another. So I have to tell you that it has seemed to me, when I've seen the two of you together, that you are in love with one another. I can't account for my ability to sense that because I've never been in love myself, and most likely never will. But that's beside the point. Sensing that the two of you are in love, and anticipating the questions you'd have for me, I've gone to the law library at the University of Chicago and looked up the laws concerning relations between members of the same family. I found that they vary a great deal from state to state. Some are very harsh and others have no penalties at all for relations between a half-brother and sister."

Damien said, "I'd like to know the laws concerning our situation."

Margaret, turning to Catherine said, "Are you sure that you want me to go into detail about the laws?"

"Yes, I'm sure."

Margaret began by saying, "In Illinois, the penalty is up to twenty-five years of imprisonment. In seven other states it is life imprisonment, and in two states there are no penalties for relations involving siblings or half-siblings over eighteen."

Alarmed by the fact that what she and Damien were doing could result in life imprisonment in some states, Catherine asked, "Why is the punishment so severe, as severe as for rape and murder?"

"I don't know, really. It's a highly inflammatory subject. I think that the laws are harsh in order to protect children from being molested by parents, and to protect younger siblings from being molested by older siblings or older cousins."

"Do you believe that what Catherine and I have done should be punished?"

Margaret responded without a moment's hesitation. "No, I don't." These words hung in the air for some time before Margaret added, "I also think that your decision to end the pregnancy is a wise one. From what I've been able to learn, the frequency of genetic abnormalities in situations like yours is higher than it is otherwise, and I imagine that that factor has played a role in your decision to end the pregnancy."

The three sat in silence for what felt like a very long time as they absorbed all that had been said in the space of a few minutes. Margaret felt very glad to be able to help these two children, and particularly glad to be able to do something that in some small way helped make up for the harm she felt she'd done Damien. He was a sweet, kind boy, and Catherine was a lovely girl whom she felt very fond of. Of course, she wished that they had each fallen in love with someone else. But they hadn't. She asked herself whether they were doing harm to themselves. This was a question she couldn't answer. If Damien and Catherine were not Rose's children, her niece and nephew, would she be disapproving? Isn't incest a breach of something fundamental to the survival of the species? She didn't know, and realized she didn't care. She asked herself again, What harm are they doing to one another? None, she thought. But they would be doing a grave injustice to a child they bore.

Damien broke the silence by asking, "So how do we proceed?"

The question didn't seem to be directed at anyone in particular. Damien hated the idea of asking Margaret for anything.

"To be on the safe side," Margaret said, "I'd suggest going to the Cleveland Clinic, a nationally recognized medical center in a state where there are no laws against relations between siblings."

Margaret noticed that she avoided using the word *incest*, and wondered whether she was doing so for her own sake or for theirs. She wondered whether she was blinding herself to something that should be obvious. Maybe it was obvious that brothers and sisters should not be having sex with one another. Margaret didn't trust her own judgment regarding the way other people should live their lives. Who was she to judge anyone?

Damien was also in a sea of confusion as he listened to Margaret explain that sex between siblings was illegal in all but two states, and that she was advising them to have the abortion performed in one of those two states. He had never been able to make sense of where he and Margaret stood with one another. Did she hate him for not being the cuddly little boy she'd hoped he would be, her little soldier who loved her, depended on her, and made her feel like a real woman and a real mother? He wasn't sure how he felt about her. The way she and Rose had behaved was deplorable, and Sybil had made matters worse. Margaret, Rose, and Sybil were pathetic, each in her own way, he thought. And he was the one who had to carry the effects of their decisions and actions. But as he sat in her living room that evening, he could feel that Margaret was offering him something more than solid, pragmatic thinking. He sensed in her genuine warmth and a sincere desire to look after him and protect him, as if he were her son, which was probably as close to love as she was able to come with anyone, except Rose.

Catherine asked Margaret, "Would you help me make the arrangements to have the abortion performed at the Cleveland Clinic?"

"Of course, I will."

The following week, the three of them took the train to Cleveland. They told Rose that they were going to hear the Cleveland Philharmonic play a program of Beethoven and Brahms. During the trip, hardly a word was spoken between them, each with their head in a book. An interview with a social worker, blood tests, and an internal exam were conducted in the hours following Catherine's registration at the clinic. Catherine then met with the obstetrician who would be performing the procedure the following day.

The morning after the abortion, Catherine was discharged from the clinic, and Margaret, Catherine, and Damien retraced their path home.

## THIRTY-ONE

E rin stood by himself on the far side of the refreshment table, trying to look busy, sipping a cup of coffee. He had watched Margaret talking with Catherine, and had seen Catherine being escorted by the young man to the chair where she was now sitting. The last family event that they had all attended was his wedding six years earlier. He had not mentioned to anyone in the family the end of that short-lived marriage.

Erin had hoped that Damien would forgive him in the course of the seventeen years that had passed since he'd left for college, but clearly that had not happened. He knew that it was he who had caused the rift. He had given his solemn word to Damien that he would stay in close contact with him during his freshman year at university, and that Damien would join him the following fall. But everything changed the day he arrived at school. Erin remembered the physical sensation of exhilaration he'd felt during those first weeks away from home. He was responsible for no one but himself for the first time in his life. He had dutifully called on Sundays for the first month or two, but the calls became more sporadic after that, he remembered, and as they became less frequent, he was met with increasing coldness at the other end of the line. Eventually, he stopped calling altogether.

He felt guilty about breaking his word to Damien, and shutting out his mother and Catherine, but the relief he felt in being free of them outweighed the guilt. He had put in his time, he told himself, and now they were going to have to take care of themselves. He wasn't Damien's or Catherine's father, nor was he Rose's husband. During his four years at university, he rarely came home for vacations or for the summer break, and when he did, he made no mention of friends he'd made, or girls he was dating, or courses he was taking. Margaret had written him to say that she understood that he had taken on far more responsibility for his family than any child should have to, but it would be kind and considerate of him to maintain some contact with Rose and Damien and Catherine, and to visit occasionally. He knew she was right, and that she wasn't asking a lot of him, but he couldn't get himself to do even the little she was asking. But feeling free of the responsibility of taking care of the family wasn't all that was going on at that time. There was much more, and he tried not to think about it.

The morning of Rose's funeral, Erin had been early and was nervously pacing in the lobby of the funeral home when Catherine arrived to make final arrangements about the ceremony and reception. She was surprised to see Erin. She hoped that her facial expression did not betray the fact that she thought he had aged significantly in the years since his wedding. His formerly blond hair was now thin and darkened to a brownish tan. His forehead was furrowed. Catherine was friendly, but not warm, to him. Damien barely made eye contact with Erin when they shook hands an hour or so later.

Erin was stunned to see Catherine and Damien conducting themselves as a married couple with their daughter, Alice. They couldn't be married, could they? Isn't it illegal to marry your sister, he wondered? Or could they have married without letting on they were brother and sister? The whole thing seemed surreal. He'd never been told they'd married, or that they had a daughter. But why, after cutting himself off from the family as completely as he had, would he expect to be let in on the personal lives of the members of the family? He certainly had not let them know about his personal life. As he stood alone beside the refreshment table, he thought, If being treated as an outsider is the cost of my freedom, so be it. But he knew that it was more complicated than that. He had been more than a big brother to Damien—much more—and Damien had been much more than a kid brother to him. Just as Rose and Margaret were the love of one another's life, he and Damien had been the love of one another's childhood.

There was no one in the family, except maybe Margaret, whom Erin could ask about the relationship between Catherine and Damien, and whether Alice was their child. He was finding that he was becoming increasingly upset about the idea that Damien and Catherine were having an incestuous sexual relationship. It was unconscionable for them to have a child who would suffer the physical and emotional damage brought about by their relationship. He didn't know how to make sense of what they had done. He didn't even know what they had done. Incest was insane—that much he knew. He had always known that Damien and Catherine were strange—they were unlike any other people he had ever met—but he hadn't dreamt that they were capable of this. He felt he no longer knew them. But he was strange, too, far more so than any of them suspected.

Margaret, after thanking another couple for coming to the funeral, surveyed the room, not knowing what or whom she was looking for. It came to her that she was looking for Rose. She had fully expected to catch sight of Rose, and go over to talk with her about her impressions of the funeral and the reception and the family and the guests. Rose certainly would have commented on Damien and Catherine's decision to bring Alice to a public event. Only Margaret knew how profoundly Rose

227

had been shaken by the idea that Damien and Catherine were having a sexual relationship. Margaret recalled how horrified Rose had been when there reached a point where it was impossible for Rose not to recognize that Catherine and Damien were lovers. Rose told Margaret again and again how upsetting it was to imagine Catherine and Damien in bed together. She had never actually seen them in bed, or even seen them holding hands, but she could not get out of her mind the image of them in bed or in the back seat of a car together.

In response to the incestuous relationship between Damien and Catherine, Rose felt a deep conviction that she had been an even worse mother than she had formerly believed. The sexual relationship between two of her children felt like the most profound indictment of a mother that there could be. Rose sometimes said to Margaret that she couldn't stand the pain any longer, and yearned for death as the only possible release from it. She felt that the only identity she had had as an adult, the identity of a mother, had not only been stripped from her, it had become a tawdry, stinking pall of shame. Margaret could hear Rose's voice speak the words "stinking pall of shame." From the moment that Rose could no longer deny the reality of the incestuous relationship, she never left her house, even to retrieve the mail from her mailbox or to have a brief chat with neighbors across the fence separating their back yards.

Margaret, still lost in thought, recalled urging Rose to see a psychiatrist. Rose dismissed the idea out of hand, insisting that what she was dealing with was real; she wished it were a figment of her imagination, but it wasn't. Finally, she acceded to seeing a psychiatrist. Margaret recalled her name—Dr. Lediard. Rose met with her for a year or two, which helped Rose diminish the self-torment, so far as Margaret could tell, though Rose insisted that Dr. Lediard wasn't doing her any good.

Rose never once visited Catherine and Damien in Cleveland during the five years they lived there before Alice was born. Margaret found Rose's behavior inexcusable, though she never said that to her face. For Margaret, it was very important not to make Damien and Catherine feel like pariahs, so she took the train or drove to visit them about once a month. She stayed for only a night or two, but the visits mattered greatly to all three of them.

A few weeks after Alice was born, Margaret spoke to Damien and Catherine about how difficult a time Rose was having with the fact of their relationship, and with Alice's birth. She added something that she had not said to them before. "You have to face the fact that you are doing something very unconventional, and it is a severe test for a mother to see two of her children live as husband and wife. Mothers are prisoners of their instincts. Although I have no maternal instinct, I know that mothers have powerful inborn conceptions of the way things should be. Rose has to do battle with that in herself in order to accept what the two of you are doing. I'm not a mother, and so I'm not saddled with the feeling that the two of you shouldn't love one another in the way that you do, as a traditional husband and wife do. That, too, is something I know almost nothing about—the love between a husband and wife. I didn't see it between my parents, and I didn't feel it in my brief marriage. I see it in the two of you, and that's worth more than anything, but you have to understand that it's not easy for Rose. There's one more thing, though—I have to tell you again that I don't think it was fair to subject a baby to the increased odds of genetic abnormalities ..."

Catherine interrupted Margaret to say, "There's something I haven't told you. You of all people have a right to know. You're the only person who understands and accepts Damien and me in what we're doing, and I'll always be grateful to you for that. So it's unforgivable of me to have subjected you to the worry you've been living with ever since we told you I was pregnant.

"I know it would have been irresponsible of me to have a baby with Damien. So I saw several gynecologists and was referred by each of them to the same clinic, where I got

229

pregnant by means of artificial insemination with sperm from an anonymous donor. I chose a donor who sounded like a person I would like and respect. It was important to me that he was from an Italian family, so that there would be some chance the child would have coloring that was a combination of Damien's and mine. I didn't tell Damien about the artificial insemination until the pregnancy was confirmed, which was a terrible thing to do to him."

Catherine paused before going on. "When I decided to have a baby, I felt defiant. I felt, No one is going to prevent me from doing what feels important and right for me to do. That was cruel and insane of me. There was no reason to think Damien would 'forbid' me to have a baby. We don't forbid one another from doing things, we talk to one another about doing things. I can't tell you why I had to do this on the sly. I was acting like a child. My behavior caused terrific pain to Damien and you, and also Rose."

Tears welled up in Catherine's eyes as she spoke, and after she finished talking, she wept.

Margaret listened intently to Catherine's words, with an expression on her face that was full of sadness—not for herself, but for Catherine and Damien. She said, "I'm greatly relieved to hear that Damien is not the biological father. I've worried about that a great deal. But I also understand that the way you went about getting pregnant has been very hard on Damien, and I'm sorry to hear that it had to be that way."

The three were emotionally depleted by this conversation.

As Margaret prepared to leave for the train station that Sunday afternoon, she asked if she could tell Rose that Damien was not Alice's biological father, and how Catherine went about choosing a sperm donor.

Catherine said, "Yes, that would be fine with me. In fact, I'd appreciate it. I should have told her myself from the beginning."

Damien was silent.

After Margaret left the apartment, Damien said to Catherine, "You actually believed the story you told Margaret, didn't you?"

"It was a story made for public consumption, not the facts that you and I have talked about at great length for the past year."

"The way you say 'at great length for the past year' sounds like you think I just rag on about some trivial detail, like you overcooked the string beans."

"Let's not go there again."

"Where should we go, to the fantasy land you were telling Margaret about? Why don't you tell yourself the truth just once, Catherine? That we were living together for four years and you decided that *you* were going to have a baby. You figured that once you told me you were pregnant by another man's sperm, I would have two choices. I could either pack my bags and leave, or I could stay and help you raise a child I never decided I wanted to have, a child for whom you would be the mother, one hundred per cent, and to whom I would have no biological or legal connection at all, and no part in wanting the baby to be a part of our lives. You have no conception of *we*. You know I've never been a real member of any family, except maybe at *Interludes*. I naïvely felt that I had finally become a genuine member of *our* family, the family *we'd* made together. But being the gullible sap that I am, I had it wrong. The family was *you*, you alone. And *your* family decided to have a baby, and the perpetual visitor could find another apartment to live in, or he could remain here as a visitor to *your* family. It would have been easier on me if you'd told me you'd had an affair, and that you were sorry about how hurt I was by it, and that you were afraid I'd leave you. That's what a couple does when they're really a couple. You don't get that, do you? I feel like I'm trying to explain the concept of human decency to you, but I'm finding that I can't do it because either a person feels it or they don't."

231

Until that evening, as Damien listened to Catherine tell Margaret the story of her pregnancy, Damien had never quite known what lay at the core of his fury. He had raged for months after Catherine first told him she was pregnant. He had thrown table lamps and chairs and dishes. He once left the apartment for a week. She had understood that he left in order not to hurt her physically. Neither of them knew at the time if that was the end of their relationship.

"I was a coward," Catherine said. "I didn't tell you because I desperately wanted to have a baby and didn't want to take the chance you'd say no if I asked you."

"That's exactly what I'm talking about. You have no sense of *us* as a family in which the two of us talk to each other about things that are important. Instead, you became a family of one and grabbed what you wanted."

"I hoped that once the baby became real—first as a pregnancy, and then as an actual person—you'd forgive me for leaving you out of the decision."

Damien's voice shook as he said, "I understand why you did what you did, but I so wish you had taken a chance on me, maybe even trusted me, and talked with me ahead of time." Catherine and Alice slept in the bedroom that night, while Damien slept on the couch in the study.

The phone rang the next evening. Damien picked up the telephone at the same time as Catherine picked up a phone in another room of the apartment. On hearing Rose's voice, Damien decided to listen in on the conversation. Rose apologized for not trusting her and Damien to do the right thing. She said, "I'm a silly old woman. I've caused the two of you a lot of pain. A mother should support her children, not try to live their lives for them. I've already lost precious time that I could have been giving to my granddaughter, and to the two of you, even before she was born. And I've robbed myself of the pleasure of being a grandmother to Alice from the day she was born, and before. I hope you'll forgive me some day."

"I forgive you today," Catherine said. "Margaret may have told you this, but I want to say it to you directly. I feel terrible about torturing you and Margaret during the pregnancy and for these months after Alice was born by leaving you to wonder if Damien is Alice's biological father. He's not the biological father, but he's the best father a little girl could ever have. It's me who should be asking for your forgiveness for what I've put you through."

"Sweetheart, let's put aside the past and enjoy the present. I'd love to come and see all three of, if it's all right with you."

Rose came to visit her children and grandchild the following weekend. She and Alice took to one another the moment Catherine put her in Rose's arms. It was as if both of them knew that a piece of life had been missing, and that life was now complete.

## THIRTY-TWO

Eleanor, a large matronly woman in her fifties who conveyed a sense of order and kindness, asked the children in her first-grade class to draw a picture of their family. They had been talking that day about the parents and grandparents in a story Eleanor had read aloud. Alice sat transfixed in front of the drawing paper. There were sixteen children seated around four low circular tables. The room was quiet as the children concentrated on the crayon drawings they were making, except for occasional assertions of "That's mine," "It's not," "Give that back."

Eleanor saw the confusion and pain in Alice's face just as Alice threw her crayon down on the floor, crumpled the drawing paper, and burst into tears. Eleanor tried to pick Alice up to comfort her, but Alice wriggled away and ran to the coat closets in the back of the room. Eleanor followed, and when Alice slid to the floor, her back to one of the closet doors, Eleanor picked Alice up and held her in her arms. This time Alice didn't resist. Eleanor carried Alice to one of the adult-sized chairs near the desk on the other side of the room. After Alice calmed, Eleanor quietly asked her what was making her so upset. Alice whispered, "I don't know."

When Catherine came to pick Alice up from school that day, Eleanor took her aside and told her what had happened. She asked Catherine if there was something upsetting going on at home. Catherine said that her Aunt Margaret, who was like a grandmother to Alice, was in poor health, and that was no doubt upsetting Alice. Catherine was painfully aware of the degree to which this was a censored rendering of the life of the family.

Eleanor handed Catherine a piece of creased drawing paper and said, "I kept the picture that Alice was drawing." Catherine thanked her and folded the paper before putting it into Alice's knapsack. Alice objected, "I don't want that." Catherine responded, "That's all right, can I put it in my bag?" Alice didn't reply and instead headed for the door, carrying her knapsack on her back.

Each afternoon at the end of the school day, Catherine and Alice walked home to the house in the Cleveland suburb in which they'd been living since Alice was two years old. They walked slowly the afternoon of Alice's upset at school, as they always did, because of the pain in Catherine's hip.

"What made you cry when you were drawing a picture of our family?" Catherine asked Alice as casually as she could.

"I don't know. I already said that to Eleanor."

Tears formed in Catherine's eyes, but she decided not to speak because she didn't want to say anything before thinking it through with Damien. As they walked, Catherine once again went over in her mind what to tell, when to tell, or whether ever to tell Alice about the fact that she and Damien were half-siblings. What an ugly sounding word—*half-siblings*.

When Catherine and Alice arrived home, Damien was there to meet them, as he often was, before going back to work for the rest of the afternoon. Catherine whispered to Damien that she was very upset about something that had happened, and that she wanted to be sure to get Alice to bed for a nap so they would have time to talk.

When Alice was finally asleep, Catherine and Damien went to their bedroom and closed the door. In order to be sure that Alice couldn't overhear what they were saying, they kept the radio in their bedroom on while they spoke. They sat down beside one another on the side of their bed. Catherine unfolded Alice's drawing, which she had not looked at until now. In the middle of the drawing were stick figures of a man, a woman with a cane, and a little girl in a dress, all drawn in red crayon. It appeared that there was the beginning of a house drawn in brown, but instead of completing the house, Alice seemed to have switched to a black crayon which she pressed very hard against the paper as she made a thick black rectangle around the three figures again and again, until the paper tore under the pressure of the crayon.

Catherine told Damien that Alice had then crumpled the paper, threw the crayon to the floor, and began crying.

"What do you make of the drawing?" Damien asked.

"I'm not a child psychologist, but anyone can see that the family she's drawing lives in a black box—a prison or vault. I may be reading too much into it, but I'm afraid that she already knows we have a secret, and that we live in a world separate from the rest of the world. It's not a happy world inside the box. I didn't realize she thinks of me as a woman with a cane."

They looked at one another in a way that made it unnecessary to say that the pressure was on them to somehow clear up Alice's confusion about her family, while not announcing to the world, through Alice, that Alice's parents were brother and half-sister. Even now, after ten years of living together, neither Catherine nor Damien had ever used the word *incest* in speaking about themselves. They didn't think of their relationship in that way. They didn't feel that their relationship was abnormal. They could forget, for periods of time, that many others viewed their relationship as ugly and criminal.

Damien said, "I'm afraid I may have said something at Rose's funeral that set this off."

237

"What are you talking about?"

"Alice asked who Erin was, and I told her he's your brother. I was really stupid and told her that he's my brother, too. I changed the subject before she could ask any questions, but she's smart—she doesn't miss things like that. I don't know why I did such a dumb thing. She didn't ask, I just volunteered it."

They sat in cold, anxious silence for a minute or so before Damien said, "Let's just think out loud, not feeling that we have to come up with an answer right away. Should I start or do you want to?"

"You start," Catherine said, relieved that Damien was not joining her in the alarm she felt.

"Okay, if we're completely honest with Alice, it would sound like this. 'Mommy and Daddy grew up in the same family for part of the time they were growing up. But Daddy wasn't really a member of the family because he had a different father from Mommy.'"

Damien stopped and put his head in his hands. "That's ridiculous. She wouldn't understand a word I was saying."

"I was thinking about this on the way home with Alice today," Catherine said. "What I was thinking was telling Alice—and asking Rose, Margaret, and Erin to go along with this—that you were adopted by Rose and Brian, so you aren't really my brother at all."

"That's much better. It's simple. Alice could understand that."

Catherine replied, "The problem with that story is that it's a lie. I don't like lies because they make everything they touch feel less real, and I'm afraid that our family will feel less real to all of us if it's based on a lie. And the other thing about lies is that they can very easily be exposed as lies. The truth is easy to defend. Everything supports it—the way a person speaks it and the context that naturally confirms it. Lies don't have

238

natural connections with the real world, so they just don't feel true to the person lying or to the person being lied to."

"That's the risk we've always known was there," Damien said, "but we decided that we were willing to live with it because we wanted to live our lives together. The tension of living with that risk got higher when Alice was born, but I don't regret for a second that she was born." Damien realized he'd come close to touching their family's raw nerve: His having been left out of the decision to have a baby, which in turn tapped into other deeply felt grievances that he nursed. He continued without a pause so as not to distract from what they were trying to think through. "We don't have to do anything now, but it's good to have your version of the story in reserve. It's a story that Alice will be able to understand when she's a little older. We've done what we can to protect our family. We've moved to a city where no one knows us and have kept to ourselves. We do live in a thick-walled box. I'm amazed that she was able to draw that feeling, but probably I shouldn't be. Alice is a very perceptive little girl. I think she knows there's a big secret, but doesn't know that she knows, so she drew it and became frightened by what she saw."

Catherine took one of Damien's hands between hers and squeezed her hands together around his as hard as she could.

# THIRTY-THREE

Catherine worried about Margaret after Rose died. They spoke on the phone every day. Margaret had not returned to work as she had planned after Rose died. She ate very little, saying that she had no appetite. She was open about the fact that without Rose, she had no reason to live. Catherine made the drive from Cleveland to Margaret's house frequently during the months following the funeral.

In the afternoon of one of Catherine's visits, while they were seated in the enclosed screen porch at the back of the house, Margaret said in a matter-of-fact way, "I have a limited capacity for love, and Damien has suffered most for that. I don't love money or material things. I am not a collector, and have never felt that there's anything I'd rather do with money than give it to Rose and her family, which I feel to be my family too. I fear that without my knowing it, that has had its ill effects. Erin asked me not to leave him anything when I die except a memento to remember me by. Such a loving boy. A number of years ago he asked me not to give him any more financial help. He asked that I give to you and Damien what I had planned to leave to him. He was gracious in the way he told me, but it was clear that he felt that supporting himself was important to him. I feel like a very old lady talking like this about my will."

While Rose was alive, she was the only person with whom Margaret spoke about her feelings. Since Rose's death, Margaret seemed to be speaking her thoughts and feelings aloud, as if Rose were listening. Catherine often felt as if she were eavesdropping on Margaret's conversation with Rose, and felt very uncomfortable doing so. Catherine would bring the conversation back to the mundane—an edited version of how Alice was doing in school, the article on *Interludes* in the *Sunday New York Times Magazine*, her new studio space, the replacement of the water heater after it flooded the basement. Margaret's mind wandered while Catherine spoke.

Interrupting Catherine, Margaret said, "Last night, I was trying to think of something I've culled from my life that might be of use to you. I couldn't think of anything that you don't already know. The funny thing is that I felt consoled by that thought. It wasn't that I had sunk into grim resignation. I found relief and even some pleasure in the idea that you don't need me any longer."

"Stop it, Margaret. Don't put yourself out to pasture quite yet."

"No, it's not putting myself out to pasture, it's an acceptance of myself that has eluded me almost all my life."

It was difficult for Catherine to listen to Margaret say this, but she, too, knew it was true. Margaret was dying, though not a word was said about it directly. She had developed the beginnings of congestive heart failure not long after Rose died, and like Rose, she had chosen not to take the medicines her doctor prescribed, and then not to see the doctors at all.

Some months later, talking became a strain for Margaret— she used an oxygen mask both during the day and throughout her sleepless nights, but her mind remained clear until just before the end. Margaret died eighteen months after Rose's death.

Margaret had not kept in touch with her colleagues at work after Rose died, so Catherine decided not to have a funeral for Margaret, and instead to simply have Erin and his wife, Muriel, join her and her family in one of the rooms of the same funeral home in Chicago where Rose's funeral was held. There would be no service or refreshments, simply a room in which to talk, and an adjoining room with an open casket to visit if they chose.

The "Sacred Departures Room" was a windowless, elongated room, lit by fluorescent light that buzzed almost imperceptibly. On the green-flecked beige carpeting sat a small turquoise couch between two brown end tables, each with a clear glass pitcher of water with lemon slices in it and a tray of glasses next to it. Four folding chairs flanked the couch, two on each end, forming a vague semi-circle around an empty coffee table.

When Erin arrived, Damien, Catherine, and Alice had already set up camp on the couch and the floor in front of it. As Erin stood at the door observing the scene, it seemed to him that Damien and Catherine were using Alice as a shield to hide behind. He walked briskly across the room and placed both hands on the back of one of the folding chairs, where he stood not knowing what to say. He seemed smaller to Catherine than she'd remembered him. Maybe he'd lost some weight. Catherine, with considerable effort, got to her feet and gave Erin a hug while saying, "Erin, it's so good to see you. It's a shame that lately we've been meeting at funerals."

"Funerals are better than nothing."

"Yes, unfortunately, they are."

Erin turned to Alice, who was unpacking her knapsack, and said, "Alice, I don't know if you remember me. I'm Uncle Erin. I don't want to take you from what you're doing, but I just want to say hello."

Alice, now almost six, said without looking up, "Yes, I remember you. I can't talk to you, I'm busy now."

Erin smiled and said, "I'll come back later when you're not so busy and maybe you and I can talk a little about what you're doing at school."

He then said to Catherine, "Could I take Damien from you for a little while so we can talk?"

"Of course. Alice and I have important things to do here."

Damien followed Erin to the far end of the room, where heavy burgundy curtains were meant to give the illusion that there were windows behind them.

Erin began: "I've been wanting to talk with you for years, but haven't had the courage to do it. Neither of us has said a word about what happened after I left home to go to university. I've felt too guilty to talk about it. First of all, I want to tell you that I'm sorry that I hurt you and let you down so badly. You were a good-hearted and vulnerable kid, and we had a lot between us, and then I went and did that to you. You didn't deserve to be treated like that. I'm sorry I couldn't do any better."

Damien tried to interrupt, but Erin said, "No, please let me say what I've waited so long to say. When I arrived at the university, even before I opened the door to my dormitory room, I felt a tremendous weight lifted from my shoulders. I felt free. I can remember the feeling as if it were yesterday, the feeling that I could breathe the air in deeply, as if the air I had been breathing until then had been filled with smoke and I hadn't noticed the smoke until it cleared. It's not that I felt you'd been a burden. You weren't a burden at all—you were my best friend. I hope you know that. I think you do. I've never had another friendship like the one you and I had. To tell you the truth, I've never had a good and close friend in my life other than you. It was the family that was suffocating me, mostly Mom. I felt that she was so insubstantial a person that I had to either try to prop her up or take on myself what she should have been doing as a parent. Our friendship may have started with my trying to do the job Mom should have been doing— the job of taking you back into the family after she sent you into exile. But even though it began that way, it didn't stay that way. I hope you know that, too."

Tears rolled down Damien's cheeks as he listened to the sound of the voice of the boy who had brought him so much joy and comfort and the feeling of being loved when they were growing up. He could see in the face of this thirty-six-year-old man the face of the eight-year-old, and the ten-year-old, and the nineteen-year-old boy whom he'd so loved and admired.

When Damien was able to clear his throat of choked tears, he said, "I've waited nineteen years to hear you say that. I don't know why I haven't been strong enough to say to you that I want you back as my brother and my best friend. I feel terrible about the way I treated you at Rose's funeral. I tried to convince myself I was justified in being aloof. I even made up the story for myself that I was doing you a favor by not pulling you back into a family that you didn't want to be part of anymore. But the truth is that I wanted to punish you for leaving me the way you did. I wanted to make you feel the way I did when you left. You've done the bigger thing, the right thing."

"I deserved what I got from you."

"Deciding who's to blame is a waste of time. Who cares? I don't. All that matters to me is having you back as my brother again. You raised me. You were my whole life after I got back from Margaret's. When you left for university, nothing was worth doing because I couldn't do it with you or tell you about it afterwards. It was as if you had died. I'm not saying this to make you feel bad; that doesn't do anybody any good. I'm saying it because I want you to know how important you were, and are, to me, but I don't want you to be afraid that I want you to take care of me. I don't need that from you any more."

While Damien and Erin talked, the rest of the room and the rest of the world disappeared. It was only the two of them there—outside of time and outside of place. But all that changed in an instant when, after a pause, Damien brought them back to the immediate reality of what was happening in the room in which they were talking. "If you haven't heard this from Margaret, I want to be sure you understand how Alice's birth came about. I'm not her biological father. Her birth was by artificial insemination with the sperm of a sperm donor. I want to tell you that, if you don't already know it, because it would be a terrible thing for Catherine and I to have a baby together. I want you to know that we wouldn't do that to a child because what you think of me means everything to me."

"When I saw you and Catherine together with Alice at Rose's funeral, I imagined the worst. I did that to make myself feel better about my life. I was feeling holier than thou. But that didn't last long. Even before I got in the car to drive back to Pittsburgh, I regretted having squandered a chance to talk with you. I got drunk when I got home, which is something I do too often. I'm not an alcoholic, but I numb myself instead of trying to do the difficult thing that needs to be done. I'm rambling. Let me tell you why I didn't call you after I left home. This isn't an excuse, it's an explanation."

"Erin, you don't have to apologize to me for anything."

"I want to apologize, but I also want you to understand what was happening during my silence after I left home. As I told you, I felt free, but the freedom brought on its own problems. All that any of the guys talked about in the freshman dorms was which girls they wanted to screw and which girls they claimed they'd screwed. It probably was no different when you were a freshman."

"Right, but I was already with Catherine at that point in my life. Catherine was living with Rose while she finished high school. In a way I was insulated from the pressure of showing off my masculinity in terms of notches on my belt. But in another way, I missed out on a period of life, and I've paid for it in my own way. But you're trying to tell me something, so I don't want to interrupt."

"I had a very hard time with the pressure to have sex with girls," Erin continued. "There were girls who liked me, and I liked them and was very attracted to them. Once we were going together for a while, we would both want to have sex, but with each girl I couldn't do my part of things. The relationship would end because I felt so embarrassed. The girl wasn't in a rush to dump me, but I just couldn't face her afterwards. This happened a few times, until I gave up in the middle of the second semester. I felt so bad about myself that I stopped going to classes and ended up with an incomplete in all of them. They were very nice not to have flunked me. I think the dean spoke to my teachers and told them I was having emotional problems.

"I felt so bad that I couldn't leave my bedroom in the dorm. My roommate brought food for me. I left the shades drawn all the time. I had sunk so far into myself that there was no room for you or anyone else. It didn't occur to me to turn to you. I felt more hopeless than I have at any other time in my life, and there were some pretty bad other times.

"A psychiatrist prescribed an antidepressant. It helped a little, and I was able to resume classes. The worst part of the story is that right after college, I went to law school, where I met Muriel, who as you may have noticed, isn't here. I liked her and she was beautiful, and I was able to do my part with her. After we dated for a year and a half, I asked her to marry me, and she accepted. I don't know what went wrong—we were both working eighty hours a week at different hot-shit Philadelphia law firms—and we didn't have time to make the marriage work. We argued constantly, and to make a long story short, she asked for a divorce."

"I'm sorry to hear it."

"It wasn't losing her that was hard; it was the feeling that I had failed yet again. I decided to leave the law firm I was working for. All I did there was write briefs for or against some person or corporation. I was sick of the arguing, at work and at home. I eventually left the law altogether. I've ended up teaching high school English in the Pittsburgh public school system, which suits me pretty well, and yes, Mr. Lerner was on my mind when I made that choice."

247

"I'm sorry that I couldn't help you the way you helped me when we were kids."

"How could you help me if I wouldn't talk to you? It was like I was living in an underground tunnel. I *was* the underground tunnel."

"I don't know. I just wish there'd been a way I could have stopped feeling sorry for myself and instead wondered, just for a few seconds, whether you were in trouble and could use my help."

The two brothers stood quietly together in that strange room with Margaret's body in an alcove.

"I'm trying to tell you almost twenty years worth of stuff in a few minutes," Erin said. "We're neglecting Catherine and Alice. It's only the four of us here—well, five if you count Margaret."

Damien and Erin laughed a deep laugh that was like the laugh they'd had together by the Richardson River while talking about Erin's project for the science fair, like the ones they'd had walking home from school, and like the ones they'd had when playing the Rocky game, although the memory of the Rocky game was now tarnished by the sadness of its final act, the one performed with Jimmy Hetch's gang under the railroad tracks.

# THIRTY-FOUR

Damien was lying on his back in bed with his fingers intertwined behind his head, looking up at the chalky ceiling. He was ruminating about the "situation" the family was in. Catherine, also unable to sleep, rolled over and placed her head heavily on Damien's chest.

"Are we sleeping or are we fucking?" Damien whispered, not wanting to be overheard by Alice or Erin, who were asleep on the upper floor of the house.

Catherine tried unsuccessfully to suppress a laugh at a line that had become a standing joke, but continued to amuse her—more than amusing her, it reminded her of why she was with Damien.

"No, we're not sleeping or fucking, we're talking," Catherine said.

"What are we talking about?"

"The same thing we've talked about for the past hundred years."

"You don't mean, What the hell are we doing? How are we going to save Alice from the repercussions of the sick way in which we've lived our lives? How the newspapers will have banner headlines about the incestuous brother–sister act going on in our sleepy little suburb of Cleveland?"

"No, something else," Catherine whispered, moving her head up to Damien's shoulder. "I'm worried about you and Erin."

"What are you talking about? Erin's the gentlest, kindest person I know. Present company excepted, of course."

"I'm serious. Stop turning this into a George Burns-Gracie Allen routine."

"All right. I'm listening."

"You've been close to Erin your whole life. He and I don't really know each other very well. He was much older than I was, at least it felt that way when we were kids."

"That's the way it felt to me, too—I mean, between the two of you."

"He and I never really got to know each other. We grew up in the same house, and I looked up to him as my big brother who could do amazing things that I couldn't do and never imagined I'd ever be able to do. You were different because first, you were gone, you hardly existed for me, and then when you came back from Margaret's, you were a stranger, a homeless kid who came to live with us. Anyway, what I was trying to say is that I don't know what to make of the trouble that Erin has been in. I feel sorry for him, but he's a mystery to me. Not just anybody gets into the kind of trouble he's had."

"Have you tried looking in the mirror lately?"

"I know that. I'm not an imbecile. But I know how we went about making our problems, and I don't know how Erin went about making his. He doesn't talk about himself when he and I are together. I talk to him about our lives since he left for university in an attempt to encourage him to talk about his, but he never does. It's not that I feel he's a danger to me or Alice or you. I know he couldn't hurt a flea. He's the kind that takes in stray dogs. But I don't understand what makes him tick."

"I'm in a bind because when Erin and I talk, we are very open with one another. We don't round the edges. We say straight out whatever it is we're talking about, but we're talking to each other, not to anyone else. He's never asked me not to tell you what we talk about. He trusts me. But I don't know where the line is when it comes to telling you what he and I talk about. If you want me to tell you, I will because you're my wife. What I'm saying is: I'll tell you, but please don't ever let on that I've spoken to you about his confidences."

"You know I won't. Anyway, who would I tell even if I was dying to repeat it?"

"Erin is such a kind soul that he seems naïve to the evil in this world. You and I are the opposite; we see it everywhere. You know he's moved a few times for no apparent reason—well, there is a reason. After he left the second law firm he worked for in Philadelphia, he taught at a private boarding school for boys in rural Pennsylvania somewhere. He was very popular among the students, faculty, headmaster, kitchen crew, gardeners—everyone. You get the picture. Erin is the same guy we knew when he was in high school. Team sports are very important at a place like that. You remember how Erin felt about team sports."

"No, I never really noticed or cared, but I don't remember him playing on teams."

"That's right, he didn't. He was well coordinated and threw a ball like a boy, not like a girl, and all that, but he just didn't see anything in sports. He never explained it, and it never even occurred to me to ask. That's just who he was, and I liked who he was.

"Anyway, the ritzy boarding schools play various sports against one another, and all the fathers come and glory in being part of an exclusive private club where their sons are gladiators. Also, these games play an important part in the fundraising efforts of the schools.

"One of the kids had been getting C-minuses from teachers when he was actually failing because the kid's father was a big shot on the board of trustees. The kid's name was Armondo. I think the family was Spanish and lived part of the year in

251

Madrid and part in New York. Erin gave the kid a D, which upset his father and other board members because the kid was a star in soccer, basketball, and rugby. According to the rules, a student is banned from participating in inter-school sports if he is failing any of his subjects.

"You can probably see what's coming. The headmaster asked Erin to give the kid a C-minus, not a D, and if the kid didn't pull it together in the second semester, then Erin could give him the grade Erin thought he deserved. Erin didn't like it, but he agreed. The kid glowered at Erin the entire semester, as if to say that he could do as he pleased and Erin was powerless to do anything about it. Erin arranged tutoring sessions for Armondo, but the kid never showed up. Seeing that trouble was brewing, Erin sent memos to the headmaster to keep him informed about the kid's grades and his failure to attend tutoring sessions. Despite the fact that Erin had taken these precautions, just before the end of the semester, Armondo accused him of trying to molest him during the tutoring sessions, which, in fact, he had never attended.

"The headmaster told Erin that Armondo's father was prepared to report Erin to Child Protective Services, which would mean that he would be put on unpaid leave until the investigation was over. The headmaster said that he sympathized with Erin, but strongly recommended that he resign immediately. The fact that the kid was huge—six-one or six-two, a hundred and ninety pounds—and could have crushed Erin like an ant didn't seem to matter to the headmaster. He advised Erin to 'disappear'—pack up his stuff and leave without talking to anyone. The headmaster said he would make up a story about a family emergency. Erin complied, but has never gotten over the humiliation of it. He interrogates himself about how he brought this on himself. He took a job in the Pittsburgh public school system, where they worry less about teachers harming students than about students harming teachers.

"Erin has never said it directly to me, but I think even in Pittsburgh he's been very depressed, I think even suicidal, though I may be wrong about that. What he said was that he goes through the motions of teaching, and has no life outside of work. It took him a long time—almost a year now—to tell me this much of the story. I'm sure there's much more to say, but it's taken a lot for him to be able to tell me this much."

It was only when he finished talking and felt the moisture on the collar of his nightshirt that Damien realized that Catherine was weeping. She said, "I feel so bad for him. He's an innocent, a kind soul, in a treacherous world. He was eaten alive."

"I'm glad you see him the way I do," Damien said, still in a hushed voice. "You know how grateful I feel to him. He's the only person I've loved, other than you and Alice."

"I know that, and to be honest, I'm jealous sometimes when I see the two of you talking to each other with such intensity. I feel that no one else matters when the two of you are talking that way. I wonder if you are ever so fully present when you talk to me."

"Hon, don't feel that way. Erin and I haven't talked to each other for almost twenty years."

"I know, but you're my whole life, along with Alice. I don't have any adult, other than you, to talk with honestly since Margaret died."

"Maybe you and Erin could talk honestly with each other. I know he'd welcome that, even though he feels so defeated."

"Maybe … but now we're sleeping, not talking or fucking."

## THIRTY-FIVE

A s Damien closed the front door of his house behind him about an hour before sunrise, the feel of the air outside the house was precisely the temperature inside. The night had failed to cool the air. There was an explosive quality to the July morning. Damien could feel that by noon the temperature would approach a hundred for the third day in a row, and the humidity would wrap the air around his body like a warm, wet blanket and draw perspiration from every pore.

Damien walked down the brick path to the gate of the white picket fence that surrounded the house. On both sides of the path were stretches of soft, Kentucky bluegrass, glistening with the drops of water from the sunken sprinkler heads that pop up silently at two in the morning and begin their work with a stuttering hiss before creating, for forty-five minutes, a semi-transparent circle of mist that overlaps identical circles on all sides. Like a woman who is almost, but not quite, beautiful, the circles of mist were almost pleasing to Damien, except for the fact that they were a requirement of the bylaws of the neighborhood association to which every homeowner agreed in writing when buying a house in this development. Damien was a renter, not a homeowner. He and Catherine and Alice had been living in this, their third house in as many years, since the previous September. He felt like Io wandering the earth as the gadfly inflicts its pain, as much through the ever-present reminder that the gadfly is inescapable as through the sting of its bite.

As he turned right on the wide sidewalk, Damien passed house after house nearly identical to the one in which he was living. He made a point of not knowing the names of his neighbors and, if possible, their not knowing his, which was difficult to achieve in the eager-to-be-of-help culture of this high-end, but not actually wealthy, community. There had been the usual homemade cookies delivered by neighbors on both sides of his house and from across the street. Each house had the same two stories, with an upstairs of either two or three bedrooms—depending on the model—along with two or three full baths, and downstairs a large "kitchen-family room," a living room, and an office ("which could easily serve as a guest room if you furnish it with a convertible couch," the real estate agent had told him).

Even language itself—"the family room"—seemed to have turned against him, Damien thought, as the round face and ever-moving lipsticked lips of the real estate agent passed through his mind. He had chosen each house they'd rented as if selecting his own witness protection domicile. The sterility of the suburban neighborhood in which he was living was at once oppressive and slightly comforting. Only "slightly" because he had no faith in the camouflage it provided. He did what he could to keep his anonymity complete. There was not a leaf of crabgrass in either his front or back lawn, not a flake of peeling paint on the wood or gutters of his house, and not a yellowing dead branch on the boxwood that ran along the street side of the fence.

Erin came to visit for the weekend a couple of times each month, using the guest room/office downstairs. He apologized again and again for disrupting the weekend routines of the family, despite Damien's telling him that he was an

256

essential element in the sanity of the family, just by virtue of his bringing a third adult mind to bear on the circularity of thinking in which he and Catherine were trapped because they spoke to no one but themselves. Catherine strongly concurred that she and Damien, on their own, lived on the edge of the precipice of insanity, and once in a while fell into that breach. But she continued to feel excluded by the tight bond between Damien and Erin. It was as if they became two parts of one person when they were together, she thought.

Despite feeling left out, Catherine both pitied and loved Erin. He would always be her big brother who looked after her when she was in elementary school, making sure she knew where everything on the school ground was, and explaining to her very clearly and carefully how to get to the school office if she ever felt bullied or lost or sick, or even if she missed Mommy very much. He was a dear, dear boy, and she never forgot that, nor did she ever forget how lost and lonely he was as an adult, living on his own, without friends either at work or outside of work. Erin had not invited them—forbidden them was a better way of putting it, Catherine thought—to visit him in Pittsburgh. She imagined that he lived very humbly in a small one-bedroom apartment, getting by on a teacher's salary. She and Damien had, on several occasions, told Erin that they thought it was only right that they should give him his part of the inheritance they'd received from Margaret, but he would not hear of it.

For Catherine, the feeling of being excluded by whatever it was that tied Damien and Erin together so tightly was mitigated by the relationship that Erin had established with Alice, a child who was very choosy about the people to whom she would give any of her time or affection. Erin had the ability to capture Alice's imagination so tenderly that it often moved Catherine to tears to overhear them playing or talking together. She didn't have a name for the way he made clear in everything he did that he not only loved Alice, he loved her as he loved no one else in the world. It was a love that was an absolutely personal gift to her.

Catherine believed that Alice could feel that her family, which now included Erin, was a family in flight from someone or something dangerous, but invisible, something that, like smoke, could kill you even while you were asleep and you didn't know it had gotten in and was killing you. Alice was an extraordinarily intelligent girl, mature far beyond her eight years. Her intelligence was evident in her ability to read and write and to play with numbers, but even more startlingly in her ability to perceive and feel compassion for the pain that the other people in her life were suffering. It seemed to Catherine that Alice could felt the deep sadness in Erin as well as the joy he took in spending time with her. Alice seemed to feel that he was different from anyone else she'd ever known, different in a way that made her feel very safe and secure, as if he held the power to protect her, and her mother, and her father from the thing that was after them.

# THIRTY-SIX

In the Saturday mail, that same stiflingly hot day in July, the event occurred that Catherine and Damien, and even Alice, had been expecting—not necessarily that day or that week or that year, but they knew it would happen. Alice ran out the front door of their air-conditioned but nonetheless warm and muggy house, into the blast of afternoon heat and white sunlight, down the steps to see if the mailman had delivered a large envelope from Uncle Erin. On the weekends when he wasn't visiting, Erin would send a book he had chosen for Alice, and maybe a magazine for girls her age or a little older, and always a long letter to her that she would read many times, and only sometimes showed to her parents. The envelope from Erin was there in the mailbox along with a lot of letters and faded advertisements printed on newsprint. It was a big load of paper that Alice had trouble holding in her arms as she walked as quickly as she could back to the front door.

Catherine was sitting at the table in the family room, waiting for Alice to return and finish her lunch. Eager to open the envelope from Erin, Alice dumped the rest of the mail on the table and headed up to her room on the second floor. Catherine called after her, telling her to finish her lunch, as she sifted through the bills and advertisements. Alice returned and picked up a half-eaten sandwich from her plate.

A letter caught Catherine's attention and sent a chill through her. She knew immediately that it contained a threat. It was addressed to Miss Catherine Keane and Mr. Damien McCardle. There was no return address. The stamps had been cancelled at a downtown Chicago post office. She opened the letter and found only a clipping from the *Gazette*, the weekly local newspaper of the central Illinois town where she and Damien grew up. The news story was about an addition that was being built for the high school because the population of the town had more than doubled in the previous decade. Nothing was written by hand on the article or on the envelope.

Catherine said, "Alice, there's something Mommy has to discuss with Daddy this afternoon, so I'd like to see if you can go to Sharon's house for a play date. It's very important that Daddy and Mommy have time to talk, so it would be a big favor to us if you'd do that."

"What does the newspaper say?" Alice asked.

"It's only about enlarging the high school that Daddy and I went to. Would you like to read it?"

Alice didn't reply. Catherine and Damien had told her more than a year ago that Daddy had been adopted, and that Mommy and Daddy grew up in the same house, along with Uncle Erin, and that it was okay for Mommy and Daddy to get married after they fell in love because Daddy wasn't Mommy's brother. By that time, Rose and Margaret had died, so it was only Erin who had to collaborate in keeping the secret from Alice.

Damien arrived home soon after Catherine had returned from driving Alice to Sharon's house. They went to their bedroom and sat on the bed next to one another. Catherine handed Damien the envelope and the clipping. Trying to keep her fear out of her voice, Catherine said, "The envelope was mailed in

Chicago, and there's no letter with it, and nothing written on the clipping."

Damien examined the letter and then the envelope. "It had to happen. We've both known that, and now that it has happened, we'll deal with it."

"I don't think that we should assume this is the first step in a blackmail scheme, or a threat to expose us, or anything of the kind," Catherine said as calmly as she could. "Until he makes another move—I don't know why I assume it's a he—there's no need for us to do anything."

"We could always stay here, no matter what happens," Damien said. "We'd let whoever wants to expose us do whatever they're going to do, and we'll handle whatever fallout there is. We haven't broken any laws in this state, and we don't have to worry about money, so we could just say, 'Do your worst.'"

"I'd love to do that. I can't tell you how much that idea appeals to me. I don't give a damn what people think of me. I don't have any ambitions. Let anyone who wants to, look at me as slime. We have each other and we have Alice and we have Erin, and that's all I care about. But it's complicated because Alice is in the picture. She's the one who has to be out in the world as a school kid. We can live in our cave, but she doesn't have that luxury. She can't just drop out of the world the way we can."

"That's true, and I hate the world for it."

Catherine, without knowing if she believed it, said, "We don't know how people will react if we're exposed. It's possible that no one would give a damn. We're not elected officials who've been hiding something from the voters, and we're not movie stars that people want to undress. We're nobodies—we don't matter to anybody. Maybe it wouldn't be big news to anyone that we're brother and half-sister."

"The parents of Alice's friends would think they had to protect their children from the disease Alice inherited from us,

261

even though she's an ordinary kid," Damien countered. "She wants to be loved by us and have friends and be liked by her teachers, like every other kid. She just wants what other kids want. She's not like us when we were kids. That's what hurts so much: She's a regular kid and we weren't. She hasn't done anybody any harm." Damien struggled to hold back his rage.

"It's like we had a female version of Erin—a normal, good-hearted kid," Catherine said. They both laughed, partly because it was true and partly because of the solidarity between the two of them that Catherine had conveyed in the way she had twisted the delicate word *we* like a pretzel without breaking it.

"I just want the fucking truth to be told, just once in my life. That's all I want. Then I'll be ready to die, no complaints."

"I'd like that, too," Catherine said, "but …"

Damien stopped her, "Just let me live for a second or two with the feeling that there are no secrets that have to be hidden before going on to the 'buts.' I know the 'buts,' but I just need a few seconds in an imaginary world where they don't exist … I'm sorry, I just had to take my frustration out on you because I don't see anyone else around here to take it out on."

They were quiet for a while before Damien said, "All right, I'm ready to deal with the 'buts.' If we say to ourselves and the world, 'Do your worst,' we could be met by the terrible hatred that is expressed by the life sentence we could get in some states for what we've done, and that hatred would be taken out not only on us, but also on Alice. Even here, where we've done nothing illegal, who knows what's going to happen if we were exposed? I hope to God people won't hate Alice for it, but I can't get myself to believe that."

"It's a very strange life the two of us have chosen to live together."

They were quiet for another few minutes before Catherine said, "If we decide not to stay here in Cleveland, and try to find a place to live where no one who wants to hurt us can find us, where would we go?"

"I don't see that there's anything to gain by thinking about that until we have to. We haven't gotten there yet."

"I give it a lot of thought, all the time, but I don't talk about it. It would make me feel better to know we have a plan," Catherine said.

"I've always had vaguely in mind the idea that we'd move to a remote part of the country, like northern Montana or North Dakota or Alaska. I imagine us taking on new names and new identities. We'd invent ourselves and our past. We'd keep secret where we were born, who our parents and all our relatives were, where we grew up, where we went to school, what jobs we've held, whether we have siblings, and everything else about us. Erin wouldn't exist. We'd have no birth certificates, no driver's licenses, no social security numbers, no passports, nothing. Alice would have to live a lie, too, and keep all these secrets straight every moment she's outside the house. Alice's name would no longer be Alice. I don't know if we'd use our real names inside our house. Everything about Alice would be a lie. For her, there would be lie on top of lie. She'd have to lie about the lie we told her about my being adopted, and my growing up in the same family as the one you grew up in. It's horrible thinking about living a life like that and the effects it would have on Alice. It makes me crazy with rage to talk about us as vermin so repellant that we have to hide under rocks."

"I'm sorry I asked. Please don't go to extremes. It's not necessary. We've received a veiled threat, and I think that the person who did it is not going to carry it any further. What they're doing is illegal, I think. You can't go around threatening people, even by insinuation. What do you think about talking to Erin about this? He's a very balanced thinker, and we both trust his judgment more than anyone we know. That sounds ridiculous because we don't know anyone other than Erin— but you know what I mean. I guess what I'm trying to say is that we're not alone in this." She put her arm around Damien's waist, pulled herself across the few feet of bed between them, and put her head on his shoulder.

Damien called Erin that evening and told him what had happened. The first thing out of his mouth was, "I can hear the fear in your voice, and I'm sure Catherine feels the same fear. That was the whole point of sending the article and the envelope it was in. It said, 'I know who you are, and I know where you live.' Imagine the kind of person who goes to the trouble of doing that. My thought is that he once felt envious of you for how popular and smart you were. And he felt that a girl as pretty and poised and intelligent as Catherine wouldn't give him the time of day. This nasty prank is the high point of his life. He somehow figured out where you were, maybe from *Interludes*, but I don't think of him as intelligent enough to read a magazine like that. Maybe someone he knew read *Interludes*, but it doesn't matter. He's a loser who lives in a basement apartment somewhere who has nothing better to do than take revenge on you and Catherine for the bad luck he had in being who he is, and the good luck the two of you have had in being who you are. He's gutless and probably harmless. There's no way in the world he knows Alice's paternity—now I'm talking like a lawyer—so for him to say that Alice is the product of incest would be libel—which is illegal. Nothing that you and Catherine have done is illegal."

Erin said to Damien that he'd like to drive up to Cleveland now because he thought he might be able to bring some calm to him and Catherine in the wake of the crude attack they'd suffered. Damien said that that was a very kind offer, but he thought it might give the letter more importance than it deserved. Erin said he thought Damien was probably right, but he hoped he and Catherine would call him if they wanted to talk over what had happened, or even if they just wanted some company.

# THIRTY-SEVEN

Despite efforts to minimize the impact of the envelope and the newspaper clipping, everyone in the family understood that the attack they had been dreading had now begun in earnest. Waiting for the second assault was as emotionally draining as the explosive effect that the first had had. The person who had sent the letter seemed to be deliberately using silence and invisibility and time for the purpose of creating an escalating state of fear. Waiting for the next attack opened a space in which the members of the family could not prevent themselves from imagining tortures far worse than what realistically was likely to happen. Alice imagined her parents and Erin being killed, and her being left alone, knowing no one, trusting no one; Catherine dreamt of being confined or tied down as she watched Alice being sexually molested; Erin feared that Damien, Catherine, and Alice would go into hiding, and that their security would require that they cut off all contact with him; and Damien imagined a military-style attack on the house in which the aim was to kill the whole family, while he futilely fought to stop them.

What made these fears all the more harrowing was the fact that every member of the family lived in relative isolation in an effort to protect the others from their fears. The effect of this additional layer of secrecy and isolation was so powerful that it stretched the sanity of each member of the family close to the breaking point. Erin found himself in the position of being the guardian of what remained of the sanity of the family, a responsibility he readily accepted, though he was not sure for how long and under what conditions he could succeed in safeguarding that precious commodity. He visited almost every weekend and would spend longer stretches of time during school holidays. He was like oil on troubled waters. Erin had no wish to usurp the place of Catherine or Damien as the head of their household. He preferred to stay in the background, often sitting by himself in the family room or living room as he read, or walking on his own. If anyone wanted to join him, he was happy to have their company, but he was the bassoonist of this family orchestra—not the percussionist, not the concert master, and certainly not the conductor.

Almost three months after the arrival of the letter, one gray October day, Catherine and Alice were returning home after school. They had stopped, as they did sometimes, to have a piece of cake while sitting at one of the tables in the bakery. They took their time as they talked, Catherine sipping her coffee and Alice sipping her hot chocolate. They had momentarily let down their guard and were feeling like an ordinary mother and daughter who loved being with one another in this quiet way. Perhaps it was this brief stay against fear that made what followed all the more nightmarish.

On arriving home, Alice pulled her orange knapsack out of the back seat of their station wagon and ran ahead to the front door, where there was a package of some sort. Catherine yelled, "Alice, stop. Don't go near that. Let me handle it."

Catherine, cane in hand, slowly approached the brown package that was carefully placed in the center of the doormat. It was an ordinary brown paper bag that reminded her of the bags out of which homeless men drink whiskey on the street.

She gingerly picked it up. Its contents were so light that it was unlikely to contain a bomb. Catherine instructed Alice to stay where she was while she brought it around to the side of the house to inspect it. Alice silently complied.

On opening the brown paper bag just a bit, Catherine saw and smelled ripe feces that she assumed was that of the man who was in the process of terrorizing them. There was no doubt in her mind that this was a symbolic statement that she and Damien and Alice were nothing but shit. A wave of feeling— a mixture of fear and anger and nausea and vertigo—coursed through her. She tried to drop the bag to the ground, but found that she had lost control of the muscles of her hand. She could not get her fingers to loosen their grip on the bag. It was as if the bag were stuck to her fingers by a form of glue that was impossible to remove. The bag was now part of her. With terror growing exponentially inside her, Catherine screamed as she violently shook her hand and arm. The bit of paper that she was clutching tore and sent the bag flying, but the contents of the bag had been so wildly shaken that with the inward con- vulsions of Catherine's arm, some of the excrement flew at her, smattering feces on her chin, and hand, and clothes. She felt the sensation of screaming in her throat, but could not hear the sound. She lost her balance, fell to the ground, and lay there on a blanket of dry leaves, sobbing. Alice, on hearing her mother scream, ran to see what was happening.

"What was in the bag? Why are you crying? Did it bite you?" Alice, now down on the ground with Catherine, began to cry.

"I'm fine. I was just scared about something that there was no need to be scared about. Someone just left a mess to clean up."

"It smells like number two."

"That's what it is. Someone very mean put it there for me to find."

"Why?"

"Sweetheart, to be honest, I don't know why anyone would be cruel enough do that. But it's over now. I'll clean up the mess. Please go into the house while I clean up."

"No, I won't. I'm going to get some soap and the plastic bucket under the sink so you can get it all off of you." With that, Alice ran to the front door, used her key to unlock it, and gathered the things she was looking for. When she returned to her mother, Catherine was sitting up, surrounded by brittle brown leaves. A light, ghostlike mist was moving along the side of the house in the breeze as dusk settled in around them.

Alice half filled the bucket with water from the hose that was coiled on a green metal frame on the side of the house, and tore off some of the roll of paper towels she'd brought. After bunching up a few strips of paper towel and dipping an edge into the cold water, she handed the mass to her mother. Catherine softly touched her cheek, not knowing precisely where the feces had adhered and dreading the possibility of pushing any of it onto her lips.

"Down a little and back toward your ear."

"There?"

"A little farther back." Catherine was grateful for Alice's composed, self-possessed way of taking charge.

"Now the part on the right between next to your nose, and down a little," Alice said, leaning toward her mother to point to the spot.

"No," Catherine said, more loudly than she'd intended. More important to her than anything else at that moment was that Alice's skin not be defiled by the feces. And then, in a softer voice, she said, "Alice, just point to where it is, don't touch it."

"Okay, it's right here," Alice said.

Catherine moved the towels to the spot Alice was directing her to.

"No, a little more to this side …" Alice grasped her mother's wrist and moved her hand to the streak of feces, and then helped Catherine lower the towel to the spot.

Catherine scrubbed the area.

"That one's off. That's the worst one. There's another by your eye." Alice again positioned her mother's hand, and Catherine scrubbed off the excreta. One by one, Alice and her mother removed all visible traces of feces from Catherine's face.

"I'd kiss you a hundred times, but I don't want to bring my face to yours until I get it all off when we get inside."

The evening light was now so poor that it was difficult to be sure that Catherine had fully cleaned the excrement from her hands. She slid out of her soiled ski parka and let it drop to the ground behind her. Alice helped her mother to her feet, and put her arm around Catherine's waist to steady her as they walked over the foot-deep leaves, and then over the lawn, and finally onto the brick path to the entrance of the house. Alice's efforts to help her mother keep her balance were of little help, but the sensation of Alice's arm on her back was soothing to Catherine, more soothing than she'd ever remembered Rose's touch.

Once in the house and seated on the couch in the family room, Catherine picked up the phone, but found that her hand was trembling so violently that she couldn't press the right numbers on the phone. Alice took the phone from her mother's hand and, without speaking a word, punched in the correct numbers and handed the phone back to her mother. Catherine quickly told Damien what had happened, and then returned the phone to Alice.

Feeling too unstable to walk very far, Catherine asked Alice to lock the front door and back doors and check to see that all the windows in the house were locked. She knew that this request would be frightening to Alice, but she had no one else to ask.

As soon as Alice left the room, Catherine struggled to her feet and made her way to the kitchen sink, where she turned on the hot water. As she waited for the water to reach its maximum temperature, she glimpsed her reflection in the window over the sink, and immediately looked away. She couldn't stand the sight of herself. When the water was very hot, she methodically moistened a corner of a kitchen towel, squeezed some emerald-green liquid soap on the moistened section, and scrubbed the lower portion of her face as hard as she could. Then, after soaking the towel in the running water, she twisted it into hard knots to remove residual feces embedded between the threads of the cloth. She then scrubbed her right hand. Catherine lost track of how many times she repeated these actions, stopping only when Alice screamed, "Mom, what are you doing?"

"I'm just getting the rest of the poop off of me."

Alice walked into the kitchen and looked closely at her mother's face and then at her right hand. The skin on the corners of her mouth and from the knuckles of her hand had been rubbed off, leaving raw patches. Alice gently took the towel from her mother's hands and turned off the water.

Alice retrieved her mother's cane from the spot it had been dropped just inside the front door. "Put your arm around my shoulder so we can walk to the couch," Alice said. She could feel her mother trembling. They walked to the couch, one deliberate step at a time. Catherine turned and let herself drop into the seat cushions of the couch. She felt like a very frail old woman who had lost control of her body and her mind.

"Thank you for helping me. You've been very calm through all this, calmer than I've been able to be. I'm very proud of you. You've done more than enough already. Why don't you go to your room while I rest here until Daddy gets home. I'll be fine. It was just the shock of it. I can feel it wearing off now."

"I'm going to stay here till Daddy gets home. I don't feel like being in my room alone."

"It feels as if it's ten below zero in here. Is it just me?"

"No, it's cold in here. I'll turn the heat up."

Alice returned to the family room carrying a pale blue blanket, which she wrapped around her mother while standing in back of the couch.

In what felt like a matter of minutes since she had spoken with Damien on the phone, Catherine heard the metallic sound of his keys jiggling as he tried several times to get his key into the lock, finally succeeding in opening the door. Catherine called out, telling him where she was.

Damien's face blanched as he saw Catherine huddled on the couch under a blanket.

"Alice, would you please go to your room while Mommy and I talk about what's happened?"

She left the room, walked upstairs, and loudly, but not angrily, shut the door to her room while standing in the hallway. After taking off her shoes, Alice walked quietly to the landing to eavesdrop. Her parents, so far as she could tell, were now both sitting on the couch in the family room. They were talking in a highly agitated way. Alice wasn't sure she wanted to hear what they were saying, but she couldn't pull herself away.

"The situation has changed," Damien said. "He or they aren't in Chicago any longer—they're here at our house. If we stay in this house, we have to make it a fortress. I'll get a high-end security company out here tomorrow."

"Are you sure that that's the best thing for us to do now?"

"To tell you the truth, I'm not sure of anything."

"It sounds as if you've declared war on him or them."

"They've declared war on us. The war has started. If we pretend it hasn't, who knows what form the next attack will take? We're dealing with lunatics."

Damien paused and actually looked at Catherine for the first time since he'd arrived home. He was alarmed to see what she had done to herself. "Catherine, you know you're bleeding."

"I am?"

271

"Yes. From the sides of your lips and from your hand."

"I had to get the shit off of me. I couldn't get the odor out of my skin. It feels like it got inside of me, almost as if I've been raped."

Alice became so frightened that she didn't want to hear any more. She quietly retreated to her room.

Damien leaned over and hugged Catherine. "You have to know at every second that you're not alone. We have each other, whatever happens. You know that, don't you?"

"I do know that. It's the only thing that keeps me going. And we have Alice. You wouldn't believe how she took charge and helped me when I was in shock." She told Damien all that Alice had done.

"It broke my heart to hear your voice on the phone. It didn't sound like you. Your throat must have been so tense that your vocal cords weren't working right. They're trying to scare us to the point that we'll go out of our minds. And to hear you tell me about how Alice helped you scrub the shit off your face made me terrifically sad and terrifically angry. She's an eight-year-old! She shouldn't have to be washing shit off her mother's face."

"Those were my thoughts, precisely."

"And to see your face and hand raw ... I wish I'd been here so you didn't have to touch the bag of shit and so Alice didn't have to watch all of it happening." He pulled Catherine close to him so their cheeks were touching. He could feel her warm tears on his face and she could feel her face burning as the salty tears entered the pores of the raw skin.

## THIRTY-EIGHT

Damien lay in bed thinking most of the night. He hardly moved for hours, so fixed was his concentration. Catherine was sleeping restlessly, thrashing as if being suffocated under a pile of blankets. He hated the fact that Catherine had been alone when the second assault was made. What he was doing in his office was of no importance to anyone, even to him. That would never happen again. It's too much for one person to handle, he thought. Damien felt a sharp ache at the pit of his stomach that was familiar to him. He'd felt it periodically for as long as he could remember. It was always connected with a feeling of being lost, as if he were in an unfamiliar place, not knowing which direction he was headed and, worst of all, not knowing where he wanted to go. He could not allow that feeling to interfere with what had to be done in the real world now.

Before leaving for home after Catherine called to tell him about the bag of excrement, Damien had called the emergency line of a security company, the insignia of which he'd noticed in stores and on metal posts in front of expensive homes. He'd arranged a meeting at his house the next morning. It was important to him to talk with the company representative alone, without Catherine, so that he could make decisions with a clear head.

The task at hand, for Damien, was that of protecting Catherine and Alice. He didn't care what happened to him. He had two people to protect, and nothing to lose—he didn't care about being injured or even killed. This was his greatest advantage over his attackers: He didn't care if he died, but they did.

Through the night, Damien checked the light in the window opposite the bed as if it were a clock. The black color of the windows began to yellow just a bit, and then, in an accelerating sequence, the morning light evaporated the black liquid that had hidden the chair and dresser, and restored the reflections in the glass under which the photographed faces of Alice and Erin and Rose and Margaret were frozen in time on the stand next to his bed.

He got up quietly and walked to the window. The sky was taking on a pink hue above the straight, uninterrupted line of the roof of the house across the street. The horizon was blocked from view. Soon, cars were pulling out of driveways; streetlights were flickering off. The long wait was nearly over.

At nine-thirty, a charcoal-gray Lexus pulled up and parked on the street in front of the house. Damien, through the corner of a closed curtain next to the front door, watched a broad-shouldered, square-jawed man in his late thirties get out of his car. He wore a dark business suit and walked with perfect posture up the brick path to the house. Damien went to the door and brusquely pulled it open as the man was reaching for the doorbell.

After they introduced themselves, Damien ushered the man to the study, where they sat in round-backed blue wicker chairs with thick gray-and-white striped cushions. Damien explained that the family was being threatened by unknown people who had delivered their threats anonymously, the second of which was the bag of feces placed on the doormat at the front door.

He showed the man the newspaper clipping and the envelope in which it came.

Jim Edwards listened carefully and took detailed notes as Damien described the events that had occurred. Damien claimed to have no idea why the threats were being made; he believed that the reasons for the attacks were irrelevant to the ways that Alice and Catherine had to be protected.

Before making his recommendations, Jim—who insisted on being called "Jim," even as he continued to address Damien as "Mr. McCardle"—asked Damien to show him the house. When that was done, Jim asked if he could take some time to look through the house again on his own and to inspect the surroundings of the house, as well as the neighborhood. Damien took comfort in the professionalism of this man.

After inspecting the house and its surround and making notes on the pad of paper he'd brought with him, Jim went over his recommendations with Damien. After he left, Damien asked Catherine to talk with him in the living room. Damien, with enthusiasm in his voice, described the different features of the security system that would be installed: Door and window sensors, infrared heat detectors, movement detectors, under-carpet weight detectors, and digital cameras, as well as an armed, off-duty policeman providing a twenty-four-hour watch of the house (three men, in eight-hour shifts) from a parked car across the street.

Catherine was more horrified than impressed by Damien's account. It sounded insane to her. They had received a newspaper clipping with their full names on the envelope and a bag of feces—that was it. She didn't say this to Damien for fear that her cautioning him about excesses would cause him to feel that she, too, was someone to be overcome or evaded. She asked him to talk with her about future decisions because she thought that they thought well together. He readily agreed, but Catherine didn't put much stock in his assurances.

Later in the day, Catherine looked out at the front yard from the window above the kitchen sink. Damien was talking with the foreman of the crew who was installing the security system. His shoulders and head were bent close to the foreman's mouth, seemingly in an effort not to miss a single word that he spoke. Damien was a man possessed. Catherine both hated him and pitied him for it—hated him for taking sole possession of the course of their lives at this delicate juncture, and pitied him for the terror that she knew was coursing through every fiber of him.

Catherine decided to take Alice to the park after picking her up from school and then to supper at Alice's favorite family restaurant because one of the men installing the system told her that, at Damien's request, they'd be working into the early evening. Catherine and Alice ate in silence, both lost in thoughts they dared not speak to the other. Catherine felt the ache of longing for Margaret, the only person with whom she'd been able to speak with complete openness and honesty.

Flashes of conversation with Margaret went through Catherine's mind—not the specific content, but the feelings she'd had as they talked. Margaret had been unapologetically different from everyone else in the world, including Rose. When Catherine spoke to Margaret, she knew that she was not going to be given what she wanted to hear; she would be given something that felt true to Margaret. Catherine had not always liked what Margaret said. She recalled a time when she'd left Margaret's house feeling angry and misunderstood, with the sense that Margaret was too strange to really know what it was to be in a love relationship—after all, her marriage had ended very quickly, and according to Margaret, it was loveless. Catherine also remembered feeling, as she'd walked to her car, that the world looked and felt somehow different—the feel of the air against her face felt different and the trunks of the eucalyptus trees, with their peeling, gray-brown bark, looked different.

God, what a loss it was to live in a world without Margaret. Catherine had talked with her quite a few times about her belief that Damien had never really forgiven her for not telling him she was trying to have a baby by artificial insemination. After Alice was born, they had both been too exhausted for sex, and as time went on that part of their lives together withered. Catherine had read that this happens to a lot of couples after they have their first child. It was ironic, she thought, that in their first years together, they pretended to be a brother and sister, not a couple; and now they were pretending to be a couple, not a brother and sister. That's unfair, she said to herself; they'd never stopped being a couple—they'd been a couple fighting for their lives and now fighting for the life of their child, or at least that was what they believed they were doing. She loved Damien—of that she was certain.

# THIRTY-NINE

D amien and Erin stood on the sidewalk, watching the security company's crew working on ladders leaning against the roof of the front of the house. Erin had arrived only a few minutes earlier.

"Catherine didn't tell me you were coming out here to help," Damien said, his eyes on the men in white jumpsuits, "but I need all the help I can get. There are things I've had to keep from Catherine because they'd frighten her, and there's no point in scaring her, but I can tell you."

Erin, stunned by the impersonal, almost mechanical way in which Damien was speaking, said, "Let me put my things inside, and we'll find a private place to talk."

"Yes, yes, you're right—we can't talk out here."

As they entered the house, Damien said, "Let's wait to tell Catherine and Alice you're here until we've talked. Let's go talk in the study."

They both took seats in the blue wicker armchairs that Damien and Jim had used when talking that morning. Because of the way Damien was speaking, the room felt more like a bunker than a study.

"I made some sightings of the intruders last night that I haven't told Catherine about," Damien said. "I got up quite a few times during the night to track them. I thought I saw a man in dark clothes and wool cap, but the light was too dim for me to make out any features. They're going to install infrared cameras that can film in the dark and are triggered by anything that moves in their visual field, but they're on order and won't be coming in until next week. I've bought a hunting rifle that I don't intend to use, but I like to have it because it gives me a sense of security."

Seeing Erin's worried expression when he mentioned the rifle, Damien said, "Don't worry, it's just a precaution. It's locked up in a cabinet in the garage so there's no chance that Alice could accidentally get her hands on it."

Erin, finally finding a moment to break into Damien's pressured monologue, said, "Slow down. I think you're getting ahead of yourself. There has been only a news clipping and a bag of shit on your doormat. Catherine told me she thought it was human shit, but it could have been dog shit."

"I know you're trying to help, Erin, but you haven't been here long enough to know what's going on. It feels eerie. That's the best word for it, *eerie*."

After allowing Damien to talk without interruption for a long time, a half hour or so, Erin said, "Damien, I think I understand the horror of what you're going through. Do you want to know what I think?"

"Sure, I do. You're the only person I can talk to."

"I think that by fortifying your house against another attack, you're building yourself a prison. If I were you, I'd be looking into moving someplace where he, or they, wouldn't bother me any longer."

"That's just it. There is no such place. I've given a lot of thought to this. They'll find us wherever we go. You're right about building myself a prison, complete with an armed guard across the street. I've tried to think of every possible option. Sometimes I think that the only thing to do is to put an ad in the paper saying that, despite the fact that Catherine and I are half-siblings, Alice was conceived by artificial insemination, using the sperm of another man, and that all I do is look after the two of them, as a brother and stand-in father." Of course, that was not the whole truth. He'd left out the fact that he and Catherine had a sexual relationship. He couldn't tell if Erin was aware that he was leaving that out.

"What do you think of that idea?"

"It's a definite possibility."

Damien said, "The downside of that plan is that Catherine and Alice would be treated like lepers. I really don't care what they think of me; I mean that. It's possible that I'm underestimating the general public in Cleveland. Maybe they'd yawn and say, 'So what.' I've lived at such a great distance from other people for so long that I no longer have any idea what the *general public* thinks. Catherine has her clothing design business, which is doing very well. She deals with people much more than I do, and so does Alice—in fact, Alice deals with more people than either Catherine or me. She's been in school for four years and has teachers, friends, and parents of friends in her life, not to mention swimming teachers, camp counselors, and on and on. And that's the rub—Catherine and I can withdraw from the hate that the world can dish out, but Alice can't. I feel an animal instinct to protect her."

"I know you do. I know you love her and Catherine more than anything."

"Thanks, and don't leave yourself out."

Later in the day, Erin took Catherine aside and said quietly, "I think that Damien is living in a world of his own, and only now and again returns to the real world."

"I know, and it terrifies me … I'm so glad you're here."

That night, after the lights were out, Damien said to Catherine, "I know I've put you through hell. I've been so shaken by the attacks on us and so afraid of what might happen

281

to you and Alice that I've cut myself off from you, which is ridiculous because you and Alice are the two people I'm trying to protect."

"You've been under unimaginable pressure. You've been asking the impossible of yourself. No one can protect the people they love from a madman's ideas and actions. They're beyond anyone's control."

"After talking with Erin, I've been thinking about how and where we might move to get away from this. We could move to northern Montana or the Canadian border of North Dakota and change our names and invent a story of our past and where we've lived. But Alice would have to be given a new name and she'd have to live a lie. It's more than an eight-year-old can do, or should have to do." Catherine became terrified as she realized that Damien had no memory of their talking about this plan several times in the past and his having rejected it each time because it would be impossible to carry out.

"Stop. We're not going to move to North Dakota like murderers on the run. I talked with Erin today, too. He told me that you had the idea of just telling the truth so there won't be any secrets. I think that's the best thing to do."

"But what about Alice? She'll be treated like a freak. The parents of her friends won't allow her to play at their houses."

"You don't know that."

"You don't know either."

"No, I don't, but I'm willing to take my chances with it."

"How do we get across to whoever is persecuting us the fact that we have no secrets? That he's welcome to tell everything to anyone he likes, and we'll be happy to fill in any details he might forget to include?"

"I don't know that either, but we'll figure it out."

"I wish I could believe that."

Damien moved to his side of the bed and stared at the ceiling. He was awake most of the night, standing at the window on the second floor landing, trying to sight intruders. Exhausted, at about three in the morning, a solution to the problem occurred to him—not for the first time, but with a force that felt beyond his power to resist.

In the morning, Catherine found that Damien had already gotten up, which was his custom, but she somehow sensed that he wasn't in the house. She quickly dressed and looked around the house, not calling his name in order not to frighten Alice. On the kitchen counter was a note saying, *"Catherine, ask Erin what's happening. He knows. Don't worry about me. Love, Damien."*

After reading the note, Catherine sobbed. She handed it to Erin who, on hearing Catherine walking around the house, had come down to the kitchen. He read the note several times, trying to figure out what each phrase meant. He then put his arms around Catherine and held her tightly.

"Has he told you what he's doing?" Catherine asked through her tears.

"He's told me a lot of plans and then circles back on himself, mixing one plan with another, using one plan as a disguise for the other. The one he arrived at last night is the one I think he's decided to act on. His idea was that if he disappeared from your life and Alice's, you and Alice would be an ordinary mother and daughter living on their own, and there would be no secret to hide. You wouldn't have to move to Montana or North Dakota and live under aliases."

"Did you tell him that that's an absurd solution?"

"Of course I tried to, but you know how he's been lately. Nothing gets through to him. What frightens me most is that he told me he'd bought a rifle that he keeps in a locked case in the garage, 'just as a precaution.'"

"I don't remember seeing a case of any kind in the garage, but let's assume the worst. What do we do?"

"I'm wary of calling the police. He's terrified and out of his mind. If the police were to find him, he'd think they were trying to lock him up or kill him, and he might shoot at them and end up getting killed. I wonder if that's what he hopes will happen. It would put an end to his agony. I apologize for jumping to the worst scenario, but I think that's the outcome we have to use all our energy to prevent."

"I know it is," Catherine said. "But if we don't call the police, he might shoot someone else—an innocent person who he thinks is after him, or possibly even a child who, for some reason, frightens him. I think we have to call the police."

Erin checked the garage for a rifle case, and to his alarm, found a black metal case laying open behind a pile of cardboard boxes filled with Alice's baby clothes and stuffed animals. He then walked to the other side of the street to talk to the off-duty policeman who Damien had told him was watching the house. There was no car parked across the street, nor was there a man seated in any other car on the entire street.

Erin talked with Catherine in the study about what he'd found. "Both things are frightening—the rifle case most of all, but also the fact that he's been imagining that a cop has been stationed across the street. I'm sure he thought that was true."

"Do you think there's any possibility that the police could handle the situation sensibly if we tell them that Damien is lost and frightened, that he has a rifle, and that they should notify us if they see him so we can help bring him to a hospital without anyone getting hurt?"

"I have no way of knowing if they'd be willing to do that. If we talk with them, the situation is, from that point on, out of our hands. But the situation is out of our hands as it is. So I'm inclined to take a chance on the police."

"I'm terrified that this will end disastrously. It's so awful to imagine Damien on the run with demons after him. I have to keep my mind on each step that has to be taken now and not let my imagination get ahead of me. Let's get Alice to the house of one of her friends without telling her that Damien is gone. We'll tell her tonight if he's not back."

## FORTY

The officer at the desk of the police station asked Erin and Catherine to have a seat while he called another officer to take their statement. The building was of modern institutional design, with cinder-block walls painted pale green, shiny beige linoleum floors, bulbous skylights, and a row of orange plastic chairs bolted to the floor opposite the police desk.

It was only about ten minutes before a uniformed man in his forties introduced himself as Officer Matthew Higgins and asked Catherine and Erin to follow him through two swinging doors into a hallway identical to the one they'd just left, except for a series of doors on the left. Higgins unlocked one of the doors, and motioned Catherine and Erin to enter as he held it open.

It was an interview room with a metal table, four metal chairs, and a two-way mirror, just as they'd seen on television police programs.

"I read here that you've come about your husband, Damien McCardle."

"Yes," Catherine said in a voice stronger than she'd expected. "We've been frightened by someone who has left a bag of feces at our front door and a letter that said, in effect, 'We know where you live.' We have no idea who it is or why they're doing this. Damien has been undone by it and has arranged for an elaborate security system to be installed, which they're doing now. But he's become so frightened that he told my brother here, Erin, that he bought a rifle 'just as a precaution.' He left the house in the middle of the night last night, and left this note for me." Catherine fumbled through her handbag and handed the note to the officer.

"What is it, Mr. … ?"

"Erin Keane."

"What is it, Mr. Keane, that Damien McCardle is referring to when he says that you know what his plan is?"

"I'm Catherine's brother and a close friend of my brother-in-law, Damien. Last night he talked about a great many plans about how to handle what he called 'the intruders.' One of the plans was to go off on his own in hopes that the intruders were after him and would leave his wife and child alone. I know that the plan makes no sense, but his mind isn't working right."

"What do you know about the rifle?"

"Only that he said he had bought one because it made him feel more secure."

"Did he say he had anyone in mind to shoot?"

"No," Erin said, hesitating before he went on. "I want to say as respectfully as I can that I don't think that the police should intervene forcefully as soon as they find him. Damien is paranoid. He will feel terrified by the police. I beg you to let Catherine or me talk with Damien before you approach him. He won't hurt us, and the whole thing can be safely brought to an end. Of course, he'll need to be brought directly to a mental hospital for evaluation and treatment, to keep him and everyone else safe."

Higgins said, "Our goal is the same as yours—to end this without anyone getting hurt. I can't promise that if we locate him there will be time for you to get to the scene before any police action is taken, but I will make clear to everyone involved

286

in the search that, if at all possible, you or your sister should be brought to the scene before any action is taken."

The interview took almost two hours. At one point, Catherine awkwardly told Higgins that she and Damien were not married, Alice was her child, and that Damien had legally adopted her. Picking up on Catherine's self-consciousness, Higgins said, "I'm here to help you find Damien, not to pass judgment on something I know nothing about."

Catherine, to her surprise, burst into tears. "I'm sorry," she said, as she rummaged through her handbag, looking for a tissue. "I was so touched by your kindness and humility. I've dreaded being looked on with suspicion and disapproval."

Higgins looked at her from across the gray metal table and said, "We'll do everything we can to help get your Damien back safely."

Since Damien, when very anxious, seemed to find comfort in taking walks by himself, particularly in the woods, Catherine and Erin spent the day driving up and down the streets leading from their house to various wooded areas and checking streets leading to the state park. Damien and Catherine had given the police the numbers of their cell phones, which they nervously checked for missed calls. They returned home after dark. The mother of Alice's friend Sharon dropped Alice off shortly after they returned. Catherine and Erin decided to tell Alice that Damien was working late at the office.

It was about three in the morning when Catherine's cell phone rang.

"Mrs. Keane?"

"Yes."

"This is the Wilton Police Department. A man was sighted on foot at a gas station at the intersection of Routes 112 and 116. The officers at that location have requested that you get there as soon as possible."

"Yes, thank you for calling. I can be there in less than ten minutes." Catherine decided not to ask questions in order not to waste any time getting there. She woke Erin and told him about the call. Erin pulled on his clothes, awoke Alice, and carried her to the car where Catherine was anxiously waiting.

Catherine explained to Alice that her father had been acting strangely and had gotten lost while walking. The police had found him, and now the three of them were going to help the police. She did not mention the rifle, hoping that that would not come into play.

"Why are the police after him?"

"The police aren't after him," Catherine said. "Police don't just catch criminals, they also help people who are in trouble or who get lost. Daddy got lost."

"How did Daddy get lost?"

"He's had a lot on his mind since someone played that trick on us with the bag of poop, and people get confused and sometimes lost when they have too much on their minds." Alice knew that that wasn't the whole story, but she didn't ask any more questions because she could tell that her mother didn't want to continue making up the story she was telling.

There were two police cars parked to the side of the pumps at the gas station when they arrived. The policeman who seemed to be the senior officer, a large man in his fifties, said, "Someone driving by in a car saw a man with a rifle walking right there on the side of the road opposite this gas station. We think that he's somewhere in this strip of trees, which is about seventy-five yards wide. We have a car on the other side of it. I can't let either of you go in there alone—it's too dangerous. We don't know what his mental state is, and he's armed."

"What do you suggest?" Erin asked, in a deferential tone.

"I wish we had the luxury of waiting until the sun comes up, but I'm afraid he'll be gone by then. There will be an officer accompanying whichever of you goes into the wooded area."

Catherine said to Erin, "I'd like to go."

Alice, whom everyone had forgotten, began crying. "Don't go, Mommy, please!" The policeman's saying her father was armed terrified Alice.

Erin said to Catherine, "I think that it's best if I go. I'm more neutral to him than you are, less likely to cause him to do anything irrational to try to protect me from the police."

The senior officer, Ray Lenguiza, told Erin to get fitted with a bulletproof vest. Minutes later, the two of them crossed the two-lane highway and entered the woods.

Lenguiza had a very powerful flashlight that lit large areas of the woods in the direction it was pointed. The sticks breaking under their feet made loud crackling noises that Erin hoped Damien wouldn't mistake for gunfire. They padded up and down beneath the canopy of tree branches for what felt like hours. The task began to feel hopeless to Erin. There were far too many places Damien could hide to be able to find him unless he made a sudden movement. As Erin trudged through the leaves, he felt terrible sadness that he was walking with a policeman in the woods in the middle of the night, wearing a bulletproof vest, looking for Damien. How had it come to this?

Lenguiza suddenly took Erin's elbow firmly in his grip. "Shh!" Erin stood absolutely still. There was no doubt that someone not far away was taking slow, careful steps. Lenguiza slowly took his pistol from its holster.

Erin whispered, "Please put that away."

"Enough."

Erin suddenly called out, "Damien, it's Erin. Don't be afraid. I'm here to help you get back to Catherine and Alice, who are waiting for you right across the street at the gas station."

Silence, and then the sound of faint crackling of sticks and leaves. Lenguiza said quietly, "Keep talking."

"Damien, I would never do anything to hurt you. I'm your big brother, and I'll never stop looking after you."

Then, from out of the woods, "Stop! Don't come any closer."

They stopped.

289

"Damien, everything's all right. No one has any reason to want to hurt you. I'm with a policeman who is a good and gentle man and who's here to help." Erin considered telling Damien that he'd never lied to him, but they both knew he had. "Catherine and Alice are at the gas station waiting for us now."

"They're here?"

"Yes, they're worried sick about you."

Lenguiza took a step forward and Erin did the same. And then another step, and another. They were now close enough to Damien that Lenguiza was able to direct the beam of the flashlight to the foot of the tree behind which Damien was crouched. The artificial light created the illusion of a cave in which everything felt ominous and supernatural.

"How do I know you're who you say you are?"

"I'm Erin. Who else would know about Mr. Lerner and the way he had kids act scenes in your class about the Japanese internment camps, and the suffragettes, and the slaves and slave owners? No one but me would know that. And who else would know about the time you got detention for losing so many library books, and the hole we dug every summer in the rock cave, every day of the summer, really expecting to hit China?"

And then there was only the sound of the wind knocking the bare branches of the barren trees against one another and the whoosh of cars on the highway behind them.

Lenguiza said softly to Erin, "Ask him to put the rifle on the ground in front of the tree."

"I don't want to bring guns into this, yours or his," Erin replied.

Because Lenguiza had the flashlight in one hand and his pistol in the other, he couldn't grab hold of Erin as he walked toward Damien. "Damien, I'm not afraid you'll hurt me. I'm coming to take you to Catherine and Alice, who are waiting to see you."

Damien disappeared behind the tree. Lenguiza didn't move, but Erin could feel his tense presence behind him. Erin kept walking slowly toward the tree.

Damien emerged suddenly from behind the tree, the rifle at his side. Erin could see that his finger was on the trigger. Damien couldn't see who was carrying the light because the beam was blinding when he looked in that direction.

Erin, seeing that Damien was trying to see who was carrying the flashlight, said calmly, "The policeman carrying the flashlight, whose name is Ray Lenguiza, is here to help you and Catherine and Alice and me."

Damien made no reply. Erin took a few more steps until he was standing right next to his brother.

"Don't lift the rifle, Damien. Let me take it from you."

Erin slowly moved his hand toward the barrel of the rifle and began to take hold of it. Damien jerked the rifle away from Erin so forcefully that the barrel swung upward. The report of the rifle filled the air as the bullet flew into the sky.

Lenguiza, seeing that the shot wasn't directed at anyone, did not return fire. Banfield, the policeman who had been watching from the other side of the strip of woods, on hearing the rifle shot, fired his pistol at the silhouette of the man holding a rifle. Lenguiza yelled at the top of his lungs, "Stop firing, Banfield, the rifle shot was an accident!"

Damien dropped the rifle to the ground.

Erin and Lenguiza walked silently with Damien through the woods to the gas station, one on each side of him, neither touching him. To Erin, Damien seemed to be peering out of a deep and narrow recess, not knowing what to make of the sliver of light he was seeing.

After they crossed the two-lane highway, Damien looked at Catherine with tears in his eyes and said, "I'm sorry. I'm so sorry."

Catherine didn't know how to say all that she was feeling, and before she was able to get a word out, Lenguiza was firmly, but not gruffly, ushering Damien to the rear door of a police cruiser, where he gripped Damien's upper arm as he slid into the back seat. Erin was already seated on the other side of the back seat.

The overhead plastic sleeve of the cruiser flashed red and blue beams of light of enormous intensity.

# ABOUT THE AUTHOR

**Thomas Ogden**, M.D., published his debut novel, *The Parts Left Out*, in 2014. He has also published twelve books of essays on the theory and practice of psychoanalysis, and on the writings of Frost, Borges, Kafka, and others. His most recent works of non-fiction include *Reclaiming Unlived Life: Experiences in Psychoanalysis; The Analyst's Ear and the Critic's Eye: Rethinking Psychoanalysis and Literature; Creative Readings: Essays on Seminal Analytic Works; Rediscovering Psychoanalysis;* and *This Art of Psychoanalysis: Dreaming Undreamt Dreams and Interrupted Cries*. His work has been translated into more than twenty languages.

Dr. Ogden was awarded the 2012 Sigourney Award for his "contributions to the field of psychoanalysis"; the 2010 Haskell Norman Prize for "outstanding achievement as a psychoanalytic clinician, teacher and theoretician"; and the 2004 *International Journal of Psychoanalysis* Award for "The Most Important Paper of the Year." He practices psychoanalysis in San Francisco, where he teaches both psychoanalysis and creative writing.